Mario Basini
Anthony Bunko
Jan Caswell
David Edwards
Boz (Philip Evans)
Phillipa J Evans
Wendy Grey-Lloyd
Ken James
Mike Jenkins
Alan Murphy
Leslie Norris
Viv Protheroe
Nigel Roberts
Chris Sullivan
Celia G Thomas
Eira Williams
Martyn Williams

'A Big Night' by Leslie Norris appears
courtesy of 'Seren' Publishers

* * * *

Thank you to Anthony Bunko and Merthyr
Tydfil Libraries for all the time and effort
given, in helping to produce this short stories
book.

* * * *

Thank you to Rhymney Brewery, Dowlais

* * * *

Thank you, also to

Juan Lozano
our front cover star as 'The King',

* * * *

Peter and Joan of
Peter Hughes Photography (01685 386876),

* * * *

Lyn Williams at Opal Design Studio
(07727155617 www.opaldesign.co.uk)

* * * *

....and finally again to Anthony Bunko for the
cover concept and book title.

* * * *

All characters and events in this publication are
fictional.

The views and opinions expressed are entirely the
work of the authors and in no way represent the views
or position of Merthyr Tydfil County Borough
Council.

ISBN 0-9547273-2-0

© Published by
Merthyr Tydfil County Borough Council, Arts Division, 2006

www.merthyr.gov.uk
arts@merthyr.gov.uk
Arts Division, Merthyr Tydfil County Borough Council,
Civic Centre, Castle Street, Merthyr Tydfil, CF47 8B

Recommended reading age 16+

Language and content may not be suitable for younger readers.

Illustration by Dewi Bowen

Contents

All Roads Lead To Merthyr

'Foreword'

Since the Royal Charter of Incorporation in1905, Merthyr Tydfil has been a borough. The borough's great heritage was built upon the heavy industries of iron and coal, helping to create a particular character and culture. Merthyr Tydfil saw the inward migration of the Irish, the English, the Italians, the Spanish and of course from other parts of Wales and further a field, all drawn by the prospect of work during the industrial revolution. An outward migration followed, as those industries ceased and young people became drawn away, in the reverse footsteps of their descendents. Today a more limited inward migration can be seen, including the Portuguese, the Polish and others, contributing to the borough's ongoing story of flux and integration.

The people of Merthyr Tydfil have a resilience born from a culture created by a history of turbulence and neglect. The notorious Iron Masters and the Merthyr Rising in response to dwindling pay and conditions. The trauma and terrible confusion of how the Aberfan disaster could ever have happened. The legacy of 1984 and the desolation that pit closures had on communities. No wonder perhaps, that some of the borough's most recognised local heroes are fighters, some with an added sense of pathos and tragedy. The town centre celebrates three local boxing champions, with statues in their honour and a local pub is named after a local working class hero, who was also celebrated in the acclaimed novel, *Fire People* by renowned author Alexander Cordell. Merthyr remembers Dic Penderyn, Johnny Owen and others with both pride and compassion. Perhaps it is now time to recognise our rich literary heritage too. Not only can Merthyr Tydfil boast the likes of Leslie Norris or the award winning Mike Jenkins, both of whom have stories included in this book, also the critic, poet and story writer Glyn Jones, who was born in Claire Street, Charlotte Guest who made a great contribution towards English language Welsh literature, by being the first to translate 'The Mabinogion'. Merthyr Tydfil can also claim the talents of all the authors who have contributed to this book, Mario Basini, Anthony Bunko et al.

As the influence of Merthyr Tydfil's rich heritage is combined with the contemporary impact of globalisation, each author displays his or her own unique voice. Their honesty produces characters that are sometimes well informed, sometimes naive and politically incorrect, reflecting the traits of some of the personalities familiar to Merthyr Tydfil. The setting for these fictional characters shifts from gritty reality and historical fact to the supernatural and comic surrealism. What binds these stories together is the experience of Merthyr Tydfil borough. Empathy, spirituality and pragmatic necessity reveal a particular sense of humour and temperament, at ease with both tragedy and comedy. All roads still lead to Merthyr Tydfil, with hope for the future. A twenty-first century centre for the south Wales valleys.

Arts Development Officer, Michael Gustavius Payne.

All Roads Lead To Merthyr

'The Inventor of South Street, 1830'

Anthony Bunko

A very excited Samuel Crocker woke-up in a tiny, cramped room of a dingy house on the narrow terraced street in Dowlais, long before the fingers of daylight had inched their way through the curtains. Darkness was still very much in attendance. Outside he could hear the noise created by the blast furnace of the giant iron works as it belched out flues into the already polluted valleys skyline.

Two of his children were wrapped around him tightly, in a vain attempt to try and protect their thin bodies from the cold air which engulfed the squalid room. At this time of year the weather was bitter and unsympathetic. It had a mischievous way of creeping into every nook and cranny, and an annoying habit of burrowing under the skin and chilling straight into the bone.

Today was an important day for Samuel and hopefully for the rest of his family. For today he was due to present his latest invention to the Church Council. He knew that if they sanctioned his creation it could be the beginning of a new way of life for them all; no more living in the squalor of South Street; no more living in a house with giant holes in the roof; and no more sharing floor space with a family of disease ridden rats, who squatted, rent-free, in the attic. All he required was the Council, and more importantly Minister Daley, to agree.

But it was Minister Daley, the head of the Church in the borough, who was the main issue. He was a heartless man, a larger-than-life disciplinarian who used his immense power to rule the town with a strict set of religious guidelines. Last Sunday, during mass, he had a poor girl branded with a hot iron just for sneezing during his sermon.

Back in the damp bedroom Samuel lay in bed listening to the sound of the long-tailed hairy vermin scurrying about beneath the floorboards. He couldn't make out exactly what they were up to, but in his mind they were probably playing some stupid rodent game such as hide and seek, touch or kiss chase.

The father's eyes strained through the blackness. He could just make out the shape of his other three, older kids nestled together under a mass of blankets in the far corner near the tall-boy. They appeared to be shivering in unison. Recently they had started to suffer from a new type of plague that had hit the unlucky town. Sadly, 1830 had been a bumper year for plagues in the borough. Epidemics, with an appetite for death, seemed to descend on the growing industrial town like raindrops falling from the dark winter skies. They were a bit like waiting for a number Fifty-three tram to Merthyr; none would turn up for ages, then six would come skidding around the bend all at the same time.

It had all started during the long days of February when a wild dose of Black Death came strolling into town looking for a dancing partner. The effects were extremely nasty; discolouration of the skin and frizziness of people's hair was quickly followed by a swelling of the lips. Soon after, the chills would kick in and the unfortunate victims would speak in strange tongues before finally dying.

Samuel's poor wife, who was prone to catching most illnesses, contracted the disease and died soon after, but not until she kept muttering over and over that *'She was Jenny from the block…who used to have nothing but now she's got a lot.'*

In the end Samuel was glad to see the delirious woman pass away just to shut her up.

Next came the Scarlet eyed fever, which was largely a self-induced illness brought on by the town's craving for neat gin mixed with the polluted Taff water. After that a flock of giant headlice with teeth like tigers rampaged through everyone's body hair. This caused the Church to demand that all residents (except for Minister Daley) have their head and body parts shaved completely. Minister Daley believed he was too important in the eyes of God to catch nits. Predictably, he did but kept his large bishop hat on at all times to hide them.

As summer came, a 48 hour illness struck the womenfolk of the town. It was aptly named 'the curse of a thousand warts on the face.' It wasn't a pretty sight and many thought it had been brought about after a travelling medicine man, called Big Ernie, claimed that rubbing frogs on the skin would cause it to become more beautiful; it would also bring good luck. At the same time, the men-folk suffered from a similar disease, but of the penis. Again the finger of suspicion was pointed at Big Ernie who swore (on the Holy Bible) that frog rubbing had strange enlarging powers.

Minister Daley wasn't amused. He made everyone of them sit in a bath of freezing cold water while they said 708 Our Fathers and 23 Hail Marys.

Big Ernie was found dead the following Tuesday. His troop of wart carrying frogs were made into a large green soup.

This month it was the turn of some illness called the Big Brown Plague, a distant cousin of the Black Death. The Big Brown Plague wasn't fatal but what made it worse was its arrival had coincided with an acute strain of itchy arse syndrome. It meant that people turned a rich dark chocolate colour. Then all night they would itch and scratch, then scratch and itch until they were red raw. Technically it should have been known as the 'Red Raw' Plague, but the bloke who thought up the names of plagues was colour blind (a result of drinking too much Taff water and neat gin).

As the daylight arrived, Samuel knew he didn't have time to lie in bed, reminiscing about the past. There were too many things to do. He limped down the freezing flag stones which connected the upstairs to the rest of the house. He could feel the black pats squelching between his toes as he searched around for a flint to light the oil lamp. Once lit the artificial glow sent the big, black intruders scurrying to the dark corners of the room where the light couldn't reach them. Samuel was sure he could hear the creatures moaning and groaning to themselves about the bright ball of light which always spoilt their fun.

He poked the remains of yesterday's ashes out of the grate and lit a fresh fire. He then started to lay out the ingredients required to produce his latest invention on the course, wooden table.

He lit the stove and put the items he required into the cooking pots. Within five minutes the smell drifted up from the oven filling the entire house with a delicious aroma. It woke the kids from their deep sleep. They came crashing down the stairwell, tongues hanging out of their mouths. Two of the children were still stuck together with the cold. They were like two icicles hanging from a rooftop. Samuel told them to sit by the fire to defrost.

'What's that dad?... it smells lovely!' asked the eldest, large balls of sleep stuck in the corner of his brown eyes.

'Sorry kids… it's not for you.' He could see the sadness etched on their faces. He quickly added 'Look I've got to give this stuff to Minister Daley and the Council to get their approval… and if they agree to it… just think... we will be able to live like Iron Masters…. Each of us will have our own castle. We will all have our own servants to cook and clean for us…. You'll see!'

He hated himself for not being able to provide for his own flesh and blood. He hated seeing them starve while others in the more affluent part of town fed until their bellies burst. It was so unfair, so unjust.

'Look,' he said 'there's still some bits of yesterday's dinner in the pantry… Help yourself.'

He felt their sadness, but there was nothing he could do. They were poor. An accident at the foundry which had left him with four fingers missing on his right hand and ensured that manual work, which meant a regular income, had deserted him. After the incident there had been no compensation, no pay off, no state pension. He had his hand stitched up, was given a week's wages (minus allowances) and booted out to fend for himself. It was hard enough for a man with two strong hands to earn a living in a rough old town like Merthyr, never mind one with only one hand and a thumb, a recently deceased wife and five children to support, while trying to cope with the most vicious outbreak of itchy arse syndrome in living memory. He wouldn't wish it on his own worst enemy.

He had to do something to keep the bailiff away from his front door. So he focused all his attention on inventing things, and, to be fair, he was quite good at it.

Back in his room he wrapped his new creation up in newspaper, placed it under his arm and headed out into the cobbled streets, walking hopefully to his appointment with destiny. He took a last look back into the kitchen where he saw his kids bitterly fighting over who was going to chew on the last piece of rat's tail in the pantry. He felt like crying and tears began rolling down his cheeks.

Outside, the whole place stunk of smoke and desperation. Everything was covered with thick black ash that constantly rained down on the Merthyr skyline. People would get filthy just by hanging around on the pavements.

Like most mornings, the streets were a hive of activity and noise. Hordes of individuals with long, drawn, grey faces, rushed about, or ducked and dived into every available inch of space. Samuel could just make out the familiar and distinctive banging sound of wooden panels being knocked together by the local coffin maker, the aptly named, Jimmy the Box. Fortunately for Jimmy and his family, business was thriving, which was not so good news for the rest of the community. People died for fun in this part of the world, which wasn't particularly amusing at all.

Samuel battled on. The first person he bumped into was Georgie Onions, the long-standing village hobo. Apparently the tramp had been born quite normal until he accidentally collided with a runaway tram that had turned the healthy young man into a empty shell of a person with a first rate honours degree in kookiness. Nowadays, he somehow made a living from persuading people to boot him in the nuts for either a couple of pennies or some scraps of food. Samuel was amazed how Georgie had survived, but to be fair to him, it was tough going (especially on his nuts), and it helped him to pay his way on the place he called home, a hole in the ground that was covered by a tarpaulin, situated up near the Bogey road.

To give Georgie credit, it had been a better plan than the late Dopey Gerald's moneymaking scheme. He dared people to hit him with a farmer's scythe. He had been decapitated on the very first day of his new business venture. This meant that Gerald not only lost his life, but also lost the brand new scythe he had put a down payment on the week before.

From the upper side of South Street, Samuel watched as the younger men of the village prepared for the long arduous shift in the depths of hell known as the foundry. The heat from the furnaces caused the young men to age overnight. Many of them were teenagers covered in old men's skin and bones. They unintentionally found themselves travelling quickly into manhood without having the opportunity to spend time in a place called

Youth. In a perverse sort of way, Samuel was glad he'd lost his fingers when he had. This now meant he didn't have to indulge in the hardship and pain that faced the young men in the fires of hell. He was glad to have broken free, even if it was at a painful cost.

Next to grab his attention, on that rainy morning, were the gangs of shrill-tongued women folk, who appeared collectively in the main High Street. They were like a synchronised dance troupe performing a daily routine, while being choreographed by someone high up in the sky. Even from where Samuel stood he could see the pain and suffering ingrained on their relatively ugly faces. Deep furrow lines scarred their foreheads. He found it amusing how they all had at least one tooth missing, which enabled them to talk without having to take their fags out of their decaying mouths.

They all stood on their doorsteps and after a silent count to three, emptied the remains of last night's bedpans into the already polluted street. The stench was shocking. A concoction of last night's filth mixed with large helpings of dysentery covered the pavement. Turds of all shapes and sizes, surfed on yellow rivers of piss, and unknowingly raced each other down the steep slope of South Street to the finishing line in Old Church Terrace. Samuel was relived he didn't live in Old Church Terrace. Only the real, real poor people were unfortunate enough to live there.

He walked on. He came across the crouching figure of Mrs Thomas, scrubbing her front step, a sharpened axe by her side. She was sobbing heavily. He had heard through the grapevine that her husband, Mr Thomas, had gone missing last Thursday and hadn't been seen since.

8

Rumours concerning the whereabouts of Mr Thomas flew about like dinner plates getting chucked around a kitchen. Some said that he had been murdered in Chinatown, his throat sliced and then his body dumped in the cold waters of the Taff. Others talked about seeing him disappearing over the slag heap mountain tops, hand in hand with Kathy Gypo, the stunningly attractive gypsy girl with beautiful green eyes and the proud owner of three of her own teeth.

Samuel stopped and offered some conversation with the woman. 'Hello Mrs Thomas… still no news I see?' He lowered his eyes to the floor as a mark of respect.

'Hello Samuel…. I'm afraid so… Terrible news… terrible … terrible news… I can't believe it.' She shook her head, tears welling up in her eyes.

Samuel feared the worst. He wondered what news Mrs Thomas would actually find the worse to have been told? Would it be the slit throat story or the tale of him running away with the beautiful diddycoy? Samuel hoped it was the former. He himself had designs on one day running away with that gypsy with the long shiny hair, even though it was crawling with lice and bits of other stuff.

There was an awkward pause until Mrs Thomas added, 'I can't believe it…. they found the useless bastard sleeping under the iron bridge this morning. Drunk and penniless. Lost all his pay in a card game… He's upstairs sleeping it off and snoring like a fat hog.' She spat on the pavement. It was full of anger and green bits. 'But I'll have my revenge!' She slammed the axe into the wooden frame of the door. 'I'll have my revenge!'

Samuel gulped before saying his goodbyes and carried on with his journey through the miserable tenement pathways. Off in the distance he saw the intimidating church steeple. His heart thumped wildly in his chest, his hands trembled.

Ten minutes later, Samuel Crocker sat nervously in the elegant waiting room of the vestry. He held on tightly to the package under his arm. Many thoughts quickly surfaced in his overactive mind and raced around bumping into themselves without mercy.

'Would the council think his latest invention could help to change the fortunes of the village?'

'Would it pass the strict guidelines imposed by Minister Daley?'

'And would it stay warm for long enough to have the desired effect?'

Whatever the answers he realised it was too late to turn back now and he gripped firmly onto the parcel. Old Farmer Morgan, who had also been summoned, was already in the room demonstrating his latest inventions to the council.

In truth, Samuel had been quite impressed with Farmer Morgan's prototype of a non-stick cooking utensil and he had wished the old farmer all the luck in the world as he strolled into the chamber, carrying his pot.

He knew the kind of ordeal Farmer Morgan would be going though behind the large wooden door at that very moment. He himself had been grilled by the Board of Council and especially Minister Daley many times over the past couple of years. It was a stressful and nerve racking time. He found that inventing things was the easy bit; getting them approved was the difficult part. It was as if Minister Daley was on some kind of personal mission to keep the area poor and depressed. The priest hadn't sanctioned any inventions, by anyone, ever, no matter how good or bad they were.

Samuel remembered the last time, when he thought that he'd cracked it. He'd invented something he'd named 'Permanent marker pens'. They were constructed by dipping a piece of gauze cloth in pigs blood and covering it with a wooden sheath.

He could see in the council's eyes that they liked it. They could see the possibilities. They had all grown up with chalk and black boards, so this would make life a lot easier. Samuel was already congratulating himself inside and picturing his entire family moving into the comforts of a new house on Wealth Street, when Minister Daley piped up from his throne at the back of the room.

'It looks like the love-tool of a peasant field worker,' he shouted out at the top of his voice. He then proceeded to shake uncontrollably before writing the word 'COCK' in large six inch letters on the wall with the marker pen. 'Look! it's controlled by the devil…. It's evil. It must be stopped before it covers the world in obscenities. Take it away!…. Take it away!'

The priest made a sign of the cross and dramatically dropped to his knees.

The council members all stared at the floor, unwilling to challenge his holiness on his rather biased point of view. But Samuel spoke up in defence of the innocent and rather practical writing devices.

'What do you mean?' he pleaded, 'It's not controlled by the devil… If it was it wouldn't draw this.' He sketched over the top of the profanity a small basket of flowers on a table top. He started to colour the petals in.

'That's nice,' one of the council members commented.

Minister Daley wasn't impressed. No one questioned his decisions. He snatched the device back off Samuel and yelled 'Look at it standing there, all erect with its pointed tip!' He again used the pen but this time to draw a horse with a giant erection. He yelled 'It shall be smashed up immediately!'

He didn't need to ask for consensus. Colin, Minister Daley's right hand man, snatched the rest of the markers out of poor Samuel's hands and beat them to a pulp with his lump hammer.

'Back to the old drawing board, Stubby,' Colin said mockingly as he handed a bag with the broken pen bits back to Samuel.

But today it would be different. He had a feeling in his water. As Samuel sat in the waiting room, his eyes wandered around the light coloured walls of the chapel's back room. Large portraits of past Baptist ministers of the Non-Conformist church stared coldly back at him. He stared at the solemn faces on parade. Their cold features sent shivers dancing up his spine and Goosebumps broke out over his skin. These were hard men with bellies full of fire and brimstone and not a trace of treacle to be found. Samuel wondered if Ministers were actually born or made out of lumps of granite.

'If these are Men of God... I wouldn't want to bump into the ones that work for the Devil,' he said to himself, but made sure he dismissed his thoughts quickly before they got him in trouble.

From inside the chamber, Samuel could hear the raising of voices. There was a brief silent pause before the sound of the dreaded lump hammer could be heard throughout the church as it smashed Farmer Morgan's non-stick frying pan out of shape.

The oak door was opened slowly and a very upset Farmer Morgan trudged out of the room carrying a bag with a deformed pot inside.

'Bleedin' religious nutcases!' he said to Samuel.

'What did they say this time?' asked Samuel nervously.

'That pinhead Daley said that from a distance, the pot looked too much like the backside of a dirty sinner from Aberdare….. then up marched Colin and disfigured it… and that was that!'

Despondently the farmer crept out of the room and into the drizzle. Samuel was shaking like a leaf on an autumn tree as he knocked on the large door and waited for his turn to enter.

Once inside, the room was large and overpowering. There were eight figures including Minister Daley dotted around. The Minister didn't bother to look at Samuel Crocker as the inventor sat down at the large table to face the religious panel that made up the core of the Inventor's Committee. He was nervous, he shivered under his undercoat as though he was racked with fever.

'What have you got this time for me to mash up?' Colin asked sarcastically, his fingers tightening around the handle of his beloved lump hammer.

'I've got this,' Samuel replied as he unwrapped the newspaper to reveal his latest creation. He laid it out on the table.

The first thing that struck each member of the committee was a delicious smell that wafted up from the strange items that Samuel had uncovered.

'That smells good!... What is it?' said Denzil, the oldest member of the council.

Samuel took a deep breath and announced, 'I call it a ' Fish and Potato Chip' supper. I've cooked it in warm oils.'

'Where did you get such ingredients to make such a lovely dish?' another asked, licking his lips. All their stomachs groaned with desire.

'I found the potato in the ground up by the cop-fields and I tickled the fish in the Taff yesterday morning.'

'You did what….. to a what?' Minister Daley shrieked from the back.

'I tickled a fish your holiness.'

'You tickled a fish… Are you some kind of weirdo?' Minister Daley cried, as he stared long and hard at Samuel. The inventor could feel himself turn to stone.

The Minister Daley had been aware that the practice of loving animals was rife in these parts. Sheep were favourite, but the odd mad cow had it's attractions and for some strange reason, hedgehogs coated in butter cream sauce were favoured as a special treat. He had made it his personal crusade to stamp out this kind of behaviour once and for all.

Samuel quickly changed the subject and suggested they sampled his dish. He handed it over to the council officers. They stared at it for a few seconds. One man prodded it and poked it. Finally with the smell driving them wild, they threw caution straight to the wind and took a taste. It was lovely, the best thing that any of them had ever tasted. They started to devour the appetising meal as if they hadn't had food for a month of Sundays.

A loud cough stopped the feast from gathering momentum. The cough of course belonged to the bigot, the one and only Minister Daley. He motioned with his long bony finger to Colin to bring him the food. Colin quickly took the fish and potato chip supper and placed it on the lap of the Minister.

They all watched as he placed a chip in his mouth. Samuel could see by the expression on his face that he thought it was nice. Next he sampled what was left of the fish. Again, his face gave away his thoughts.

'At last!' thought Samuel, 'something he likes.'

'At last!' thought the board of council.

Many of the council members had began to think that, for some reason, Minister Daley didn't want any of the inventions to be accepted. Over the years he had rejected all of them put in front of him. They all recalled, with much regret, the thing that Reggie Black, the town's blacksmith, had designed and had called a 'Space Hopper'.

'What use is a space hopper?' someone asked Reggie that fine bright morning.

'It's a way of transporting yourself to places without using your legs.' Reggie was so chuffed. His smile was as wide as the Taff itself, as he demonstrated it by bouncing clear across the great hall of the church and back.

'Well I'll be blown!… that's great,' one man yelled, asking could he have a go.

Members of the panel giggled while waiting in line to have a bounce on the wondrous thing. Then Minister Daley spoke. 'It looks like the deformed testicles of a sex-starved elephant,' the words spat out of his mouth.

He commanded Colin to slash the obscene orange ball with a knife, and then he sentenced poor Reggie to only eat bread and dripping for three years.

It got worse when, less than six weeks later, a man from a neighbouring village copied the design. It brought instant wealth and riches to the village. All but one in the council was gutted. Minister Daley was secretly pleased.

The man of the cloth was part of the old school of religious thinkers. He had been taught that prosperity was a one way ticket to a station called Decadence. It was a place where the preaching of God was left in the shadows as greed and false desire took control until all was destroyed. Minister Daley had a burning ambition to make Merthyr Tydfil the purest town in the land. He believed that by ridding the diseased infested, shit-hole of its evil and temptation he would protect the church and himself, from losing the stranglehold they had on the town. He was ruthless in his approach and driven by strict discipline. He believed he was destined for greatness and to spend eternity sitting at the table of the almighty.

From where Samuel was positioned it had started to look quite promising. He began to count his lucky stars. It was going to be a watershed day for the town. The day Minister Daley had finally said 'Yes.'

'I'm going to be rich,' Samuel said to himself. 'I'll open a Potato and Fish store and maybe sell deep fried rat's tails and little field mice in batter as well. Maybe I'll have a home delivery service.' His imagination reached up to the stars and was merrily jumping over the moon when he was brought back down to earth with a crash.

They were all smiling in the chamber. Minister Daley nodded his head in approval at the fish and chip potato supper and relaxed back in his chair. He thought it was rather tasty but maybe it could use a little salt.

As Minister Daley scratched his nose, everything turned a nasty shade of horrible. Suddenly his face changed. He was smelling the pungent aroma on his fingers left by the fish.

'Hang on!… what's this?' he screamed and he sniffed some more. 'This is disgusting… If I'm not mistaken… this fishy thing smells like the undercarriage of a common whore from Pontlottyn…. and those chip things look like the fingers of the devil himself who's been playing with a thousand harlots who apply their trade down by the docks of hell known as tiger bay.'

The room fell quiet as the remaining scraps of food flew across the floor.

'Fish and potato chips will never be allowed in my town… end of story. Colin get out your lump hammer.' Minister Daley turned and departed. His long cloak swooshed behind him.

Several moments later, Samuel found himself out in the high street carrying a newspaper of regurgitated mush. The rain was lashing down. He shrugged his shoulders and gave himself a rye smile as he thought what Minister Daley would have made of his other new invention, a bag of snacks that could be eaten between meals, called 'Scampi Fanny Fries.' The Minister would have had Samuel's legs chopped off and the rest of him deported to Abergavenny.

Samuel threw the rejected mess into the street next to the non-stick pan. He began his trek home to tell the kids the bad news that he was giving inventing up for good.

During his journey he bumped into a young man called Dic Penderyn.

'Where are you off to Dic?' Samuel asked.

'I'm off to see Minister Daley and the council.' He had a wide smile on his smug face. 'I've just invented this.' He showed Samuel a long glass filled with sand and sealed at both ends.

'That looks good…. What does it do?'

'It's an egg timer. If you turn it and wait for the sand to flow to the other end, you can make the perfect egg. It's a certain hit. The council will definitely pass this… definitely.' He was so pleased; he felt like a schoolboy who had just received his first gold star.

'I wouldn't bank on it, the Minister's in a very bad mood.' Samuel didn't really want to throw cold water onto Dic's fire, but he thought it was his duty to maybe damp him down a little, before he got soaked to the skin by Minister Daley.

'Well if he does reject it…. there will be a bloody riot,' Dic stated and marched purposely off in the direction of the church.

It had already been a long day and it was only noon as Samuel entered South Street. He saw a crowd gathering at the top. He stopped to see what was going on. He pushed in amongst the circle of people and saw a thick-set youth facing Georgie Onions, the town's hobo. Then, without warning, the young man took a running jump and kicked poor Georgie straight in his love sack. Samuel winced; Georgie flew three feet in the air and then hit the ground, poleaxed. He was writhing around in agony. The young thug then paid the hobo for the pleasure by popping half a carrot into the poor man's mouth before walking away. The crowd dispersed laughing.

'There's got to be an easier and safer way of earning a living,' Samuel said to himself as he reached down to help poor Georgie up from the dusty road side. 'Maybe I could design some kind of box to protect him.' He rushed home to start sketching his idea.

All Roads Lead To Merthyr

'Punch-Drunk'

Mario Basini

The woman's bellowing laugh riveted Geraint Gower. She was gazing into the eyes of a youth half her age, his jet-black hair thickly brilliantined, his earrings glinting dully in the lemon-yellow light.

Her red hair spiralled in a narrow flame from her coarsening features. Her heavily lipsticked mouth gaped as she drew deeply on her cigarette. She was listening as if every word from her companion was a gem of wisdom or wit. She laughed again and sank back, her thickening body spreading like a stain into the imitation red velvet of the bench seat.

The boxer's misshapen knuckles tightened around his glass as he watched her from his seat in a far corner of the crowded bar. She smiled at the youth invitingly, her legs parting against the constraint of her tight black skirt. She leaned forward to whisper something in his ear. She giggled and placed a hand behind the young man's head drawing him to her.

'Ave a drink with me then, champ?'

Gower looked up. A tall man, his powerful body still evident beneath the layers of fat, rocked unsteadily on his feet, his round face collapsed into a crooked grin. His massive fist offered a handshake. The action threatened to unbalance him, bringing his huge frame crashing on to Gower. The stranger paused and straightened like a pilot pulling out of a nose-dive.

Gower grinned and patted his midriff.

'No thanks. Got to watch my weight. In training, see.'

'C'me on, have a pint with me.'

'No. Thanks anyway.'

The drunk bent and thrust his face into Gower's. The folds of skin quivered with anger.

'Wassematter with me then? Not good enough to buy you a drink? Too high and fucking mighty to have a glass with a fan these days, are 'ew?'

Gower gazed steadily into the man's face now contorted with anger.

'Look, I'm here for a quiet drink, no trouble.'

Out of the corner of his eye Gower saw the woman stand up. She glanced towards the drunk's voice. Gower turned away. He looked back as she was turning to leave, the youth close on her heels.

The boxer winced as his antagonist thrust his face closer. The drunk's breath was putrid with rotting teeth and stale beer.

'I just wanted you to have a drink with me, that's all. But not high and fucking mighty Geraint Gower, world fucking boxing champion. Bloody 'as been more like.'

The man straightened and raised a fist. The boxer half rose to parry the blow. A hand snaked out from behind the drunk to grab his arm and swung him round. The drunk bellowed with anger and groped for his attacker. The man, short, square-shouldered, his large head topped by a mass of wiry black hair, thrust a hand into his chest above the huge belly. The drunk staggered back before collapsing into a bench seat. A shock rippled through the bar.

The short man hooked a thumb towards the door.

'Now bugger off.'

The drunk, whimpering, pulled himself to his feet and staggered away. Gower's rescuer turned to the boxer and grinned.

'I see they got the committee out to give you a proper welcome home, Geraint boy!'

Gower laughed and stood to shake the hand extended to him. Carl Ryder sat down heavily in the chair next to the boxer's, unbuttoning his jacket. His stomach spread gratefully over the waistband of his trousers. The barman hurried across to them.

'Sorry about the disturbance, Mr Ryder.'

He oozed deference to the man who owned the bar and much of the town. Ryder dismissed the apology with a wave of his hand. He turned to Gower.

'What can I get you?'

'Tonic water. No ice.'

'And a large gin and tonic for me.'

The barman backed away, smiling. Ryder gazed at Gower, his small eyes softening into affection.

'Great to have you home where you belong.'

'Having a world champion like you around will de the town a power of good.'

'Ex -champion,' Gower muttered.

'It's been five years since I held the title.'

Ryder laid a hand on his arm.

'You'll always be the champion here. The town's so proud that you left a great career to come back to us.'

Gower smiled. Great career? Once, maybe. Before the strength and speed had gone out of his legs and his arms had become as supple as perished rubber, before he had been reduced to fighting no-hopers in bottom-of-the bill bouts for money that could not keep his wife in cosmetics.

'That's why we wanted to give you a civic dinner. It's all arranged. Leisure centre, next month. That's what I came to tell you.'

'Thanks.'

A look of distaste drifted across Ryder's face.

'And Bernice? Will she be there?'

Gower laughed.

'Of course. She's my wife.'

Ryder took another drink. 'I thought she might be with you tonight.'

Gower looked across to where a few minutes earlier his wife had been making love to the youth.

'She had to go and see a friend who wanted her help. Something about a brother in trouble with drugs, I think.'

Ryder laughed.

'Bernice Roberts, a social worker!'

'She's just trying to help'

Ryder's lizard-quick eyes clouded with contempt. He knew all about Gower's marital troubles. Who didn't? The businessman finished his drink and turned to shake Gower's hand.

'Got to go, boy. Lovely to see you home. Anything you want, ask the barman to put it on my bill.'

Watching the figure weave and sway and punch across the huge screen dominating the far wall Bernice Gower felt as if she was watching the child she never had. The eager, dancing Geraint Gower choreographed pure ambition, the innocence of the undefeated.

She glanced down the long table to where her husband sat four places away, his shoulders hunched, the handsome face puffed and swollen with scar tissue, morosely tinkling a spoon against his unused wineglass.

She stiffened as she felt a hand clammy against the small of her bare back. She turned to see Benny Benjamin, Geraint's manager, looming over her, his eyes devouring the swell of her breasts against the cut of her red gown.

His tongue moistened his lips and his mouth parted into a grin. He pulled at his cigar and billowed smoke over her.

'Good night, eh Bernice?'

'Yes, Benny. Lovely.'

'Our boy deserves every moment of it. What a tribute to a great career.'

His hand moved caressingly across her bare back and down the side of her arm absent- mindedly, a gesture of ownership. Her skin prickled. Once, that reaction would have been accompanied by a frisson of fear.

'Looking good, aint he?'

She nodded.

'I told him he was givin' up the game too early. Still a lot of money to be made in the ring.'

'It's what he wants.'

'It's his decision,' Benjamin sighed.

He bent towards her, his eyes licking her.

'Maybe we'll catch each other later,' he whispered.

She watched him weave through the crowd almost overbalanced by the weight of his stomach to the table at which his cronies sat: Crowe, the thin-featured trainer; Flynn, Benjamin's heavily-joweled assistant; the baby-faced journalist Jarman who churned out publicity stories for the manager.

Her eyes turned as if magnetised by the intensity of Carl Ryder's gaze. The businessman sat on the far side of Geraint. She remembered that devouring look from when they were kids together. 'There is nothing in this world I cannot own,' it said then, as it did now. To her surprise, he broke into a smile.

He gave an imperceptible nod to the dance floor, a half circle radiating from the dais at the side of the hall. She got up and followed him. As she moved into his arms, she felt his hand, firm as steel, clamp her naked back.

Geraint Gower braced himself. The councillor, a garrulous man who had already monopolised one conversation with him, was heading for him once more. Gower wondered whether he had time to escape. Too late.

'Fantastic night, Geraint boy. Just shows what this town thinks of you'

He sat next to Gower.

'That fight with the black boy – what was his name? – Moses, Ernie Moses, 'Go down Moses', they called him. That was your hardest in my opinion……..'

Gower relegated the voice to background noise. He looked around the huge hall which formed the heart of the town's leisure centre. The impatient silence that had accompanied the dreary formalities had shattered into an incessant chatter.

He glanced across to the crowded dance floor and suppressed a giggle. Ryder, short, square shouldered, moved with his wife around the crowded space with the bluntness of an army assault. Bernice, taller and trim-looking in the flow of her scarlet evening gown, resisted by surrounding him, enveloping him in her embrace. As he studied her a sob died in Gower's throat. She was still beautiful. Her red hair cascaded around her shoulders, gathering the hall's harsh light and softening it. Her green eyes glowed within its flame.

He was glad to see them together. He owed Ryder. He had been drowning in a mire of badly paid bouts against poor opponents when the businessman had thrown him a lifeline, an offer of a job working in publicity in his property and construction business.

He turned back to the councillor, still droning into his right ear and nodded his agreement.

'You're looking radiant tonight, Bernice, a credit to the occasion.'

Ryder's hand guided firmly into the leaden beat of the band.

'Wonderful evening for Geraint,' he continued.

'He's come along way since we were kids together.'

'So have we all.'

'We didn't all become world champions.'

'He paid his price. We both did.'

'You've had to put up with a lot. It couldn't have been easy coping with the morons you get in boxing. Not much place for a woman in all that sweat and baying for blood.'

He broke into a precise imitation of Benny Benjamin's flat London vowels. 'Boxers' wives, who needs 'em? Only thing they're good for is a quick bang in the back of the motor.'

His black eyes bubbled with laughter. She joined in.

'Not many women would have sacrificed so much for her husband's career.'

'I did what I could.'

He stopped dancing. His eyes swallowed her.

'I'm your future now.'

'And we're grateful.'

She could feel the hand tighten on her back and her skin prickled.

Gower pushed his chair away and got up to leave. His ear ached with the drone of the councillor's voice.

'Excuse me. Call of nature.'

He walked through the echoing hall. The soundless television clips of his world championship fight looped endlessly across the huge wall screen. He glanced at the dance floor crowded with couples. They did not include Ryder and Bernice. He pushed through the swing doors leading to the toilets. He entered a narrow concrete corridor and turned right into the men's lavatory. He relieved himself and washed his hands. He walked to the mirror and passed a comb through his close-cropped blond hair.

He walked out of the lavatory and into the corridor dotted with a series of doors marked private. He realised he should have turned left. He turned and was about to retrace his steps when he heard noises coming from the room on his right. They were unmistakable, the grunts of sexual excitement and the short, sharp cries of orgasm. He opened the door.

A pair of trousers down around the ankles. A shirt-tailed backside pistoning in and out between the gaping white thighs bent over the table. He recognised the flow of red hair covering the face, the forearms laid flat on the table to support her.

Gower's head exploded with the pain of a blow harder than any he had taken in the ring. He pulled the rutting man away from his wife. Chris Ryder's startled face crumpled into shock. He staggered away and stumbled over the trousers shackling his ankles.

Gower hit him hard in his soft belly. Ryder grunted and doubled over. The boxer hit him again on the side of the jaw and winced with the pain shuddering through his unprotected hand. Ryder moaned. Gower hit him again and again, to the ribs, to the face, to the body. The adrenaline roared in his ears. Above it, he could hear the crowd baying for blood.

'Kill him. Kill him. Kill him!'

Ryder moaned and crumpled on the floor, blood flowing down his face. Gower bent to continue his beating.

'Geraint stop. Please don't.'

The voice was faint, almost a whisper. Gower ignored it and rained more blows on to the prostrate figure in front of him. A hand grabbed him by the arm and tried to pull him away. He shrugged it off, turned and looked up.

Her mascara tears streaked her face. Her green eyes pleaded.

'Don't hit him anymore. It's me you want to hurt.'

He raised a fist as if he was about to smash it into her face. Then he dropped it and turned stumbling through the door.

'A whisky, double.'

The barmaid looked at him hard before turning to serve him. He looked into the mirror behind her as she put the glass to the whisky optic. The shirt was blood-spattered shirt, the collar open, the bow tie askew.

He swallowed the drink down and ordered another. And another. He offered his glass for one more. The barmaid refused. She was right. He was drunk, as much with emotion as much as alcohol. He slipped off the stool and left. He turned into the street and headed in the direction of the flat he and Bernice had rented.

The street climbed towards the oasis of light thrown out by the lamps and traffic signals of a complex road intersection. Opposite, darkness shrouded the entrance of the side road leading to his flat. A horn blared as he stepped into the road and into the path of a car. He ignored it and headed for the flat.

The darkness engulfed him. Something thudded into his back. He staggered and fell. A figure hurried past him, then stopped and turned. A boot snaked out to catch Gower in the ribs. He moaned. A second figure appeared, a third, a fourth. Kicks rained into him.

He put up his hands to protect his face. He caught a boot and twisted. The figure fell to the floor with a grunt. Gower pulled himself to his feet and set his fists into the boxer's guard.

'Come on, you bastards. Come on.'

They hesitated then advanced. Gower's hands pumped out. A right hook. A left cross. An uppercut. He winced as each blow struck home, the pain shooting through his unprotected hands.

An attacker fell to the ground, moaning. Another sank to his knees. Gower's fists pistoned in and out. The adrenaline pumped. The crowd roared. He had never felt as alive. His senses, as alert as radar, absorbed each sound, each smell.

Someone tripped him from behind and he fell once more. His spine jarred against the tarmac. He looked up into the silhouettes emerging from the pools of streetlight. Boots found his face, hammered into his ribs, caught him flush in his mouth. He tried to struggle to his feet. This time he could only pull himself to his knees. He could taste the blood in his mouth. A fist caught him on his nose. He shook his head. Another followed into his face and another. His head sank on to the tarmac. A figure knelt to whisper in his ear.

'A present from Carl, Geraint boy.'

The crowd roared, 'Gow-er, Gow-er! Gow-er!' as he sank into unconsciousness.

She walked up the hill towards the flat, the skirt of her long dress trailing in the dirt of the pavement. She shivered against the cold night air, drawing the upturned collar of he coat more closely around her face. She felt empty. She was so tired she felt herself staggering off a straight line. She if wondered if Geraint would be home. Probably not. He would be in a pub somewhere, drowning in a sea of whisky. It was a pattern she was familiar with. Fool! He was such a fool to react like that.

She crossed the floodlit crossroads with its tangle of traffic lights and into the side road leading to the flat. It was shrouded in darkness. She froze as she heard a sound like a child whimpering. She looked around. Nothing. She moved on. Again a moan, this time louder. She stopped and peered at the bushes lining the road. She heard it again. She walked to where she thought it was coming from. The spot was faintly lit by the light coming from the window of a house which backed on to the bushes. She saw the jacket, crumpled and dirty, half hidden in the bushes. Beyond she saw a body lying in foetal position beneath a tangle of branches and leaves. She parted them and stepped into the space she had created above the still-breathing figure. She bent to examine the body, gently turning the face to her own.

'Geraint,' she whimpered and fell to he knees next to him. She lifted his bloodied head and cradled it in her lap. His eyes were pins buried in the monstrous black and red swelling that was now his face. She felt the familiar pain of nights spent waiting to hear whether he would be coming home or whether she would have to go to the hospital or worse.

Her tears mingled with his blood. 'It's all right, my love. I'm here. I'll look after you now.'

'The Last Waltz
(Or 'I'm Not Strictly A Come Dancing Celebrity
...But Get Me Out of Here!')'

Martyn Williams

Dancing 'The Last Waltz' with my mother at weddings became something of a family tradition. We were a partnership of compromise, thrown together by the synchronicity of two facts. The first was that whenever the disco started my mother and father always performed the same polished routine. They would rise from their seats in perfect step. She would head straight for the music on the dance-floor. He would head straight for the beer at the bar. Once she arrived at her destination, her feet never stopped. Once he arrived at his, his feet never moved; hands that had long ago held her now content with holding a pint. I always imagined they had some unspoken agreement: he gave up his dancing energy to her and in return she gave up her drinking capacity to him, an arrangement that suited them both. And at the end of the night, they'd meet and go home together, partners again.

Having inherited neither my mother's twinkling-toes nor my father's beer-belly, I couldn't understand either form of social behaviour. As a matter of fact, I have trouble understanding *any* form of social behaviour, which brings me neatly to …

The second fact was my chronic failure regarding the female sex. I have given the matter considerable thought over the years; it is, after all, the sort of failing that leaves you with a lot of time on your hands. And I have gotten to the root of the problem: too much Subbuteo in my youth. Yes, there were other factors (too numerous to mention here without going way over length, though soon to be available in a three volume edition: *My Failure With The Opposite Sex*, *My Failure With The Same Sex* and *Let's Face It, My Failure With Any Kind Of Sex!*). But my table, or more often floor, football obsession was without doubt the major one. Looking back at the league formed by myself and several school-friends provided the most damning evidence of this. Taking the final league positions (showing me on top, triumphant, of course) and reversing them transformed it into a frighteningly accurate table of our success with girls (showing me at the bottom, relegated, of course). It never occurred to me that while I was practicing flicking a ball around a four-man wall, my opponents were putting their fingers to equally skilful, but more intimate, uses.

By the time we moved from County Grammar to Pen Y Dre High, I was already a lost cause. Even though our group had progressed from childish players of Subbuteo to adolescent players of music (with my oh-so-delicate flicking mutating into not-so-delicate drumming), my lifestyle was not so much sex, drugs and rock'n'roll as celibacy, sherbet lemons and rock'n'roll (mind you, those sherbet lemons did have a heck of a kick).

My romantic shortcomings are best illustrated by the following example. When I asked one girl out, she didn't say 'Yes' (naturally). She didn't even say 'No' (surprisingly). Her much more disturbing reply was 'Why?' (embarrassingly). It was as if she didn't see me as a member of the opposite sex at all, but as a member of an entirely different species – like a slug asking a cat on a date (and if that statement upsets any slugs who are reading this, then you know how I felt when she said 'Why?'). Those three letters express the extent of my hopelessness with females far better than any lengthy explanation. So, we have reached our own unspoken agreement – I don't bother them, and they don't bother me. Which is why I always ended up dancing 'The Last Waltz' with my mother at weddings. She ignored by her husband, and me ignored by the entire female half of the guest list.

My mother's family split neatly into two halves: herself and two brothers in Merthyr, and two sisters and a third brother in London. During the Seventies and Eighties there seemed to be an almost continual procession of weddings as their various sons and daughters came of age and found partners (non-Subbuteo-playing partners, obviously).

These celebratory occasions were more akin to military operations. Highly organised logistical support was required to handle the invasion forces of regiments of relatives convoying up and down the M4; the stockpiling of enough provisions to last through a six month siege; and the meticulous planning of sleeping arrangements. Down to the last duvet (somehow I always ended up on the floor).

This particular summer it was Wales' turn to play host to the London host (if you see what I mean). One of my Merthyr cousins was getting married. Younger than me, her wedding was another indication of how the dating and mating game was passing me by. When my elders were marrying, I received the usual good-natured comments from my relatives: 'It'll be your turn one day.' When my peers were marrying, they became more anxious: 'When are you going to find someone?' Now my younger cousins were marrying the remarks were becoming increasingly desperate: 'What are we going to do with you?' It was as if even my relations realised the situation was beyond my meagre capabilities and required their direct intervention. But that would have to wait. For now, my cousin had their unbridled bridal attention.

On her Big Day we, the dearly beloved, gathered in the sight of God to join together this Man (handsomely besuited in black) and this Woman (beautifully dressed in white) in the (wholly mystifying) holy mystery of matrimony. The ceremony went off very smoothly, apart from one tricky moment. When the vicar inquired if there was any just cause, a baby girl cried out. She certainly put her case loudly enough, but it was ignored as nobody could interpret the precise meaning of her protest (something along the lines of 'Wah! Wah! Wah!'). Besides, the baby was a *girl*, and the vicar had quite clearly stated if any *man* can show any just cause, which disqualified her on a technicality (and if that statement upsets any baby girls who are reading this, then you know how I felt when …).

Anyway, the point is, the vows continued. The couple's entire future together (from this day forward) was reduced to just five transitive verbs (take, have, hold, love, cherish) and three pairs of opposites (better/worse, richer/poorer, sickness/health), all rounded off with a chilling reminder of their mortality (till death us do part). The vicar next issued a threat: Those whom God hath joined together let no man put asunder (which presumably meant that *women* were allowed to put asunder till the cows came home, and maybe even after that). Then came the bit involving the ring (without a hobbit in sight), Man and Woman became Husband and Wife, and the bride was kissed – which was the moment everyone was waiting for as it signalled the end of the stuffy formal proceedings and the start of the fun stuff.

For those interested in the wedding's competitive team events, we won the singing (4 hymns to nil), they won the hats (17 feathers to 14), leaving the all-important decider, the drinking (for which my father had been training all year, well all life, really), still to come.

My next few hours centred around traditions that were personal rather than family ones: me failing to get my whole head into any of the photos – professional or amateur; me running the gauntlet of the receiving line leading into the reception hall, devolving with each step from urbane wit at the beginning to gibbering idiot at the end; me sitting down to the first course of carrot and coriander soup, ruing my decision not to shave off my unruly moustache and thereby condemning my light-grey suit to soon becoming my orange-spotted light-grey suit;

and me, failing to locate anything non-alcoholic for the toasts, taking baby sips of champagne, which still got me so tipsy that I laughed in all the wrong places during the speeches. Thankfully, by the time we reached the cutting of the cake, family tradition had returned, and we joined together to sing 'Me and My Girl', while the groom's family looked on in polite puzzlement.

The Wedding Ceremony and Wedding Breakfast behind us, we moved on to the final ritual of the Big Three, my least favourite – the Wedding Disco. An endless evening of people who really shouldn't be dancing, dancing to music that really shouldn't be played, played at volumes that really shouldn't be possible (and if that statement upsets any people who really shouldn't be dancing who are reading this …). Our DJ, Disco Dick, produced all the classics from his Box O'Discs (it must have been like the TARDIS in there). Everything from 'Agadoo' to 'Y Viva Espana'. Presumably there were no 'Z' songs bad enough to make it into his extensive collection, a small consolation.

I remained firmly in my seat, which proved to be an excellent observation post for studying the guests. My findings were that although it is impossible not to enjoy dancing to these songs, it is equally impossible to enjoy listening to them. I reached this conclusion by comparing the expressions of those who danced (joyous) to those who merely listened (suicidal). I would have joined the dancers to prove my theory, but I suffer from the psychological condition of chorophobia (fear of dancing) and the physiological condition of twoleftfeetitis (actually, on those rare instances I do hit the dance-floor I give the impression of somehow having more than just the two. A lot more). Anyway, my mind, body and all my feet were focussing on an altogether more important artistic endeavour.

When Disco Dick and his Box O'Discs took a much needed break (much needed by me, that is), the real entertainment began. My mother's family were born party-makers – the brothers brilliant entertainers and the sisters sensational hostesses. If they had ever joined forces they could have carved out a hospitality empire to rival Butlins at its peak, turned Merthyr into Wales' answer to Las Vegas (Llas Vegas?). Sadly for the world, the brothers became shopkeepers and the sisters, homemakers. Their true talents surfaced only occasionally, at events such as weddings.

This particular reception was treated to a rare collaboration between the brothers – The Three Bards. Sort of like The Three Tenors, but without the foreign accents, and only two of them sang, and they hadn't recorded a World Cup theme tune (okay, maybe not that much like The Three Tenors, but there were three of them). The Comic Bard, The Poetic Bard and The Romantic Bard. Featuring, for one night only, a special guest artiste: me. I had written a poem especially for the occasion (it was either that or a drum solo, and my poem fitted into my jacket pocket a little easier than my drum kit did). And I was looking forward to sharing it with the wedding party and their guests, in those odd moments when the idea of standing in front of a roomful of people wasn't making me want to throw up.

The Three Bards were an irresistible combination. The Comic Bard opened the show, engaging us with a selection of songs old and new, and gags old and older.

The Poetic Bard followed, enchanting us with rich rhymed reminiscences of his childhood, making Merthyr magical to both visitors and residents. The Romantic Bard came after him, enthralling us with passionate renditions of timeless love songs, his mellifluous voice needing no accompaniment.

After finishing his last song ('Begin The Beguine') The Romantic Bard smiled, bowed modestly and was applauded back to his seat at the table next to ours. The Three Bards having completed their spots there was only mine to come. To be honest I hadn't expected top billing in the presence of such seasoned performers. How am I going to follow that? I asked myself, a question answered by The Comic Bard – acting as MC for the show – as he announced: 'And now without further ado, as there's been quite enough ado already, back to Disco Dick and his Box O'Discs.' I wasn't going to follow that at all! Even worse, I had been usurped by Disco Dick!! Before I could so much as lodge a complaint, he had put on 'The Birdie Song' and invited everyone onto the dance-floor.

I just sat there. Mind you, this wasn't my standard I-don't-do-dancing sitting there. Oh, no. This was a special I'm-too-shocked-to-even-think-about-not-dancing sitting there. But I couldn't remain seated. I had a wrong to right. I stood, shakily, and singled out The Comic Bard on the dance-floor, determined to give him a piece of my mind (before I lost it completely).

'How could you do that?' I demanded to know, but found it difficult to maintain my outrage towards someone acting like a mad giant mutant bird. 'I was supposed to recite my poem!'

'Thank you,' he replied bizarrely, clearly mishearing me and highlighting the near impossibility of carrying on a disco conversation, especially a mobile disco conversation.

Even a social misfit like me knew that sitting, shocked, at your table during a dance is acceptable, barely, but standing, shocked, on the dance-floor during a dance is not tolerated in civilised society. So I found myself part of the dance, adding to my chagrin. My brain knew it should be reciting. My body knew it was dancing. As an inevitable result of this confusion, the signals between brain and body got crossed, all my feet got flustered and I fell over. My humiliation was complete. I had become the Fourth Bard after all – The Tragic Bard.

Unlike The Romantic Bard's earlier triumphant applause, it was laughter that accompanied me back towards my seat, my face redder than a Liverpool shirt. Unable to stand the prospect of sitting surrounded by ridicule I carried on walking, past my mother too busy Birdie-ing and my father too busy boozing to have witnessed my downfall, and out of the hall. I had to get away from Disco Dick and his Box O'Discs, The Three Bards and the rest of their co-conspirators. The legion of negative thoughts and feelings possessing me at that moment was very persuasive, convincing me the entire wedding was an elaborate hoax staged purely for my embarrassment.

Outside, I was so wrapped up in myself that I literally bumped into a female guest walking towards the reception hall. Her presence rescued me from my foul mood.

'Sorry, I didn't see you there,' I apologised.

'Are you all right? Only you were talking to yourself.'

'At least I can hear me,' I replied, glaring through the hall wall at my enemies as if I had x-ray vision.

'What?'

'Sorry, er ...' I tried to place her. She was strangely familiar and yet unfamiliar.

'I'm a bridesmaid. I just live down the road, so I went home to change.' That solved the mystery – a familiar face in unfamiliar clothes. 'Thought I'd wear something easier to dance in.'

I shuddered involuntarily at the mere mention of the d-word. Then I shuddered again as I recalled our earlier meeting. She'd been near the end of the receiving line, by which time I was just mumbling the first thing that came into my head.

'You asked me if I came here often,' The Bridesmaid reminded me.

'Sorry ... again.'

'I thought it was quite funny,' she smiled. 'Have I missed much in there?'

'My uncles. The Three Bards, as I call them.' Another smile.

'Any good?'

'Terrific. Well worth catching on the wedding video. I wouldn't be surprised if it's in the shops for Christmas.' This time, she laughed.

'So why are you out here?'

'I was just about to recite my poem when Disco Dick,' I gestured disdainfully (and obscenely) in his general direction, 'came back on instead. He stole my spot. So I came out here to ...' I wasn't sure exactly what.

'Sulk?'

Hurt by her suggestion I replied, 'No.' Sulkily. 'I wanted to make a real contribution to the day. Like being a bridesmaid.'

'I could lend you my dress if you want.'

'Peach isn't my colour.'

'Listen, this is *their* day, not yours. You're not entitled to sulk. You're meant to be happy for them.'

'And I am. I just wanted to play a bigger part.'

'Ah. You wanted to be the centre of attention.'

'No,' I protested, briefly. 'Well, yes, but only for a few minutes. I reckon I deserve that much after all I've been through. I'm a bag of nerves, hardly eaten a thing or spoken to anyone all day (although, come to think of it, that's pretty much a normal day for me). I've spent hours getting myself into a state waiting … waiting … and for what? 'And now back to Disco Dick and his Box O'Discs'!' I made another gesture. 'Suddenly I'm surplus to requirements, like the leftovers of the buffet.' I thought it a poignant analogy, deserving at least a little sympathy. The Bridesmaid didn't.

'There wasn't a buffet,' she pointed out.

'So what am I supposed to do now?' Nothing is more frustrating for a performer than expecting to and then being prevented from performing (sort of like your partner saying 'Get off!' when you want to get it on, only much worse, I imagine). I was bursting with pent-up nervous energy, aching to be released in some form.

Muffled disco music supplied the answer to my despairing question. Unfortunately, it was the wrong answer. 'You could always dance,' The Bridesmaid said, taking my hand with the clear intention of leading me back inside.

'And I could always step in front of a bus,' I replied, slipping free.

To The Bridesmaid's credit, she didn't give up on me. After a few seconds thought she provided a better solution. 'Why don't you recite your poem to me? And in return, we have a dance. One dance for one poem. Deal?' She held out her right hand to seal it.

I weighed up the pros and cons and decided that I loved performing more than I hated dancing. I shook her right hand gratefully, while my left hand nervously removed the poem from my inside breast pocket.

It was all over in a few satisfying minutes and we rejoined the reception. Any idea of me immediately completing our deal vanished as 'Y.M.C.A.' finished and Disco Dick selected 'Endless Love' from his infinite Box O'Disks. I had no intention of smooching my way through my half of the bargain, so I excused myself to the toilet – my most nimble bit of footwork all evening. The Bridesmaid's parting reminder of our contract sounded ominously like a threat to me: 'You owe me a dance.' Which had me considering spending the night in the Gents.

I was in a difficult position (no, not on the toilet). Since 'Begin The Beguine' ended I had worked myself up, been let down, nearly had a bust-up, then fallen down, picked myself up, wondering how I'd live this down, got chatted up and was now coming back down from the high of reciting my poem. A real rollercoaster ride that left me feeling exhausted and nauseous (but then so much of life does). To be honest, I hardly had enough energy to make it to my seat, let alone dance. So instead of enjoying the rest of the evening, I wasted it anxiously watching my would-be partner, wondering when she'd pounce like a praying-mantis and drag me to my dance-floor doom. However, The Bridesmaid was having too much fun with her friends, being a well-rounded human being (*very* well-rounded) rather than simply an extensive collection of fears, failings and phobias stuffed and stitched into an over-sensitive skin like me (*very* over-sensitive).

When Disco Dick finally exhorted everyone onto their feet for 'The Last Waltz' I rose, having recovered enough to fulfil my long-standing obligation with my mother, who hadn't sat down once the whole night. Before we'd taken a single step, I felt a tap on my shoulder. Twisting my neck, I saw The Bridesmaid standing behind me.

'You haven't forgotten our deal, have you?'

(And those of you who have read this far know what's coming next, don't you? All together now …) 'Sorry, I always dance 'The Last Waltz' with my mo-'

'No, it's all right. I'll find another partner,' my mother interrupted, handing me over to The Bridesmaid with a smile of betrayal.

While The Bridesmaid led me to a clear spot, my mother made a beeline for my father, excitedly drawing his attention away from his pint to the unique event unfolding (much rarer than any mere wedding). He was so stunned to see me dancing with a girl that he was powerless to prevent my mother prising him away from his safe haven. Thwarting his pathetic attempt to reach for the bar-rail by grabbing his hand, she waltzed him onto the dance-floor.

Because it was the single dance I did, 'The Last Waltz' held a deep significance for me, making it as important as a full dance-card of ordinary ones. It had an almost magical power, much greater than the sum of its words, music and movements. Did The Bridesmaid somehow feel the same way? I had to know. Ironically, my inquiries began with the very word that had haunted me for years.

'Why?'

'Why what?'

'Why 'The Last Waltz'?'

'So you couldn't say no. I figured you'd find a way to put me off if I'd asked you sooner.'

'Wow!' I nodded, impressed by her powers of deduction. 'You're probably right.'

'And after hearing your beautiful poem, I really wanted to give you this dance.' She looked straight into my eyes, and I was suddenly aware of how close we were to each other at that moment. If she hadn't been holding onto me, I reckon I'd have fallen over again right there and then; and not even have heard the laughter this time.

If a picture is worth a thousand words, how many is a poem worth? Simple – just count the words, right? Actually, it's a trick question. The number of its words is only the starting point. You have to multiply that by the value of reciting it and add the effect of hearing it to arrive at the poem's true worth. The final result is often surprising, and impossible to calculate precisely. Take my poem, for instance. I had recited its 186 words to The Bridesmaid for my own purely selfish reasons, but it had still touched her, which resulted in her now touching me. And the promise of a dance suddenly promised much, much more.

Taken aback by the intensity and intimacy of The Bridesmaid's look, I glanced away from her and across to my parents, who were staring at me. Their mouths said it all without a word: hers spread in a beam of pure pride; his open wide in absolute astonishment. Then there was a wonderful moment when, embarrassed by me looking at them looking at me, they glanced away and became aware of how close they were to each other at that moment. Bodies remembering what they had long forgotten, the years faded away with each step.

For my mother, this really was 'The Last Waltz' – she was dancing with angels before the next family wedding. But I didn't regret not dancing it with her. Far from it. By insisting that I partner her instead, The Bridesmaid gave me not only the gift of that dance but also one of my most precious abiding memories: my mother and father as I had heard about, but never seen before, or ever could again. Bodies in rhythm. Hearts in rhythm. Memories in rhythm. As Engelbert sings, 'The Last Waltz should last forever.' And in my mind it does.

What about me and The Bridesmaid I hear you ask (okay, I don't really hear you ask, but I know it's what you're thinking – okay, I don't really know it's what you're thinking, but I'll tell you anyway). It all ended in tears (mine) when she trod on my beloved league winning Liverpool Subbuteo team (I had even painted a little moustache on the Ian Rush figure). She claimed it was an accident. I didn't believe her because it was one of the few times that I was actually playing table football on a table, and she had to climb onto it to trample them!

(Oh, and by the way, the reason The Comic Bard never introduced me was simple. I was so psyched up about reciting my poem that I forgot to tell him I had a poem to recite! If I had – well, that's another story.)

All Roads Lead To Merthyr

'The Spirit'

Phillipa J Evans

It was a balmy June afternoon in 1976. The Williams family was on holiday in Scotland. The heat of that summer had not yet penetrated this far north but the summer would be memorable nevertheless. The holiday would see the first of a series of events that would remain in the family's memory without fade for a long time.

Their family home in Merthyr Tydfil was called 'Bronton'. The agent had told Maggie and Jim that it had been named after the Scottish village from where the original owner had descended. As part of their trip Jim had decided they should visit the village to see if they could find out any information about the family. Maggie had been reluctant but Jim had gone on about it so much she had conceded.

Maggie and Jim had been married for 25 years in 1976, for the most part, happily. The unexpected conception of Susan and her arrival in 1969, nine years after Ruth and eleven years after Andrew, was testament to that happiness.

Jim manoeuvred the Ford Cortina into the space. 'Why are you struggling to park here when there's all that space there?' Maggie snapped.

'The shade will keep the car cool for later.' Jim soothed. The trees brushed the top of their luggage, piled high on the roof rack. The neighbours had commented on the excessive amount of luggage. ' Moving up there are you?' Tom had laughed. This had scared Susan. She didn't want to move. She loved her home. They weren't moving but the luggage included clothes for six of them for three weeks, two sets of golf clubs, a spare artificial leg and a wheelchair for Pop, Maggie's dad, and some bedding, just in case. The car was bulging. Susan thought it an adventure to sit on the floor behind the passenger seat during the trip. She wasn't bothered that she saw little of the dramatic Scottish scenery. Three pairs of legs and a picnic basket were dramatic enough when you were only 3 feet tall.

Jim had not planned the day. It seemed that Thursday was the weekly half-day closing in Bronton. The granite village was all but deserted. There wasn't even an open shop that could sate Susan's vocal appetite for ice cream. They trundled out of the car, nevertheless, and decided to explore. 'What was his name again?' Jim managed to release the wheel chair from the clutches of the other luggage so that Pop could join them on their wanders.

'Who?' Maggie asked as she rubbed sun cream into Susan's face.

'The guy who called our house Bronton.'

'Oh. I don't know. South something?'

'That's right. Southon. Not that we'll find anything about him today. There's no one about.'

'What about looking in the church?' Ruth pointed through the wooded area beyond the car park.

'Good idea, sweetheart. The golf course is down that way too. We'll check that out son. What do you think?' But Andrew had already darted off in the direction of the church.

The 16th century Kirk was now too big to serve the small Scottish community that remained. So it did not serve as their place of worship except for particularly significant religious festivals or visits by a member of the royal family when they were in Balmoral. It was set a little away from the village in a clearing in the ancient wood, which now overlooked a golf course, which was neither royal nor ancient. The graveyard had not witnessed a burial for many years and the church had few visitors according to the book that lay open on the mahogany table set at the back. The church was pleasantly cool. 'It's smelly,' moaned Susan. It was a mixture of the dank air and cigarettes. 'Strange,' Maggie thought. 'There's no-one else around.'

'You need to speak quietly in a church Susan.' Ruth whispered.

'Why?' Susan quizzed. 'There's no one here and I want God to hear me.'

Maggie smiled 'Oh, God will hear you even if you whisper.'

Ruth took Susan's hand and led her down the aisle towards the front of the church. The otherwise dull grey church had been blessed with the most beautifully ornate altar. The golden image of Christ, arms outstretched, glistered in the light and the three arched stained glass windows were alive as the colours danced in the rays. 'That's lovely.' Susan whispered. The girls wandered around for a short while with their mother and Susan insisted on signing the visitor book on the way out.

Not really interested in interiors, Andrew had been looking at the gravestones whilst Jim was still trying to negotiate the un-maintained path with the wheelchair, the smoke from Pop's pipe wafting into his face. 'I've found it.' Andrew called suddenly. Maggie turned towards the call, adjusting her eyes in the bright sunlight after the cool darkness of the church. 'Found what?' answered Jim. Andrew was bending over a dirty marble stone, legs astride the grass patch that lay at its front so as not to walk on anyone's grave. He rubbed his finger along the faded gold lettering in an attempt to remove the many years of moss growth and gathered dirt. He read out 'Henry Southon – beloved husband of Isabella and loving son of Thomas and Esme. Born 10th April 1909, Died 26th March 1958. He died the day I was born.' As he revealed the final letters, Andrew pulled away with a start, jumped onto the path and ran from the cemetery. Everyone else just stood still with surprise for a couple of seconds and then through her nervous giggles Maggie called after Andrew 'What's the matter love?'

'He's some athlete but I've never seen him move that fast.' Jim joked. Andrew did not mention anything about it during the holiday and not for a long time after that.

The scorching summer ended and Andrew and Ruth went off to university. Susan became, to all intents and purposes, an only child. She quite liked it. But it was always good to see her older siblings. As the Christmas break approached Maggie and Jim began to look forward to the return of both their older children for the holidays and were busy preparing for the festivities. The smell of Christmas was all around. Their breath was brought to life by the cold air as Maggie and Susan walked towards Cyfarthfa Castle. It was the first week of December and there was a Christmas fete in the castle museum. It was only mid afternoon but already dusk was approaching. Susan held tightly onto Maggie's gloved hands as they walked up the long tree-lined drive to the castle. The 19th century folly was foreboding at the best of times but in this natural half light and illuminated but unnatural white flood lights it reminded Susan of the haunted houses she had seen in her books and cartoons and she was a little frightened. The only outward sign of her fear was a slight tightening of her grip around Maggie's hand. 'You Ok?' Maggie asked instinctively.

'Yes.' she said bravely. 'Will Santa Claus be there?'

'I don't think so. He's probably too busy.'

Maggie was slim and very smart. She bought most of her clothes second hand now as money was not a plenty but you could never tell. She had a penchant for hats and gloves and at the first sign of winter she had rescued her vast collection from their attic. She drew her black and orange woollen hat tightly over her head, pulled Susan a little closer and she shivered at the recollection of the day she had retrieved them. She had tried to forget it but it kept returning to her at the strangest moments. They walked silently into the museum. Maggie's mood lightened as Susan let go of her hand and bounced towards the nativity scene set up in the reception area.

Andrew was more morose than usual. He had only been home once since term began. Jim had reassured Maggie that this was because he was enjoying student life but Maggie was not so sure. She felt he did not want to come home but for now the matter was not discussed.

The Parish Church was a similar size to the church at Bronton. It had been the place where Maggie and Jim had married and the children had been christened. Saint David's Church had replaced it some years ago as the regular place of worship for the Church in Wales congregation and it was now the Chapel of Rest. It was also opened for special services and festivals. Maggie was always pleased to go back and worship there. The carol service welcomed a full church but Maggie remembered the times when she had been the only person taking holy communion at the early Sunday services. No hymns were sung at those times but tonight the programme was full of old favourites and new carols to please the mixture of believers, non believers and the undecided that filled the warm, light church. Jim sat amongst the undecided with Ruth and Susan. Andrew and Pop had decided to stay at home. Maggie was in the choir and she was very pleased to see her old friend in the congregation. Ralph was very much a believer and Maggie was going to seek his advice. After the service old friends mingled and new friends became acquainted. The young children received a Christmas gift and Maggie and a few of the other choristers checked the flowers.

'Can I write in the book Mam?' Susan questioned.

'Yes of course. Let's go and find it.' Maggie walked to the back of the church with Susan hanging on her arm. She helped Susan sign and then had a cursory glance at the other pages. The book fell open on June 26th 1976 and one particular entry stood out. Scrawled in red, it was an entry by Henry Southon, Bronton, Scotland and the comments read, 'It feels like coming home.' Maggie slammed the book closed, not really comprehending what she had seen. It simply couldn't be true.

'What's the matter boy?' Pop had asked Andrew after the rest of the family had left for the service. Andrew had never been able to hide much from his grandfather but Pop knew he wouldn't tell him anything if the others were around. So he took this opportunity. Andrew had sat down on the floor in front of the man he loved with all his heart. He looked into the pale eyes set back in the weathered face. It was a face shaped and worn by the experiences of 76 years.

'I think I'm being contacted from the other side, Gramps.' Pop stifled a laugh. This was obviously worrying the boy and he did not want him to feel he wouldn't take him seriously. Pop had long known that the house that they had moved to over fifteen years ago was haunted. He had always been susceptible to the spirits and in fact welcomed the distractions they caused. He especially liked it when his Sarah visited. 'Is it your grandmother?' Andrew looked astonished that his grandfather was being so cool, but it seemed to calm him a little.

'No Gramps. I think it's the man who used to live here.'

'What makes you think that?' Pop looked puzzled.

'Well, it started when we were in Scotland in the summer. Do you remember the cemetery in Bronton?'

'Of course.'

'Well when I was looking at the gravestone…. well it moved.' Andrew's voice shook.

'Well it had been there since 1958. Gravestones do tend to move. Your grandmother's always moves when I'm putting flowers on it.'

'But no Gramps. It was solid as a rock. I fell against it before I looked at it properly and it didn't move at all. Do you believe in ghosts?'

'Depends what you mean by ghosts.' Pop moved his leg from side to side in perfect rhythm.

'You know, spirits, dead people coming back to haunt us.'

'I definitely believe in spirits but I don't like the word haunt. Your grandmother's spirit visits me often but that's not haunting. Haunting seems to imply badness but I only know of good spirits.' Pop paused. 'I don't believe those who say they've seen ghosts. You've never seen anything have you lad?'

'No no. Just felt something I suppose. A presence. It's hard to explain.'

'So you think it's Henry Southon? He must still be troubled.'

Andrew, startled, looked at Pop, with a worried expression. 'What do you mean?' The door to the living room flew open. Susan launched herself into Andrew's arms. 'Look what I've got!' Susan brandished a half wrapped present. The Christmas paper was falling off where she had excitedly ripped it, revealing a book of carols. 'Mam's brought an old friend home. He's a vicar.' The rest of the family were close behind Susan, still wrapped against the bitter air that had, for a second or two, followed them into the room. Andrew shivered.

'Pop, you remember Ralph?' Maggie led Ralph to a fireside seat.

'I do indeed'. Pop stood quickly and swapped his stick to the other hand so that he could greet Ralph with a firm handshake. 'What a nice surprise?'

'Who wants tea?' Maggie removed her hat and gloves.

'Or would you prefer something stronger Ralph?' She disappeared into the kitchen and started to prepare the pot of tea and the Scotch for Ralph and Jim. Ruth helped her mother, cutting the fruit cake that Maggie had made for 'just such an occasion'.

'Did you enjoy the carol service?'

'Yes, lovely. I liked those modern carols. Shame Gramps and Andrew weren't there.'

'Yes. Is Andrew OK? He seems a bit miserable. Has he mentioned anything to you?'

'No. He rarely talks to me. He's always miserable.' Ruth poured the tea.

'I'll ask your dad to speak to him. Take these to Ralph and dad.'

The room was cosy with family warmth. Even Andrew had stayed to chat although his thoughts remained on the earlier unfinished conversation. After a couple of hours, Ralph bade his farewells. 'I'll walk you to the car.' Maggie offered. Ralph agreed so that he could talk to her alone. He helped her on with her coat and as they walked along the path that ran between the bay window and the sloped lawn he took her arm. 'You're very fortunate to have such a close family and such a lovely house. You always wanted to live in one of these houses didn't you?'

Maggie recalled the long summer days when she and Ralph would play tennis in Thomastown Park and sit and talk for hours. She would say 'I'm going to live in one of those houses over there.' pointing at the 6 large semi-detached Victorian houses that overlooked the tennis courts. And so when 'Bronton' had come up for sale 10 years after they were married she had begged Jim to let them buy it. By scrimping and saving and with help from Pop they had just about managed it.

'What's wrong Maggie?' Ralph referred to her current worried expression but also to her earlier quietness. She had changed little in the passing years and he knew her quite well.

'I can't live here anymore.'
He pulled her closer. 'What do you mean? Is it Jim?' Ralph secretly hoped.

'No, no.' Maggie insisted, pulling away slightly. Ralph was tall and his greying hair and age lines had only enhanced his good looks but the love he felt for Maggie was not reciprocated. She loved him as the brother she had never had.

'What then?'
She took his hand. 'I feel so stupid.'
'Tell me.' He pleaded.
'I think… I think the house is haunted. I'm scared.'
'Haunted? Why do you think that?'
'It's Harry.'
'Oh,' He wrapped his arms around her. 'Does Jim know?'

Maggie knew what Ralph was asking her. The answer was no, on both counts. There was much that Jim did not know but it had not worried Maggie until now and it seemed to concern Jim even less. His philosophy was 'live for today'. He had fallen in love and was still in love with Maggie and he was happy.

'You have to tell him.' Ralph said as he got into the car. 'You have to.'

Maggie laid awake, Jim's normal comforting presence just a snoring irritant lying next to her. She remembered the day she had met Harry. It was just before her 17th birthday in the milliners on the high street where she worked. He had walked in nervously. She had been immediately attracted to his smart dove grey flannel suit and the way he had removed his trilby when he walked through the door. He was a little older than her she had thought. He was looking for a hat for his mother. He seemed to relax a little once she started to help him but he did not buy anything that day. She was pleased as she thought this meant he might come back. He did, several times that week, eventually buying a bottle green felt hat and matching gloves and stealing Maggie's heart. They had gone for coffee in the Italian cafe near the shop. He smoked John Players. She had asked to try one and she could hear his response right now 'Absolutely not.' He'd insisted. 'These are not for girls.' She smiled now as she had then, seeing his face as clearly as if it was yesterday. His name was Henry Southon. Or Harry as she had always called him. She knew Harry's family would think him 'out of her league' but inside she had hoped that she could win them round and make them accept her for what she was, a bright, intelligent girl who loved Harry. She never got that opportunity.

There was a sudden crash downstairs. She sat upright. Jim snored on. She wrapped her dressing gown around her and crept downstairs. 'Oh' she cried in fright. Andrew was already down there. 'You scared me. What happened?'

'Don't know. You heard something too?'

'Yes. It sounded like glass breaking.'

The door of the front room was open. They walked in and Andrew put on the light.

'Andrew what's going on? What have you been doing?' Maggie walked towards the marble hearth. There were pieces of aqua blue glass scattered all over it. 'My vase.' she sighed. She bent towards it pulling her hair off her face.

'Mam, what d'you mean? I haven't done anything.'

'Have you been smoking in here? It smells.'

'Mam, no. I just heard the glass like you and I came down.' Andrew defended himself adamantly. He bent beside her and started to pick up the pieces. He knew it to be his mother's favourite vase but it was way beyond repair. 'How did it happen?'

'I don't know. Sorry I jumped to conclusions. You get to bed. I'll clear this up.'

Andrew wanted to stay and talk and Maggie wanted him to but neither said anything except a cursory good night. Maggie cleared the remains of the delicate vase that Harry had given her on her 17th birthday and she went to bed.

Jim disturbed her fitful sleep further when he brought the morning cuppa. He was oblivious to the night's events and she didn't enlighten him. However, she knew the time was close when she would have to reveal all.

Andrew spent the following afternoon in the public library. He had happy childhood memories of Saturday mornings browsing through the endless shelves in the children's corner and then as he got older reading similar books to Jim. Never happier than when he had his head in a book, Andrew was always coming up with some unusual historical, geographical or scientific fact. He had not changed but that day's visit was not really for pleasure. The library was beautiful. Standing in the centre of High Street since 1936, it dominated that part of town with its 13 sets of leaded windows and the grand stone steps leading to the glass and oak rotating doors. Andrew pushed his way through the heavy doors and turned immediately right up the stairs to the reference library. He stopped at the entrance and realised he did not really know what he was looking for. He felt a little stupid but went in nevertheless.

'Hello Andrew. How are you? How is University?' His old history teacher stood before him. Andrew's heart sank. He was never very sociable especially with his teachers and he really didn't want to discuss why he was there.

'Good, thank you. How are you? Do you work here now?'

'Just a little part time job to keep me out of mischief in my retirement. Call me if you need any help. I'll be in the office.'

Relieved, Andrew sat down and gathered his thoughts. He wanted to find any information he could about Henry Southon. He only had an hour. He was meeting Gramps for coffee before he went to his regular Wednesday matinee. He hoped they would finish their conversation.

'What have you been up to?' Pop asked as Andrew put a milky coffee in front of him and gave him his change.

'I've been to the library. Looking up Henry Southon'.

'Have you? Find anything?' Pop lit his pipe, taking in the air in great big gasps of breath.

'Some stuff. Not much. He was the son of Thomas Southon who was a local businessman.'

'That's right.' Pop interjected. 'Scottish. Owned the newspaper business round here.'

'You know this. Why didn't you tell me?'

'Didn't really get a chance did I?'

'What else do you know about him? Tell me.'

For the next fifteen minutes or so Pop told Andrew everything, well almost everything he knew. Intrigued, Andrew asked lots of questions. ' So who was the girl?' he asked finally. 'Did Henry ever come back?'

'I don't know who she was. Not sure if he ever came back. Son, I have to go. I'll miss the start of the film.'

'So do you think it might be him? Why would he contact **me**?' Andrew continued as they left the café.

'I don't know. But if he is I don't think you need to be scared about it.'

A little reassured, Andrew changed the subject as they walked down High Street and turned left towards the Scala cinema 'What are you going to see?'

'It's called Jaws. Roy Scheider and Richard Dreyfuss.'

'Oh yes. A Spielberg film. It's supposed to be really good.'

'Can I meet you from work Jim?' Maggie had not met Jim from work for as long as he could remember, probably not since before Andrew was born.

'What's up?'

'Oh nothing. Just thought it would be good to meet for a coffee.' She lied.

'OK. I'll finish a bit earlier. Be outside at 4.30pm.' He kissed her at the door as always, but held her for a little longer. 'Are you sure you're OK?' She smiled a weak smile.' See you later.' All day Maggie fretted. She snapped at everyone and couldn't concentrate for more than a few minutes at a time. Jim fretted all day too. What did his wife of 25 years want to talk to him about? 'Ridiculous.' he thought, but it was true. May be he didn't know her that well after all. At 4.15pm Maggie was sitting on the bench outside the library talking to the statue of Lord Buckland that stood proudly in the courtyard at the front. She had done this in times of trouble or confusion since she was a teenager. It was a strange, very public place to come when you needed to clarify your thoughts but it always seemed to work. Always that is until that day. Her mind was still a melee when she got up to walk to the Tax Office where Jim worked. The tax office in contrast to the elegant library was, some thought, Maggie included, an architectural abomination, a bland 1960s built structure with as little character as a blank piece of paper. Maggie was not thinking about the merits of Merthyr architecture as she waited for Jim but whether, when she went home that night, she would have a marriage. Jim bounced down the steps trying to hide his worry at 4.29pm, reliable as ever. It was already dark but Maggie suggested they walk a while before they went for a coffee. 'Kids OK?' Jim asked.

'Fine. Andrew's still miserable though. I think he met Pop for a coffee today and went to the library. Ruth's doing some of her University work and Susan's as happy as always. She made Christmas cards in school.' The small talk continued for as long as Jim could stand it, which was not very long. 'Maggie you haven't met me from work for a very long time and I don' think it was to talk about the children.'

Maggie took a deep breath, let go of Jim's arm and walked towards a bench that stood close by. The river flowed in front of them as cold as her thoughts but she knew the time had come. Jim sat beside her trying to imagine what she might want to say. In their 28 years together they had always talked openly about any problems but there had been few as far as he could remember. They were a good team, sharing most things since they had been together.

'Are you having an affair?' He blurted suddenly in an attempt to make things easier for her.

'No.' she said quietly but finding an inner sense of calm she continued, 'I did. Many years ago.'

Jim said nothing. He sat there and just listened. He was always a good listener but now Maggie wished he would interject now and then, so she knew he understood what she was telling him. Of course, he understood in literal terms what she was saying but could not comprehend why she had done it. Reading his mind as she often did she said 'I expect you're wondering why I'm telling you this now.' He still said nothing. He stared straight ahead not moving, not touching her. She felt more distant from him than at any point before and yet she wanted him to stay as close as he was.

'He's come back again.'

'I thought he was dead.' Jim suddenly responded.

'He is. But he's haunting the house. He's in Bronton.'

'For God's sake Maggie.' Jim stood up 'No - you're right. He **is** in Bronton. He's six feet under in Bronton. We saw the grave.' Jim's voice got louder until he was almost shouting. He walked away and then stopped, turned and looked at her. Now quietly he said, 'Is he Andrew's father?'

Maggie stopped exhaling. She turned her head away, and screwed up her eyes to stop the tears. 'No. No. You are Andrew's dad. Always will be.' She realised what she had said. 'He has your eyes.' she called feebly trying to recover the situation, but Jim had already turned and walked away. The truth was that Maggie did not know for sure who had fathered Andrew but it seemed unlikely and would have been very unlucky that after just one last night with Harry when he had returned out of the blue in 1957 that Andrew would have been conceived. But she could not be sure. In many ways Andrew was like Harry, nervous, shy and moody but in other ways he was like Jim, patient, caring and kind. She wanted him to be Jim's son because whilst Harry had been her first love Jim was the love of her life. She realised she had omitted to tell him that. Now he was not there and she did not know if he ever would be. Maggie sat for a while until she realised she was stiff with cold. She looked at the watch Jim had given her for their silver wedding. It had stopped at 4.30pm. She got up and started to walk back towards the High Street. May be there was a bus she could catch. It was too cold to walk. She caught the 7.10pm, which took her the long way around Twynyrodyn and Vernon Close eventually dropping her at 7.30pm. The lights of 'Bronton' beckoned but she dreaded going in. She wondered if Jim was there. She wondered if Harry was there. Neither was. Ruth and Susan were preparing supper and Andrew and Pop were in the lounge. Ralph was with them. 'Just because I'm a vicar it doesn't mean I'm qualified to talk about this kind of thing.' Maggie heard him speak as she hovered by the door. She composed herself. The room was dimly lit and the glow of the fire illuminated the faces of her father, her son and her holy friend and she felt better suddenly. Ralph rose to greet her noticing how pale she was. 'You're freezing. Get by the fire.'

'Where've you been Mam? We were worried.'

'Sorry love. Just a few things to sort out.'

'Is Dad with you?'

'No. He's working late. How are you Ralph? What brings you here?'

'Sit down Maggie.' Pop said softly. 'I asked Ralph to come over. We need to talk to you. Andrew you start. Tell your mother what's been going on.'

'You OK love?' Maggie asked worriedly.

'Yes Mam. Just listen for a minute.'

Listening had never been one of Maggie's strong points but for once she just sat there, too cold and tired to do much else. After a while Andrew paused and she moved forward in the chair. 'So since Scotland he's spoken to you several times?'

'Well I've heard his voice. What he says doesn't make much sense? But yes. And then there was last night and the vase breaking. He gave you that didn't he?'

'How do you know that?' Maggie shot a glance at Pop and then Ralph wondering which one of them had told Andrew. She was worried how much Andrew knew but she wouldn't have expected him to be so calm if he knew everything. Only Ralph knew everything and she didn't think he would have betrayed her. 'Yes he did.' She conceded. 'For my 17th birthday. Um. He's contacted me too.'

Pop and Andrew looked at her, surprised. Ralph smiled, relieved that she had shared what was obviously a burden. 'It started back in October. I was up in the attic getting the winter clothes - hats and gloves and things. I found the hat that I wore when I went on my first date with Harry. That's what I always called him. He liked the hat. He said it matched my eyes. It's red.' She laughed.

'You still have it?' Andrew was interested.

'I was trying it on and there he was. Looking at me, smiling.'

'You saw him?' Andrew and Pop exclaimed together.

'Were you frightened? Andrew touched his mother's arm.

'Frightened? I nearly fell out of the attic I was so scared. I was in the house on my own. Well, I just went out and didn't go back in until I had picked Susan up from school. I haven't seen him since but he's spoken to me a number of times.'

Ralph got up 'I'll make us a cup of tea.'

'Gramps has been telling me what he was like.' Maggie became a little uncomfortable but smiled

'Oh, what's he been saying?'

'He said you went out with Henry, Harry, for nearly a year but were never accepted by his family. He said he was as handsome as you are beautiful'.

Maggie laughed. 'He was handsome.'

'I know he left suddenly without a word when the family moved back to Scotland. What a scandal! His father, Thomas, getting one of his workers pregnant and then her losing the baby during an argument with him.'

'Well, we don't know exactly what happened but that was the rumour.' Maggie defended.

'And all that time the family lived here. And that's why you wanted to live here so much because you loved Harry.'

'You make it sound all so simple. If only it were.' Maggie sighed.

'And do you know that he came back to see your mother many years later?' Jim was standing by the door, his cheeks red from winter and whisky.

'Jim, please.' Maggie stood up and pleaded with her husband.

'Dad, are you OK?'

'Fine son. I've had a bit too much Christmas spirit, I admit, but I'm fine.'

Ralph came back in with the pot of tea with Ruth following with a tray of sandwiches and Susan carrying the remainder of the fruitcake.

'OK to eat in here tonight Mam?' Ruth asked, oblivious to the developing saga.

Jim staggered to the chair nearest the fire. 'I want to talk to you all' he stumbled over his words.

'Jim. Please don't.' Maggie almost begged him.

'No Maggie, the air needs to be cleared. Things need to be said.' Susan climbed onto Jim's lap and kissed him.

'What's that smell?' She said taking in his alcohol-laced breath.

'Your dad has had some whisky. That's what you can smell.'

'Mm. It's nice.' Everyone laughed but the atmosphere in the room was not light or warm. Henry was in the corner by the window. Andrew looked towards where he stood but did not see him. Nobody saw him.

'Yes' Jim continued. 'Henry Southon esquire returned to Merthyr in 1957, 12 years after he had left your mother with not even a goodbye. He wanted to pick up where they had left off even though your mother and me were married by then. But your mother loved me.'

'Loves.' Maggie wiped a way the single tear that was making a track along her cheek.

'Loves me. And so she said no. He killed himself some months after returning and now it seems he is haunting my house. Our house.'

Ruth was utterly bemused. 'Mam, what's going on?'

'We've got a ghost.' Susan screamed, snuggling her head into Jim's bony shoulder.

'Nothing to be frightened of.' A chorus of voices reassured. She was not convinced.

'Why now?' Asked Andrew, directing the question to Henry but it was Maggie who answered.

'I think we disturbed his spirit when we went to Bronton and he could not rest until he had settled old scores.'

The seven of them stayed in the room for a while talking through what they should do. They concluded, with Ralph's advice, that they should do nothing; that Henry's the spirit was not harmful and would probably go as quickly as it had arrived. Jim announced through his drunken haze that Henry was welcome in his home but he should not distract or disturb or frighten.

Maggie lay awake again that night. She knew then for the first time Henry was Andrew's father. Why else would he have visited him? Jim knew it too but was comforted by the fact that only he and Maggie knew. That was how it would remain.

It was early September in 1989. Jim and Maggie were having their first holiday alone since Andrew was born. Home was still 'Bronton'. The years had taken Pop but he visited Maggie quite often. The children had all left home but they visited regularly too. Henry remained a presence at the house. 'Are you sure you are OK with this Jim?' 'Of course. It's something we both need to do.'

Jim manoeuvred the Golf into the space. Maggie grabbed the flowers and they walked towards the graveyard. They both remembered exactly where Henry lay. Maggie knelt at the side of the stone and arranged the white chrysanthemums in the metal flowerpot. She said a small prayer. Jim leant on the stone. It moved. Maggie smiled up at him. That was the last time Henry visited.

'A Terrible Beauty is Born'

Viv Protheroe

Saturday night in Merthyr: a night for booze and birds, for getting away from it all. But this was a special Saturday night because events had forced upon John the action he should have had the courage to take earlier of his own volition. An existential happening of possible momentous consequences, that was the way in which he now saw it. A happening following which 'everything is changed, changed utterly.'

His resignation from his job at ICI was in the post, his union and Labour Party membership cards were torn in two and the first strike in the history of the Merthyr factory was about to make him a hero or a despot. This was the final act in this melodrama: the breaking of his parents' hearts. He was at last a poet, alone, naked and vulnerable.

I'll write slushy romances for women's magazines. I'll go to university on a mature student's grant. I'll graduate in Eng. lit and become a book reviewer for the Sunday Times. They'll like that. That will elevate me to the realms of respectability to which they aspire. But I want to be a poet and if I do that I'll never be a poet. So then I'll be a petrol pump attendant, a barman, a door-to-door salesman, a drifter. But that will break their hearts.

Christ it's Saturday night. There's a pound in my pocket; there's beer in the bar, lovely lithe young ladies longing to be loved and destinies to be fulfilled. Fuck tonight Sunday is a better day for breaking hearts. And so his brave new world began with a coward's kiss. 'Fuck tomorrow,' he called loudly now, through the open window across the wet depressing rooftops to a world that wasn't listening. The faded curtains of the bedroom window of his exhibitionistic neighbour fluttered revealing glimpses of her young voluptuousness. A deific reply to his baying at the shrouded moon.

The sullen clouds had drifted from what was now a high night sky, chased away by a sharp wind. Pinpricks of light flickered through the alto strata and a thumbnail moon slid in its thin aura of luminescence like a Phoenician boat drifting slowly on a dark sea. It was cold and clear and beautiful, like the night which haunted his dreams with such significant regularity. The narrow streets of Dowlais, that 'battered bucket on a broken hill', echoed and amplified his footsteps as he picked his way through the complex maze, ever downward to where the tang of spilt beer scented the air with as much allure as the perfumes of Arabia for the shipmates of the Arethusa. The grey moral sentinels of the Bethanias and Bethesdas muttered their silent remonstrances.

At last the friendly pool of light, warmly yellow, cast out onto the pavement from the portals of the Dowlo, grabbed and greeted him and dragged him in. He made straight away for the room at the end of the long passage labelled unpretentiously 'Backroom' unlike so many of its contemporary 'Lounges', which were back rooms where the beer cost an extra three pence a pint.

The room did not even boast it's own bar and it's customers had to buy their drinks from a serving hatch which accessed the main bar from the passageway. John tapped an impatient coin on the scarred dark oak counter, interrupting the tight skirted archetypal buxom barmaid from the orgy of violence which issued from the jam jar screened televisions set, the Dowlo's only concession to mid twentieth century technology.

'Ullo John love, usual?' she asked and answered with an expert movement which scooped a pint mug from under the counter and pulled on the long pump handle with the grace of Gilbert Parkhouse stroking the ball to the mid on boundary at Saint Helens.

'And one under the counter for my lean anaemic friend who should be along presently,' he responded perkily.

She pulled again on the pump handle and the brown old-fashioned ale squirted frothily into the mug, the head rising and spilling over the sides leaving a thin healthy head over the top - just right.

Three men sat in the corner playing cards, with their illegal money scattered untidily on the shelves underneath the table. Two more flung exotically flighted darts at a battered board and another sat quietly sipping his beer, a faraway look in his mournful eye, the sleeve of his cardigan in a black wet pool.

It was early. Later the room would be crammed with boisterous boozy men and the occasional liberated woman and the hatch would be soggy with spilt beer floating the cardboard mats like miniature Kontikkies across its old oak top. The air would ring with laughter and music and the real world would become a distant thing experienced through an intoxicated haze.

'A pint for you and a transfusion under the counter for your anaemic friend,' she smiled, pleased at her own humour, placing the pint on the shelf before him. He handed her a pound note. 'Have one yourself Brenda,' he offered. 'I'm celebrating.'

'Oh aye and what have you got to celebrate then,' fishing among the tarnished coins for change. 'I'll join you with a little G an' T if that's alright.' She raised her glass and toasted him.

'I don't know. Something. Everything. A terrible beauty is born.'

'Go on with you, you daft bugger. Dunno what you're talking about half the bloody time. But you do have a nice way of saying it.' She handed him his change and he retreated into the solitude of the backroom dolefully sipping the froth from his drink.

In a few minutes she followed him in. 'Better get the fire cheered up a bit. Can't have my favourite customer suffering from the cold now can I?' She gave his pale cold cheek a playful pinch.

'You're fire enough for me Brenda,' he responded to her banter putting an arm around her soft waist and pulling her down onto his lap.

'Ooh,' she squealed with exaggeration. 'Leave go you

sexy bugger,' and she jumped up smiling with delight. 'You're a randy one John Davies,' she laughed, brushing the sides of her rumpled skirt. 'Young girls are not safe with the likes of you around.'

'What about the older girls.' he teased. Their eyes met and she smiled the suggestive smile of a ripe sensual forty year old with more than just an eye for younger men. He reflected regretfully that another five years would see her attractive voluptuousness turn to fat. The hints of ridges underneath the eyes become prominent and the already heavy breasts grow pendulant, flaccid and sag. But as she bent to pick up the black shiny coals from the scuttle in the hearth to replenish the fire's dying embers she displayed to him the ripeness of her mellow fruitfulness. He had an irresistible impulse to touch her gently, even perhaps implant a soft kiss on that sacred spot.

Was she perhaps performing some atavistic ritual to retrieve from him through contact, performed or contemplated, some seed of his youthful vigour. If he could have achieved this he willingly would. He reached out and gently brushed her buttocks with his fingertips. The banter over, she arched her back and squatted erotically as he cupped his hand under the dark valley of her skirt.

Brenda had married young to an older man no longer able to satisfy the demands of her autumnal desires. And although the temptation to assuage them with someone young and virile was great, she would never go beyond this vulgar flirtation. Her husband would be too much hurt by such infidelity now. Some years ago it might have been different when he had such self assurance. Now impotence had bred an insecurity she would not exploit.

She had learned to live with it, satisfying herself with Bloom like fantasies triggered by such rare moments as this.

She stood up and turned to face him, shaking her head with mock disapprobation, tut-tutting as she walked slowly out with an exaggerated rotation of her haunches. She turned at the door and gave him a smile. 'In any case here comes your anaemic friend,' she shrugged.

A few beers and whisky chasers later the fire had shaken off its earlier despondency and its vaporous red orange flames reached up the soot black chimney like the tenuous fingers of a probing hand. Tonsils had eased and the topics of conversation flitted cyclically from sex to god and infinity and back again. Dave's philosophy, like John's was moulded by Merthyr's history, the dialectic of the enlightened street, voracious reading and discussion. Both subscribed to a radical existentialism, essentially socialist, of which Sartre was of course the leading exponent and Camus the icon. They saw Stalin as an aberration and the assassination of Trotski as the death knell for Soviet communism. They reacted against the throttling of the individual, which was a consequence of the industrial revolution and feared the degree to which the new technological revolution now ensuing would exacerbate that trend unless control of its development and use was wrested away from the burgeoning multi - national corporations.

John sought to give expression to his views as much through his scribblings as his political affiliations. Dave had long since abandoned overt political activism for expression through his art.

Their aesthetic development like their friendship was

something which had matured steadily through their adolescence, they had been friends for as long as either of them could remember, but initially the writing and the painting had not been a mutual interest, which made its simultaneity all the more remarkable.

It had begun in both cases secretly, almost furtively and for a while even threatened a rift in their friendship. Then when each discovered the other's artistic ambitions their work for a period became a sublime dialectic. Their relationship blossomed into an intimate and beautiful thing, devoid of any physical expression for both were blatantly hetero in their sexual orientation. And yet, what they experienced emotionally was beyond normal friendship, more like the love of David for Jonathan.

John began to get published in obscure unread periodicals, while Dave's paintings were hung in equally obscure galleries, more often the backrooms of local pubs and working men's clubs. Recently the growing maturity of their work was receiving critical notice, and it was beginning to sell, albeit for very small beer. A recent slim volume of illustrated verse with blasphemous content had resulted in a confrontation with the Archbishop live on Monitor, and their broadcast notoriety had made them a hot property on the burgeoning underground press, beyond the strict confines of the Welsh valleys. They had dined out, or at least drunk out, on their ill repute.

The little backroom was filled to overflowing now and warmer than an Avana oven. The Dowlais five were holding court. The leading lights of which were John and Dave with their recent success elevating them to star billing. Geraint, fair haired and fresh faced was an ardent

Nationalist forever being dragged before the magistrates for defacing English language road-signs. His heroes were Saunders Lewis and Gwynfor Evans who, although both nationalists were diametrically opposed in methodology; Gwynfor the non violent protester who through his hunger strike was later to secure the fourth channel for Welsh Language broadcasts, Saunders Lewis jailed for sabotage during the Fascist War. Geraint exemplified the schizophrenia that was the Welsh Nationalist movement of the time. He was the frequent butt of the more sophisticated politics of the rest of the group.

Bill was the veteran, a bachelor in his late thirties who felt he had much more in common with his young confederates than members of his own age group. He was a widely read autodidact steeped in the philosophies of the East. He quoted freely from Khayam and the Sufis, Hafiz, Confucius, the Buddha, Po-Chu-I and Karl Marx. He was forever extolling the virtues of Eurasian women, with one of whom he had undergone a marriage ritual and lived with until her untimely malarial death. He still succumbed to recurring attacks himself. His skin was the pallid yellow of a South East Asian and his face badly pitted from some tropical pox. Yet he seemed irresistibly attractive to women. He was making a moderate success in photographic journalism and had done some freelance work for Magnum which he hoped would soon free him from the tool-room; which it ultimately did with the advent of the Vietnam war which he covered to international critical acclaim.

Ted was a tall thin cynic wedded to Tolstoi and Kropotkin and whose favourite characters in literature were the mad bomb carrying professor in Conrad's Secret

Agent, whose perfection of the human bomb (himself) presaged the horrors of the present 'suicide bombers' and who's plot to blow up the Greenwich Observatory as an attack on Science had a particular appeal; and Souverain in Zola's Germinal, who blew up Le Voreux, the coalmine which brooded like a decaying monster over the lives of the villagers of Montsou. In criticising Marx who he misinterprets as an 'evolutionist', Souverain chillingly chides Etienne.

'Don't talk to me about evolution! Raise fires in the four corners of cities, mow people down, wipe everything out, and when nothing whatever is left of this rotten world perhaps a better one will spring up.'

This summarised Ted's dangerous nihilism and it is hardly surprising that he went on to achieve infamy in the sixties when, like Conrad's Stevie, though lacking his innocence, he succeeded in blowing himself up in a botched attempt at sabotage on the nuclear reactor at Trawsfynydd.

This then was the nucleus of the Dowlais (the Merthyr) 'avant garde' for were they not synonymous. Held in ignorant awe by their contemporaries they were labelled Marxists, Trotskyists, anarchists, Leninists, Diabolists, or any other 'ists that a wary Welsh community could lay it's tongue to. The Dowlo was it's principal meeting place and consequently attracted to it a strange ménage of the curious, the adoring and the sinister. It had assumed, among the Merthyr, and the wider Welsh intelligentsia, the status of The Mermaid. Even Special Branch took a fleeting interest until their Super realised that the topics of conversation were somewhat over the heads of his operatives who in their reports had all and sundry listed as dangerous revolutionaries, which in Ted's case proved unwittingly to be correct.

The Dowlo was their stage and it consequently attracted all kinds of strange and interesting people to its backroom. It was not unusual to walk in and find some self confessed genius on his feet passionately espousing his philosophy or reciting his poetry before retiring once more to his retreat in the bleak Welsh hills or dark brooding valleys. What the Dowlo's regular denizens made of all this is unrepeatable and poets and preachers were often sent on their way with friendly advice to, 'Stop talking crap and fuck off back to where you came from.'

Tonight a small group of undergrads were the only strangers, sardined adjacent to the serving hatch. Attracted by the reputation of the place they sat uneasily sipping their drinks alertly waiting for the big event. Bill brushed past them with a tray-full of drinks. John in serious mode had just explained the strike situation and cautioned them with threat of violence not to raise the subject again that evening. Sunday was the day for politics, he opined. Sunday, Welsh and respectable, ideal for insurrection and rebellion.

Young Paddy Macarthy was trying to sing some lullaby of old Ireland to his white haired mother in the corner, but was barely audible above the general din. The Macarthys were Irish as poteen and porter and the tears shone in her old green Irish eyes as he sang in a fine lilting tenor, 'I'll take you home again Caithlin to where the hills are fresh and green.' It was a Jungian memory as far as they were concerned as the closest they had been to Galway Bay was Swansea, since their ancestors swapped the famine of peasant Ireland for the impoverished slum of 'China', the immigrant area of metropolitan industrial Merthyr.

Bill's own one quarter Irish ancestry had him joining in and soon the five added their own accompaniment signalling that intellectual discourse was over and the maudlin gamut of backroom vocalising about to begin. Soon the whole pub, front room and back were in tune and by some indefinable process the songs slid seamlessly from Irish to Scottish to Welsh until the Gaelic oeuvre had been exhausted, and it was assumed, patriotic fervour assuaged.

Suddenly a dark slender member of the collegiate was on her feet and vainly trying to get general attention. John's attention she already had. There was something indescribably sensual about her. But it was an understated sensuality owing everything to a kind of languid poise. Hers was not the brash attraction which generates wolf whistles in the street but soft silent sighs in the hearts of the cognoscenti. In one of those windows of silence which inexplicably occur in the middle of a cacophonous hubbub she was heard clearly to proclaim. 'What about the English?'.

Before the inevitable barrage of catcalls which would otherwise have automatically ensued John, the shining knight, leapt to her rescue. 'Now then,' he called, commanding immediate attention. 'Fair is fair. And this young rose of England is certainly fair, though dark. Welshmen have always sung the praises of the English rose. After all you can't blame a rose for the ground in which it nourishes its roots. Of course it took a Welshman to compose the song equal to the loveliness of this rose.' He addressed her with the drunken confidence of an aficionado of too many romantic crooners of the silver screen and broke into a sugary sweet rendition of Novello's 'We'll gather lilacs in the spring again.' The catcalls soon subsided into equally inebriated accompaniment. He winked at her. She winked back and he was lost.

'Oh very sick,' muttered Ted after the strains had died. 'Poor Geraint has turned green, and it's not the beer.'

Geraint scowled from behind his pint. 'What sort of Welshman writes a song about walking down English lanes. What sort of name is Novello anyway? Sounds like a bloody spick to me.'

'There we have it,' retorted John, 'the irrationalist nationalist racist mind.'

'Fuck you and your alliteration,' Geraint spat back. Dave thought it prudent to inject a little levity.

'Perhaps it was an English lane of some special significance to Ivor,' he suggested. 'Might he have lost his virginity there?'

'More likely his knickers,' Geraint snapped scornfully.

'Well what it wasn't was the idiom of the people was it,' John persisted. 'I'm sure the combined talents of so much creative genius can make an improvement on it. Now let's see. Yes..

My English rose is driving me insane
when we go walking down the Goetre lane
she brings her knee up gives me such a pain
that's why I love her so...

and on and on he went composing verses increasingly more bawdy culminating in a great cheer from the rapt audience and a gale of laughter.

'Surely the work of a major poet,' Bill applauded

sarcastically.

'So delightfully sick,' Geraint growled.

'So excitingly anarchic,' Ted added.

'Will rank with Eskimo Nell as one of the great ballads of our time,' Dave announced.

Oh you bawdy Baudelaire and a bit, you ribald Rabelais, you randy Rimbaud he thought to his inebriate self. You are a one and doesn't this lithe lovely think so.

He clambered onto his chair, a little unsteadily, to the groans of those who recognised an imminent peroration. He held up his hands as he imagined Trotski about to address the proletariat.' She will always be remembered as 'the dark lady of the ballads', he said, 'but who was she in reality? This is the mystery that future literary historians will grapple with. Was she the seemingly shy Jenny Prendergast Pring? Did she sport a pair of black leather panties beneath all that organdie and lace? Or was it dedicated to that mysterious English rose, the black rose of Trecatty? Did she conceal a thorny stem behind her flowery facade? Oh antic love why hast thou played me false? Some have it that she was an old woman with a padded bra and that the original phrase from the first folio contained in the Black Book of Pengarnddu was...oh antique love why hast thou played me false? .. Has the time now come to tear open the tomb of the Bard of Taff Fechan. What terrible secrets lie hidden in that musty coffin? What catastrophic disaster is implied in that cryptic warning on that cracked and faded headstone. 'Leave well alone you Dowlais vandals, lest you unearth some dirty scandals.' '

'He's off,' Dave chuckled to Bill. 'Found a bird to impress. Wont shut the bugger up all night now.'

He half stumbled from his rostrum and like the consummate performer he was transformed his error into a grand running exit, sweeping past her and not stopping til he found himself outside in the cold sobering air gulping in icy draughts. He sat on a crumbling low stone wall slowly recovering a measure of composure and sobriety. Soon she followed sitting alongside him with a quizzical expression on her austerely beautiful face. 'I'm Josephine,' she introduced herself holding out her hand palm down like a courtly Guenivere expecting him to brush the back of it with his lips. So he did.

'John Davies my lady,' he responded. 'Where are your friends?' Her shrug was coldly careless.

'Jolly Roger and co,' she answered. 'He's taken Jean and Sam to see some local architectural masterpiece carved out of solid coal by the gnarled hands of the miners to welcome their King. Edward the Abdicator I believe it was. Now there's a paradox, the Merthyr miners, socialist to the core, throwing their hats in the air for a fascist numbskull.'

'Not the miners exactly,' John corrected. 'Oh they carved the Coal Arch alright. Hardly a masterpiece though just a good example of the mason's craft. A curio which stands appropriately outside the dole office. You know the place the unwashed go to get a job, and where they used to go to beg for assistance at the time of His Majesty's visit. The people petitioned and pleaded more than they cheered. But they cheered old Georgie not the abdicator, he came in 1936. The poor dimwit was apparently quite moved. 'Something must be done', he said, but very little was.'

'Actually something was,' she contradicted, if a little

wistfully. 'Not by or because of the royal dimwit but strangely enough by the little moustachioed corporal he admired. The exodus of Jews from Germany and Poland in the thirties brought my late father to unlikely places like Merthyr to set up business with a little direction from central government.'

'And what business was that?'

'Knickers,' she laughed.

'What?'

'Knickers, well and other associated underwear.' She waved her hand vaguely in the direction of a plateau in the middle distance lit by red argon,. 'Mason's Lingerie, Poliakoffs that was', she explained. 'That's our factory - mine and Mum's. Not that I take the remotest interest in it, mum's the business brain. Changed it's name and its fortune long before dad's death. Modernised, new chic, sexy undies for the masses, that sort of thing. With dad they were still making boned corsets.'

'My God,' he reacted. 'A fully fledged bloated capitalist.'

'I'm afraid so. Not English at all you see. A little dark eyed Welsh Jewess. So what are you going to sing me now?'

'I'm sure I'll come up with something, but what was all that for in there then'. 'That,' she said, 'all that Celtic yearning, all that Hiraeth, all that bloody crap.'

He looked at her seriously for a moment. 'There's nothing wrong with us Welsh,' he insisted, 'we're emotional, tactile,' he reached across and touched her hand. It was a manoeuvre straight out of the handbook. Pull her hand away she was remote and prim, leave it there and it was an invitation.

He burst out laughing and she, momentarily wrong footed, joined in. 'Come on then,' he invited, ' I'll show you the true monuments of this 'battered bucket on a broken hill', not involving the great coal arch.'

'I don't know,' she feigned hesitation, 'Roger warned me about you.'

'Roger, what does Roger know about me?' John looked up at the sky. The weather was holding. 'You wont want that symbol of your opulence, he said as she made to open the door of her elegant sporty Volvo, midnight blue, so out of place in the drab Dowlais street. 'My God you are a rich little bitch aren't you?' he mocked.

He led her along Balaclava Road, the smell from the rubbish tip adjacent to it wafting up despite the cold, and began the ascent of Regent Street, steep as an Alpine ski slope. The windowsills of the front rooms so low to the ground because of the gradient making the interiors visible behind the aspidistras and potted geraniums, sharing their intimacy with all and sundry. But front rooms were seldom used and most activity was confined to the middle room and the back kitchen. Front rooms were preserved for weddings and funerals and visits from posh aunts from Muswell Hill. In some of the houses a flickering blue light advertised the ownership of a jam jar screened television. What was the point of possessing such a status symbol if it's light was to be hidden under the bushel of the middle room.

'Do you know,' he said with the intonation of someone about to impart some words of inestimable wisdom, 'that most Dowlais prols live in kitchens which are triangular, and have developed feet which subtend an angle of forty-five degrees with the ankle.'

She laughed uneasily because the banter was tinged with a bitter irony. 'Does this bloody street go on forever,' she complained taking in great gulps of freezing air. He half dragged her to the top and they stood hands on hips panting in unison. Above them stretched another street, and above that another. Dowlais had been thrown together clumsily on the steep hillside it's higgledy piggledy architecture defying Newtonian mathematics. Up they went ever higher, along Station Road, past the Stables and the Market and the classically porticoed memorial hall to John Josiah Guest, the iron master without whose huge ironworks (the biggest in the world in that explosive birth of the industrial revolution) Dowlais might never have been. Onward and upward they climbed, deliberately avoiding the Coal Arch and the possibility of Roger and co, past the Ivor Works, a foundry named after John Josiah's son, and the last remnant of the great Guest empire, to Penywern and up an icy moonlit dirt track to the Top Pond. Beyond what must have been it's eastern perimeter a small cluster of tiny houses seemed to huddle together throwing tiny pin pricks of light out onto the ill made dirt track.

'That's Pengarnddu,' he said. 'Not much further now. Pengarnddu is the edge.'

'The edge of what?'

'The world, the abyss, the known universe. Can't you feel it, see it, smell it?' He spun her round. 'Look, look down there. Isn't this the edge of eternity. Imagine it,' he said,' as it was; whitewashed hill farms silver in the cool moonlight; bubbling streams meandering, cascading luminous ribbons into trout filled pools; free, fresh, clean green grass with roots deep in a rich tilth, waving, dancing a sensual Eastern dance in a keen breeze. And now, and now, 'a battered bucket on a broken hill', the Morlais a stinking chemical sewer, not a minnow to it's name. The ghosts of Guest and Crawshay lurking in the black shadows.

'And did those feet in ancient time walk upon Dowlais' mountains green. And was the holy lamb of God in Merthyr's pleasant valley seen? And did that countenance divine shine forth upon our clouded hills and was Jerusalem builded here among these dark satanic mills?'

His voice clear in the cold night like a muezzin calling the faithful to prayer.

She felt small and insignificant standing there above the black abyss and her instincts warned her to run, run away now from this mad poet before he completely captivated her: but she stayed. The Phoenician boat slid out from its dark harbour and in one magic instant painted the scene in shimmering silver as if the mad magician had waved his wand. At that precise and awful moment she felt his cold lips brush the back of her swansdown neck. She turned away sharply, too sharply, as if afraid of her own reactions. It brought her face to face with the view of Dowlais and Merthyr spread out in the valley far below.

'Ugly isn't it,' he muttered, 'this black body with a silver shroud.'

Was all this alliteration and metaphor a poetic form of seduction. It was working. She knew from the strange way she trembled. Or was that just the cold? Was confusion part of the process. She could make out the High Street from the red orange river of argon which slashed its way up from the town to the dark lop sided hillside hovels like a bleeding gash. Lesser luminaries of pale yellow patchily lit the tributaries, growing ever more sparse in the outer extremities where the little houses huddled together for company, hunched and ramshackle.

'Why should you venture out of your protective central heated closet to become a part of that : that is the question?' And it was. 'Well I'll tell you. Down there in all that grime and confusion beats a heart, a broken heart, a bleeding heart, but every pulse of it is amplified and echoed in my own. There are people there, real and alive, and me I'm real and alive and burning. And isn't that what you want too - to live and burn? But to live you have to suffer pain, to love your heart must bleed a little. That cocoon of yours is a little too secure, too cosy. You're an unborn child with a glimpse of the outside world where everything is new and alive and exciting - but frightening. How much easier to sink back in and let the vaginal opening shut tight behind you.

'Below us, beneath our feet, at this very moment men are scurrying about like moles in the blind earth. And there in that red glow men still sweat in the heat of the furnace. What for? They are the real monuments my spoiled little bourgeois. Do you understand?'

His blunt insults served now only to fuel the flame. Her eyes sparkled as she saw the fire that lit his. 'Just so they can hang on to the little that they have down there, because as the wise man said, they've never had it so good.' He waved an arm expansively taking in the criss crossing streets drab and dirty down below them. 'Untidy wives, belligerent husbands, crying kids, pubs and cinemas, bingo and television, and chapel. Fantastic isn't it that out of that mad ménage emerge real people, heroes and heroines, exciting and alive. Not the impotent observant Rogers of this world with his blazer and his scarf, but the doers and the livers. I am one of them, they are my people. I love and hate them. We live though all around us dies.'

In the awkward silence which followed she fought against her desperate desire for him. She was, despite the obvious absurdity of it, prepared to accept almost everything this mesmeric Welsh bard said or did. It was a complete reversal of the relationships she had previously experienced with men, with Roger for instance. She had run the gamut of witty debs escorts and was not exactly naive or without experience. But never before had she met such a phenomenon as this, who could rouse her to such passion. There was an aura of intense, almost insane genius about him which, while it signalled caution, if not fear, aroused her in a way which she did not quite understand, not just sexually but in a manner entirely new and beyond her comprehension.

'I wish I had such a simple faith,' she replied. 'Not necessarily in a deity, but some immutable base, an absolute truth which qualifies every action.'

'Faith, ' he snorted disgustedly, faith. So much Kant, he punned. 'An absolute imperative. But I do believe confessor, I really do - in many things. In freedom, for those people down there, and people everywhere, political, economic, religious, racial. But those are beliefs in what should be not in what things are. I believe in man the individual and man the mass, now there's a paradox. I believe in sex as part of a wider relationship and as an end in itself. I believe in good and in bad, in pleasure and in pain. I believe in beauty and truth and love, components of which are necessarily ugliness, lies and hate. Nothing is simple. Nothing is absolute. Everything is relative. Yet there is good and there is evil. Life is a paradox. There's so much more in heaven and earth my dear than is dreamt of in your philosophy. Anyway, why bother with all this shit when all you have to do is wait for some useless Roger to honour and cherish you and keep you in the bourgeois manner to which you are accustomed.'

On this bleak wild mountain outcrop the damp wind gusted dark scurrying clouds across the sky. He walked her quickly down to the single yellow lamp lit corner of the tiny hamlet. They paused for a moment and he shielded her from the icy blast with his body. He felt the spray of her loose dark hair in his face and caught the tang of her expensive perfume in his nostrils. For the first time he really studied her face, peculiarly illuminated by the weak yellow lamplight which the gusty wind caused to flicker like a wan flame. A general description of her features he supposed would be that they displayed a haughty sensuality. The haughtiness attributable to a somewhat aloof expression in the eyes emphasised by a head tilted slightly back on a slender neck, the sensuality almost entirely due to the full pouting Jewish lips, fellatial lips he thought them. The cheekbones were high and the cheeks hollow, the look of inbred quality, and yet paradoxically there was a certain animalism too. Not just the loose flowing hair, it was more than that. A glint in the eye, a resolution of the chin, no sign of weakening there, definitely a proletarian chin. A stubborn-ness, a wilfulness which he would have to come to terms with after this strange night of metamorphosis.

The descension was certainly quicker than the long haul up to the summit and they were soon welcomed back to the suffocatingly warm backroom of the Dowlo with knowing nods and winks in John's direction. Roger and co had departed in high dudgeon on their return from the coal arch expedition to the absence of Josephine. Which pleased John no end. They were quickly supplied with drinks by Dave and all around people were babbling heartily, but for old mother Macarthy who cried silently in the corner as she did every Saturday night for as long as anybody could remember. Nobody knew why she cried except perhaps her Cymro Irish son who sang softly to her of the 'old country'.

Betty the buxom barmaid came in with a cheerful smile to collect the empty glasses and gave John a mock remonstrative scowl. 'Come on,' Dave called, 'drink up or we'll be too late for the dance.'

'Dance. What dance?' asked Josephine.

'What dance? What dance? The dance to end all dances of course: the danse macabre.' No Saturday night could be complete for any self-respecting hedonist without a visit to the Dowlais Catholic Hall dance.

Outside in the street he held her hand tenderly then pulled her close. A single teardrop welled and rolled down his cold cheek. 'Don't you see it,' he asked looking intensely into her face. 'I love you,' he said simply. 'All is changed, changed utterly. A terrible beauty is born.

'It Could Be Paris'

Alan Murphy

He watches Miranda's left leg drawing little arcs in the air as it pivots on her right knee. Her toenails are painted black and a thin silver chain bracelet dangles over her ankle. She walks to the fireplace and lights a candle, staring at a Van Gogh print of boats hanging on the wall.

'Where you from, love?'

'Just outside Merthyr.'

'A friend of mine lives there. Used to live here in Riverside but had a gutsfull of Cardiff. Found a fella from Merthyr and shacked up with I'm. He goes mental on cider...does drugs too. I've told her to leave I'm, come back to the city.'

He notices that the room displays a passion for purple.

'But she says she loves him. You're a tough lot up there.'

'Products of industry.'

'Ecstasy more like.'

The candle flame is growing tall and is starting to flicker. He is becoming anxious.

'I've never done anything like.... you know..... like this before.'

'Don't worry love. It's not as if you're visiting the dentist is it?'

He notices her looking at her watch as she walks to the sofa and stands behind him. Her perfume smells of pear drops. Now she's beginning to massage his forehead. He'd prefer to talk more. Now he can feel her fingers circling his temples as his eyes are drawn into the burning candle. He sees a high forehead, a nose, now a mouth, that mouth, eyes accusing. He holds his breath as Christine's face materialises, haloed in the flame.

'No!'

'Ok love, you want me to stop? You're a nervous one aren't you?'

'Yes.... no... I mean I am nervous but I don't want you to stop. I was thinking aloud, that's all.'

'Oh, we've got a thinker here have we? It's dangerous to think, love. I stopped doing that years ago. What were you thinking about, anyway?'

'Nothing.... Look, it's no good, I don't think I can do this.

'There you go.... thinking again. Christ! I'd hate to be your dentist! Wife is it, love?

Girlfriend? Boyfriend?'

He doesn't answer.

'Oh, fellas come here with all kinds of baggage. I've heard things not privy to priests. I like to think I help them in some way.....well I like to think I do. They'd have to pay a hell of a lot more for a counsellor and I don't have a waiting list. Oh, I could write a book, love. I could write a bloody book.'

He wants to laugh but nothing happens. She moves her hands along his jaw and now her hair is falling on his neck. It smells of apples. Her hands are on his chest.

'Do you mind if you blow that candle out?'

'Not at all love. Don't like the smell?'

'Um.... no, no I don't like the smell. I hope you don't mind.'

'*You're* the one who's paying love.'

As she extinguishes the candle, he gets lost in the Van Gogh print and at last, he's able to let go, sinking into the sand on which the boats are beached. She plays some music; a sax slurping into his ears, yes, that helps.

'There.... don't worry now. Just relax. That's it... just relax.'

Miranda begins to unbutton his shirt. He looks at the ceiling, eyelids fluttering, butterflies skimming a stream, jaw loosening, sighing now, release. If he pushes himself gently from the sofa he thinks he will levitate.

'That's it, just let go.'

Her voice is making his body even lighter; floating now, rising higher, parallel with the print. He can see a sea gull above one of the masts, higher now, looking down on himself and

Miranda. He propels himself towards a sash window. He opens it and prises himself through and there they are.... the steps, each one a concrete slab clustered in groups of three and four with a wide gap to steady the walker.

A salt breeze, the gentle splash of waves. The steps curve away from him and descend to water. Diving. His clothes are making him anchor-heavy, accepting the invitation to sink. Limbs octopus in slow motion dragging downward. Eyes bulge in salt sting. Looking upward, he thinks he can see Christine on the steps, refracted and remote, waving.

'Why does she have to spoil it? '

Miranda places her finger in front of her mouth.

'She'll go if you let her.'

His neck sinks into the sofa. That's better, much better. Under water again, he looks upward to see if she's still there. No-one.

Swimming in a clear sea to the sound of a dolphin descant. A warmth wraps around him, tumbling, heaving, thrusting through waves, controlled by the current, no responsibility, pushing, coaxing him towards the curve of the shore. Finally, he moors on shingle shaded by boats.

'How was that?'

She places a cigarette in her mouth. Her hands are perfectly shaped to play the piano. He imagines them skilfully running along the keys, the clicking of her nails.

'I have no words for it.'

She's putting on her dressing gown and retrieves her lighter from the fireplace.

'I'll take that as a compliment I think, love.'

She's blowing out smoke without giving him eye contact, running a shower, beginning to sing. He doesn't recognise the tune. He dresses.

A man is speaking on a mobile as the train leaves Cardiff General. He feels the eyes of the passengers on him, guilt in his gut. He sees his reflection in the window and hardly recognises the face of an old man. He hasn't been looking in mirrors lately. Maybe he shouldn't have gone, should have stopped and thought about it.

The train moves....should have, should have, should have, should have ....snaking along the valleys. The man is on his mobile again, he'll be late, they'll have a takeaway...stop, start stop, start, Abercynon, Quakers Yard, Pentrebach, Merthyr Tydfil.

Getting out of the train, he surveys the town, reading the past carved into the peeling plaster on the facades of its buildings. Seven generations of his family have lived here. Ironstone runs through his veins. Now he yearns for a transfusion. As he walks through the shopping precinct to the bus station, he hears an accordionist. It could be Paris.

Miranda is waving her fingers in the air to dry her nails. Today they are purple and remind him of sweets he enjoyed as a child, the sticky fingers. She parades in her sun-bleached dressing gown, drinking, sliding out a shoulder, hair slipping over one eye.

'Had a good week, love?'

She lights the candle.

'Oh sorry love, I'll blow it out.'

'I can't help noticing your hands. Do you play the piano?'

'It's funny, one of my other clients asked that?'

She's laughing, cupping hands up to her nose is if to pray. He had prayed too. He had prayed for Christine to die.

'Block the thought... la la la..... a heart attack .... perfect.... Fuck off! Fucking fuck off! Sit down. Think of something.'

He notices the drips of dried wax on the candle and feels salt on his tongue. Miranda is rocking him.

'It's all right love. There, there. It's all right.'

He absorbs her warmth. Now, she's undoing his collar button. The music is different today. A guitar plucks frenetically, devoid of melody. He lies back, shuts his eyes and waits for her voice to drip milky rivulets into his ears and overflow down his neck into the hollow of his shoulders, melting muscles.

Floating to the ceiling again, the little window, the steps, descending, the water, diving. He resists turning around to see if Christine is there. If he doesn't look, he won't see her. Swim out more, increase the distance. She can't swim this far. He waits for the current. It takes him.

Miranda gets off the bed, withdrawing eye contact. She needs to get him out of there, he can tell.

'Have you ever, have you...?'

'What, love?'

'Doesn't matter.'

She runs the shower but she doesn't sing today.

The train, the return journey, stations passing by, flicking backwards through chapters of a book, Merthyr on the final page, the precinct, the accordionist. It could be Paris. The key turns, cat slinks against legs. He feeds it then it runs away. He avoids a photograph on the wall. He can feel her eyes following him around the room.

'It's only sex. It's only fucking sex!'

Holding the remote he stares at a blank television screen broadcasting his face, distorted and grey. His stomach convulses a wave to his throat, finds its way through the sinuses and orbits of his skull. The face contorts and seizures in the television screen. He switches it on, an invasion of colour and laughter. He presses the button and it's gone....on, off, on, off... So easy. *C'est facile.* He lies on the bed unable to sleep, voices burrowing through brain.

'I want you to be happy.'

'And he lived happily ever after'.

'Don't be facetious. It's want I want.'

'It's not what I want. I want you not to leave me. Oh I'm not making fucking sense. None of this makes any fucking sense!'

'It's not supposed to.'

They are in Cyfarthfa Park. He is imagining the sound of brass instruments blown by bushy-whiskered musicians in the band stand. She is looking at a Copper Beech, tracing its branches.

'The longevity of trees.'

'What? Oh yes.'

'They need only soil, sun and rain and they live forever.'

He points at the scene.

'What is the meaning of ....all this?'

'Maybe there is no meaning.'

'We take so much for granted; walking, breathing....time. We never think of the hour glass inverted.'

'Only the moment is important when you think about it.'

'That's the trouble. I never have until now. Should have savoured them.....should have, should have, should have. Do you want to go?'

'No let's stay here and eat sweets. I'll have a citrus orange and think of Israel.'

'I'll have a blackcurrant and think of... what can I think of?'

'Dowlais? Just enjoy the taste.... Aren't our senses fantastic?'

'Yes. The only currencies with any value now.'

They listen to a blackbird and witness the changing colour of the grass as the sun dips.

'You look different today.'

He is startled by her statement. Miranda has read him. He has felt different since the moment he has woken up this morning. He looks at her legs as she sits down and moves her finger over the rim of her wineglass. The bracelet has gone from her ankle.

'What do you think is different about me?'

'Don't know.'

'Maybe it's my socks?'

She laughs loudly. She's been drinking heavily. She's placing a cigarette to her lips. He notices the imprint of her lipstick on its tip. He follows the trail of her smoke, sensual ellipses, disappearing in slow motion above her head.

'So when did you... you know... when did you start.....'

'Selling my body, love? Become a prostitute, a whore?'

'Either one of those will do.'

She laughs again.

'Well, it's hard to say really. Fellas would take me for a night out, a meal, a club and if they were remotely attractive, we'd have sex.....a kind of 'thank you for shopping here' I suppose. After a while, I thought it would be hypocritical *not* to become a prostitute. I suppose I liked the attention..... oh, I don't know...... why did you ask me that?'

'Have you ever loved anyone?'

Miranda holds in the smoke reflexively then exhales. It reminds him of holding his breath to run through the gauntlet of smokers outside the entrance to Prince Charles Hospital.

'I don't know really. I suppose I have. Yes, once.'

'And was he a client?'

'Right first time... hey you're bloody good you are. Next question.'

'I thought you weren't supposed to fall in love with your clients.'

'Rule number one, love. Of all the rules to break, I break that one.'

'What happened?'

She's getting up now, walking to the CD player. He's upset her. He looks at his shoes.

'Why are men heartless selfish little pricks?'

'Not all men, surely?'

'I've seen enough to know, love.'

'Where is he now?'

'Haven't a fucking clue.'

She selects some music, turns up the volume, drinks from the bottle. She lets her dressing gown fall and dances, lost in the tune. Her head bends back and she moves her arms like the necks of swans.

'Come and dance. Come on!'

He shifts uneasily in the chair.

'Please.'

Reluctantly, he gets up and slowly walks to her. She puts her arms around him, drawing him in. He remembers Christine's feet on his, taking her weight, guiding her around her hospital room as they danced.

101

'That's all I've got left of him.... that!'

'Boats at Saintes-Maries-de-la-Mer, Van Gogh.'

'Is that what it is? I knew you were educated. Don't even like it. Said that if ever I felt like escaping I could imagine I was sailing in one of them boats, just up anchor and away. He stopped visiting me not long after that. Just stopped. Art teacher, that's what he was... thought he was Andy fucking Warhol. I began to repulse him.... saw it in his face. Oh, not these. *These* were good enough for him all right. '

She holds her breasts.

'And this.'

He feels the warmth.

'But the bastard didn't want this. Oh no.'

She moves his hand upward. He feels rapid beating.

Christine's heart beats against his palm, the pulse on her neck, a wing of a bird fluttering to gain height, the bedclothes lightly-draped on the angles of her body. The nurses have left him with her. She has moved beyond their science. He manages to sleep now and then. She's quietly dying beside him, well mannered even in death and he wastes his time by sleeping. Where's the importance of the moment now, eh? He closes the hospital window. Too hot. He opens it. He feels her hand to judge her temperature. What if she is too cold? He doesn't know. The rhythm of her breathing is altering...allegro, adagio, allegro...then a cadence. He can't think of anything to say, so he sings to her.

The music stops.

'You men are all the fucking same. I hate the bastard lot of you. Oh look, I'm too pissed for anything today love. Go home to your wife. They all do.

'She's dead.'

'Oh, I'm sorry... I didn't....'

'It's alright..... You know, I still can't stop the longing....there's nowhere for it to flow. It rises up in my throat and almost drowns me.'

She breaks away and places the empty bottle on the table and stares at the print again.

'You know something....you are one lucky bastard.'

'I am?'

'Yes, you fucking well are!'

'And would you tell me why I'm so fucking lucky? I'm dying to hear this one.'

'Dying.... that's it!'

'What's dying got to do with it?'

'Everything. She's dead. Gone! End of!'

'Good of you to remind me.'

'*He's* not! He's out there somewhere not wanting me.' She tries to pour from the empty wine bottle.

'Oh, I'm sorry love. It's the wine. Come on.....let's keep on dancing.'

They move to an unheard melody, swaying in their solitude, supporting each other like Thirties marathon dancers. She falls asleep on his shoulder. Eventually, he unlocks her arms from his neck and carries her to the bed, laying her down, rocking her, fingers moist with tears, smudged lips, melted mascara. She curls to the wall as he places the money under the pillow, leaving her to dribble and dream on the duvet.

The accordionist welcomes him home. He throws some coins into the hat then waits for the bus to Pontsticill. A woman passes, clutching her bag as if her life savings were inside. A man in a shirt and tie steps unconsciously to the rhythm. Now an older woman with highly polished spectacles is mumbling the melody. He thinks of worker ants.

Drinking alone at the Aberglais he marvels at how alcohol can clarify things and French words and phrases, long forgotten, flow into his mind. Almost fluent, he walks to the bridge.... *voici le pont.*

He remembers their summer walks along this river, shading under the viaduct, watching the Dippers catching flies. He studies the limestone boulders bordering the Blue Pool, wondering how long it takes for a rock to become a pebble. Above the rush of the river she speaks.

'C'est seulement l'importance du moment present qui compte.'

He breathes in the night air, savouring the seconds before climbing down steps carved by ancient currents. Standing by the pool, he can see her smiling at him from beneath the surface; that mouth, the high forehead. She beckons. He's taking off his clothes, folding them, placing them on a rock, noticing how translucent skin appears under the moon, pushing away from his foothold, yelping when he makes contact with the water. He calls out, looks around, locates her and dives.

Through the purple-black water he swims, sensing her. He feels for her, weaving between fish..... *les poissons.* He descends, delves in the silt bed.

'Qu'est -ce-que c'est?'

He clutches something. Fingers... *les doigts. Elle parle.* 'It will only take a moment... *un moment mon chere.'*

Fingers interlock with his, hold him down. He returns to her, old suns and moons orbiting, footsteps retraced, faces rejuvenatcd, her face, *son visage.* He bathes in her bubbling laughter, listens to the strength of her heartbeat. She kisses him; a struggle, he needs breath; lungs crave, bursting. He tries to surface but she vices him. Suddenly, music; a distorted accordion, notes rippling through reeds, sinking into nostrils.

She coaxes him to breathe as she tightens her grasp.

'*Aspire... un, deux, trois et expire..... un, deux, trois. Lantement... c'est facile.*'

He begins to breathe again, each breath synchronised with the rhythm of the instrument's air chambers. His breathing is slowing down now to that pace which precedes sleep.

'*Dors mon chere. C'est seulement l'importance du moment present qui compte.*'

Now, if he shuts his eyes, if he lets go that few degrees more... it could be Paris.

All Roads Lead To Merthyr

'The Italian Lob'

Boz (Philip Evans)

It was 5.30pm on a dark miserable Merthyr evening; when he bent down to lock his shutter doors. His Estate Agency, like most other businesses in Glebeland Street were closed for the night and the street returned to its night time 'Ghost Town' image.

'Bon Soir Des Res..... everything organised for our Tour De France yet?' Came a voice from behind him. Des Res turned towards the familiar voice. It was his business neighbour Perrier the owner of the baguette shop Café De Glebeland also in the process of shutting shop. He was clad in a white apron, stripy designer 'Ken' all-weather T-Shirt and French Beret. He looked ze part.

'Ello Ello .....I will say this only once 2.00pm Con Club Car Park, don't be late.' Laughed Des.

As he walked along the street, he peered through the closed Depress Newspaper Office door and could just make out a Sales Executive holding up a copy of the

Racing Post with a telephone embedded in his dimpled chin.

After a short rap on the glass Des held up a pre-printed 2.00pm sign to the shaggy Irish Newshound Brent O'Lee who raised two fingers before raising his thumb in acknowledgement.

Passing the third-generation Italian fish shop, Des could not make out any sign of life in the shop because of the all the steam from the frying fish.

However the owner, Mario, had written on the condensation- filled window…

2.00pm Con Club Car Park Grazie and had signed it with a flourish 'The Codfather'.

On reaching Post Office Lane and his car he checked his Nokia and after scrolling through the 30 Bin Laden jokes sent to him by his inner circle of mates he was confident that he could relax and that his 'Six Nations' trip to Italy was well and truly on schedule.

'It's bloody 2.00pm already…!'moaned Brent O'Lee as he shuffled his feet impatiently. 'We should be under starters orders by now….'

'Don't a worry he's-a-never on time…!' laughed Mario I always micro-de-wave his cheeps in my shop…!' 'Here he comes now….'announced Des Res to the boys.

All 'tourists' wore the required Red Cotton-traders Welsh Rugby jerseys and obligation 'Where's Wally (Wales)' scarf and bobble hats.'

As the Union Jack emblazoned new mini-cooper screeched to a halt in true Top Gear style… expecting to see Clarkson…..they saw a Midge Ure look-alike who although he was 'Slik' still had his works overalls on.

He said in a Michael Caine voice…. 'Titch Hatchey here and not a lot of people know that and I'm the designated driver for the English Stage of the Tour!!!'
'I'll give you 20-1 that we CAN get to Rome in THAT!' O'Lee offered licking his finger and pencil and opening his black book'. A Mini-Cooper –du cinque home – incredible!!!' gasped Perrier. 'It's got a large boot though … –enough for our beer storage lads!!!' enthused Brent O'Lee.

'Why do I getta the feeling that we got this car hire cheap through one of your old employers O'Lee' queried Mario rubbing his moustache suspiciously.

'It's a lovely car-. Super-Mario…..-and it will get us to the Game Boy in plenty of time I'll bet you!' said O'Lee mocking his friend.

'Well, I can't see us driving passed the Vatican in this O'Lee City vehicle-man, we wouldn't even pass the Pope-mobile in that !!!!' laughed Perrier.

'Merthyr Tydfil folk have great traditions of Roman Runs'…laughed Titch out the car window…. 'besides I'm confident that that in my Mini…-me and even you shower can pull the Italian girls in this Austin-Powered Shaguar'.
The four looked at each other wondering which one would pull the ugly bird on tour as they began loading the beer crates into the spacious boot.

'Why are we taking these continental bottles then Perrier?' enquired Mario… 'surely cans would be better'.
'Well you see Mario, this isn't only a junket …as far as the tax goes this is in fact a business trip and as such is tax deductible…my accountant assures me that I can write off my fifth providing I get receipts-besides we will stop off at Lourdes on the way in order that I can refill the

empty bottles to sell the Holy Water in my shop - and together with the cheap French loaf-sticks which I will tie to the roof then I will be stand to make some bread one way or another'.

'Do you think that I could get some fresh fish for my shop over there?' asked Mario

'Loaves AND Fishes at Lourdes on a roof rack – that would take a miracle of some kind!…' said Perrier thinking of his Profit margin.

The five nationals set out on the A470 towards Cardiff heading on a 3000 mile trip to Rome to watch the last game of an otherwise uneventful Six Nations.

If Wales lost to Italy for the first time ever then they would take the wooden spoon for the first time this decade although it seemed only a matter of time since the WRU had split Welsh Rugby into two Provinces- North, West Mid & South Wales and Cardiff.

'If Italy lose do they get the Wooden Pasta Ladle?' laughed Titch from his Pole Position behind the Union Jack steering wheel. 'Is this car a bloody prop from Spice-World-the Movie?' asked Des Res climbing into the back. 'Why?' enquired Brent O'Lee from the spacious front passenger seat 'Did Ginger Spice sit her asked Brent sniffing the seat?' 'Well I got Victoria Beckham's space'. moaned Des 'cos I can't chuffing move in the back!!!' 'Steady on Posh Spice…. just cos your used to that Posh space in that Castle of yours' laughed Titch looking in the rear mirror.

'Si, I know that an Eengleeshman's home is his castle… but did you have to buy Crawshay's castle for yourself?' asked Mario. 'Look I've told you before …I put the highest bid on the Internet Auction site and to me it was just another Four Walls For Sale.....I do have some Trading Standards you know.!!!!'

'But to bid a million in Turkish Lira…. Wasn't exactly fair trading or cricket old boy was it?' I had my bread lined up to buy the place only to be 'Dez-Umped!'

'Enough talking shop … anyway lets have some rugby songs we are on tour' said Des changing the subject swiftly. 'How about the National Anthem…. Mae Hen Gwlad…' he sang with gusto with the car occupants all joining in ….until they all released nobody spoke Welsh or knew the second line.

They finally settled on a rousing chorus of 'We are the cheeky boys !!!…' which lasted some two hours and three Counties and three crate of lager beer.

Each chorus was followed by buttock raising Mexican Wave the evade the likelihood of Deep Vein Arsebosis.Raucous laughter was met with every bout of flatulence and due to the close confines of the car each inhabitant could determine which one of the Celtic brethren had cut their own brand of Gaulic Green cheese.

After arriving at the Ferry port the drunken trio in the back of the car were awoken from their slumber and struggled from the back of the Mini.

'We must be in Dover!!!' Sighed Des Res glad to be back on his paternal home soil.

'What makes you think its Dover …asked Mario opening one eye…the White Cliffs or Vera Lynn being pushed around in that bath chair over there?'

No. The Refugee Asylum Camps give it away!' 'Are we going over on the hovercraft then …its cheaper?' asked McTitch rediscovering his Scottish ancestry.

'You tight git snapped Brent O'Lee ….. You can P & O if you want to …but I thought that with an Estate Agent Baguette & Chip Shop owners and me a Newshound on Tour …we are Heralds of Free Enterprise….and it won't go down well with my employers if we don't use our Sealinks…I've got coupons off the Ferry from the Depress this week –with four paying passengers I get to go for a Pound!!!!'.

As they approached Customs & Excise, Perrier suddenly began to sweat.

'See that one bloke there with the brown hat on….'said Perrier pointing to the Customs Officer with the long flowing Status Quo hair… 'I'm sure he was in school with me and is batting on the other side.' Before Perrier could utter another word the finger of a suspicion had been pointed back at him. 'Please remove your French Hat Sir…Anything to Declare?' asked the camp Customs Officer'.

'No-aren't you Handy Andy from Penydre School?' enquired the nervous Perrier.

'Look boys a pop star-better search him thoroughly' he said gleefully tossing his hat towards the X-Ray machine… 'Chuck Beret!!!' laughed Titch as the ashen-faced Perrier was led away by the professional shirt-lifter. After a half-hour of probing Perrier was released to the care of his cat-calling Countrymen. 'Do you want your mini-baguette back?' called Andy. 'It must have got lodged when I sat in the back of the car with those two…!!!' muttered Perrier embarrassingly. 'Before or after your home video?' laughed Des Res.

'Titch…. How can you drink some much when you weigh less than Mahatma Ghandhi?' asked Perrier.

Downing his Fifth Can of Duty Free Stella Titch stood firm despite the pitch and roll of the Ferry. 'I'll let you know my secret ….see I worked for the Japs for 14 years in senior management and they made it clear that if your own standards didn't reach their own high standards you were out….' (scratching his forehead) 'as a high- profile executive if I didn't cut it in the Board Room or Directors Bar then you faced the saki……….and if you didn't want a Nip in the Air then you conformed…. I can now drink like 'em think like 'em even builds bridges like 'em…till them yellow monkeys made redundant…. but I had them back…. industrial espionage…I am the equivalent of James Bond in Valleys circles…. I've pinched the blueprint for their new vacuum cleaner for children— some would die-son to get their hands on it. I'm going to sell the idea to my contacts in Italy…it's easy money like taking Baby from a Candi!!!' 'How will you smuggle the blueprint out of the UK?…It's odds on you'll get caught…' enquired Brent O'Lee. 'Perrier …you're an expert on tailpipes…how many exhausts does your average Mini Cooper have?' asked Titch touching a raw nerve. 'One' came the reply Perrier wincing at the memory of his recent body invasion.

'So why does our car have two?' questioned Mario…not putting one and two together. 'Precisely Mario-when it comes to blueprints on vacuum design – there is a sucker born every minute!!'

Arriving at Calais, the Mini passed through customs without any opposition. Perrier on the other hand with his youthful looks and freshly toned body was stopped at the other end by a Frenchman who enquired 'if he had anything to declare and whether he worked out?'

After a further half hour dealing with tax returns he was released by his inquisitor who had obviously been primed by his English Customs counterpart. 'It's no good being self-employed…' moaned Perrier….. 'You're a marked man!!' 'You're definitely a marked man…' laughed Titch. 'We should call you Lord of the Rings after today's performance!' As they left the harbour port, the four friends and a John Wayne walk-a-like strode off into the French Sunset.

'I'd let you drive Perrier but I've only just recovered from a vasectomy operation and its taken two years for the swelling to go down' muttered Titch. 'Brent, do you think you could swap seats ……only until we reach Paris…!' asked the barely retentive Perrier. 'I had a feeling you lot would be jockeying for position and that I'd be the one becoming the back marker before the Prix De Arch De Triumphe….. shift up Mario!!!'

After the car had a brief stop at the beer hyper-market, the drinking session continued apace.. with Mario becoming adept at reaching into the built -in easy access through the rear seats and removing some golden Artois bottles without disturbing the seats or it's occupants. 'It's a good job I'm an amateur gynaecologist….!' He declared as his hand disappeared from sight again between the two seats, 'You missed your vocation in life…Codfather… you should have been a Customs Official' chuckled Des Res watching Perrier shudder once more, 500 kilometres of grey French motorway was livened up by frequent urine stops and the five artists made murals of 20 legged elephants on the side of French over- passes by the five Welsh pee-rs of the Realm.

After the first leg of the journey, they were three hours behind schedule and a committee decision decided that toilet stops would be limited and that they should use the empty bottles for 'excess moisture' unless they passed a designated French toilet area. Bladders were stretched as the empties were refilled quicker than new bottles were drunk. Titch who didn't drink and drive (in case he spilled any) drank any bottle warm or cold… whatever that was passed to him. 'Stop!' cried Perrier 'There's a Toilet' Shouted a soon to be relieved Perrier. Pulling into the lay-by, the fans made their way to the Homme end. 'Where's the toilet's gone? ….it must be closed ….there's only a hole in the floor here!' declared Mario 'It's no wonder these French Rugby Players are so accurate with their drop-outs ….!!!!' laughed Des Res.

After arriving in Paris, the colourful Mini containing the Pride of Wales turned many heads as it sped through the Montemarte and they all had an Eiffel of the Tower of France. As the mini mean machine entered the Latin Quarter the Anglo-Welsh Jones boyos sipped the last of their bacardi breezers as dusk set in the French Capital.

After checking in their hotel 'Le Fleapit', on the banks of the River seine the five tourists were in party mood, true their 3 star accommodation wasn't exactly up to scratch but having selected the Hotel from 'To Let Magazine' - (the Estate Agency Bible) what did they expect. As they unpacked their bags the Tour Party changed gear into the obligation Welsh second strip of

Sweater Shop Polo-neck, casual slacks and white Donnay socks.

As the 'Old spice' brigade headed towards the action they suddenly realised that they were in the more seedier part of Paris –the West Bank.

Looking at the dilapidated hotels, boarded up cafes and pubs, they all felt a little homesick for Glebeland Street. 'Look we're in actual Avenue De Clichy' laughed Perrier. 'Yeah, but ours has more red lights!!' laughed Des Res looking round at the array of brothels but no traffic lights to control the kerb crawlers. As their Welsh accents echoed in the evening mist – an ageing prostitute attempted to entice the party towards her establishment. 'Excusez-moi mon cheri…parle vouz-Francais?'

Titch, being the most experienced linguist and all-round master of the tongue headed toward the Madame.

The streetwalker was 60 if she was a day and had obviously used Plaster of Paris as make-up. Even so Titch was curiously aroused.

Mario had never seen such a site before and was a little anxious at the prospect of entering a back street bordello in a strange City. He therefore placed his wallet down his underpants ….so that if he was mugged at least he'd enjoy it!

After Titch had negotiated the deal handed over the 'kitty' notes the gang followed him into the house of ill-repute which strangely had an entrance hall filled with old French oil paintings.

Clearly this woman was an artiste in different oils and other secretions. The main room was dark and dingy with a low-ceiling and was full of drifting smoke both tobacco and the dry-ice kind that precedes a stage artist entrance.

Having selected the table closest to the stage, the group were treated to a round of Stella as they peered at the stage to glimpse the entertainment.

Both Perrier and Des applauded loudly as the paid- up voyeurs realised it that the artiste was in fact a stripper. Brent O'Lee was the first to agree that the performer was in fact worth the clap but only because she was ginger. Perrier however was already stood on his chair and was doing his own 'Express Yourself' version of Pole Dancing.

As the scantily clad Madonna gyrated towards their table Mario's sense of unease grew further as the smoke began to clear and he could make out men present at the bar in white vest tops, leather hats and 'Freddie Mercury style moustaches'.

On the stage in front of Brent O'Lee, the now topless stripper gestured to Brent to place a note in the knicker-line.

Carefully selecting the lowest denomination from his money belt, in doing so sending several previously thought extinct moths in the direction of the red strobe lighting.

Placing the 5 Franc note in his teeth, he proceeded to crane his neck towards the Stripper.

Titch nudged Des and whispered something inaudible in his ear. Mario reading the mind of the deadly duo released a split second before Brent the anticipation bringing a lump to his throat. Brent had his own unexpected lump to contend with, as he passed the note into the Ginger collection box. Brent recoiled in horror as he suddenly realised that he had an eyeful of another Paris

Tower. 'He's a Transister!!!' cried Brent outing the hermaphrodite.

'Its got a nob!' shrieked the traumatised paper boy. Perrier went limp…. as he jumped down of the chair trying to cover his embarrassment with his Sweater shop jumper.

Mario could make out further shapes looming out of the smoke…like a surreal nightmare….an Indian Chief, a telephone engineer- 'We're in the YMCA!' squealed Mario noticing four other poofs sitting on an upturned bar stool. Both Brent and Mario raced towards the door in an effort to retain their own stools. Des and Titch had to be helped up of the floor in hysterics by Perrier who was trying to be cool by pretending he knew all along about the joke. 'That's why you were pointing at him' Laughed Des staggering to his feet as they left the bar with Perrier nervously bring up the rear.

As Titch slipped the Madame a 5 Franc Service Charge for her part in the humiliation she replied in her native Port Talbot voice. 'For five more you can kiss me where it smells!' 'I'm not taking you back to Port Talbot luv!' laughed Titch. 'Besides your no oil painting and I'd have to be 'In-Seine)'to go on a Two Louse La Trek with you!!!'

As the gang headed for the Moulin Rouge they searched vainly for Dirrty Christine Slaguilera's of their own. As they entered the Internationally- acclaimed cat-house they sat back to enjoy the dancing can-can girls. They became can-can boys as the Stella flowed and they became under the influence of the demon drink. Des became entranced by the dark-haired caged dancer who seemed to be staring at him.

'I'm sure that's Demi Moore' mused Des. She's been looking at me all night!' 'Don't talk to me about cat-houses... sobbed Brent O'Lee ....I'll never be able to stroke a ginger pussy again after tonight!....my pet kitty will have to go when I get home!'

'Speaking of Kitty ...laughed Titch...pay up you lot.....I'm thirsty.....'

As the beer flowed Mario, was enjoying his own Virgin flight of fantasy to Disneyland Paris as he witnessed two pensioners dressed as rodents copulating intermittently on swing trapezes high above the stage.

No more Mickey-Mouse establishments for these boys.

After a night in 'Le Fleapit'Titch discovered why it was only a three-star hotel.

As the rain had finished dripping in through the holes the holes in the roof he could make out Orion, Venus and Betelgeuse in the Paris sky above.

As he awoke he emitted a belch that Barney from the Simpsons would have been proud of. Even this didn't manage to block out the thunderous snoring of Des Res, which threatened to make the Hotel into a Five-Star. One by one the occupants unintentionally recreated the camp-fire scene from Blazing Saddles as the flatulence awoke the slumber party members.

'See he is always up before me in the morning tickling me under the chin!' boasted Titch doing his own stand-up routine. 'Don't remind Brent about last night...!' teased Des. In their semi-drunken state the boys tried not to laugh too much as the had a Hair of the Dog from 'Le Fleapit's Mini Bar'. The ribbing of Brent was merciless as Mario suggested that had almost eaten the 'Lunch-pack of Notre Dame'.

After each of the party had sworn on the Hotel Room Bible not to reveal details of Brent's humiliation. The usual Centuries old unwritten Welsh Male Oath of 'No Tales on Tour' was adopted. Perrier did literally get the book thrown at him by Brent when he asked the boys what they thought of the 'Sword-swallowing Act' last night.

Des was oblivious to events he could only see a vision of Demi Moore dancing in a cage...beckoning towards him.....I wonder if she was doing so research for 'Showgirls 2' he thought. Still ....she looked different without 'the pause button' on.

As the group resumed their internal 'Traffic Jam', the Estate Agent became the Des'ignated driver as the Tour De France set off towards the mountain stage of the journey.

Wearing his yellow 'Lacoste' from the former Co-Op store in Merthyr (Lacoste of Living) the Tour Leader headed south towards Lyon like a man on a mission and a Playstation 2 Steering Wheel.

As the Mini sped along the French motorway they reached incredible speeds which seemed even faster in kilometres.

As they finally arrived at the mountain region between France and Italy the group had almost exhausted their own 'Mini-Bar' and decided to 'refill' the empty bottles at St Berrnard in the Alpen Springs. The Spring Water was promptly loaded into the boot and Christened 'Eau'de Chien' by Perrier the entrepreneur.

After stocking up on local breadsticks which they tied to the roof the car was well and truly over-loaded and looked to the locals like a vehicle commissioned by the Hovis Expeditionary Ski Force. After a further hour on the 'Beer' the four passengers had polished off the last of the 'Gold' Label lager they parked the car up for the night and the five Welsh-men settled down for a night in the Alps. Due to last nights snoring Des Res was voted a back- seat place as punishment. Brent O'Lee had voted driver to ensure he couldn't dodge the 'Toll' at the border. The vote also ensured that Radio 4 was left on through the night to drown out the likely snoring of Des Res.

As each of the businessmen left reality, the 'Archers' theme blurred into the background.

Titch was unsure what sound had awoken him first,…Des Snoring or the announcement on Radio 4. Either way he was grateful.' Rover- the manufacturers of the Mini have decided to recall all models following a discovery that they may be technical problems with the handbrakes.' Came the Radio Broadcast. Looking down at the 1000 foot drop into Italy six inches from the Mini Titch agreed.

He looked back at the Party and wondered whether he should open the Mini-door and save himself-after all it is a 'Self-Preservation Society' he thought.

The Mini had rolled to its present position in the night partly triggered by the vibration snoring of Des and the rear wheels and boot were perched perilously over the edge of a Mountain Pass. Brent O'Lee was the next to wake and soon realised that the odds on survival were slim. Assuming he was going to die, the news-hound's life passed before his eyes in the shape of Merthyr

Depress Headlines 'Downhill all the way for Rugby Fans on the Piste'. 'Des-aster as Estate Agency Crash hits Peak'……….Perrier Springs Eternally' Who would have thought that the sound of a Welsh Ringtone could be fatal as the inevitable fumble for mobile phones in the back of the Mini nearly caused an avalanche tipping the car over the edge of the edge of the Alpen Peak. With every intake of breath the Mini rocked back and forth with Des snoring. As Mario and Perrier realised the 'gravity' of the situation, Des continued to snore blissfully on. 'We need to lighten the load in the back' whispered Titch to the still, white, Perrier in the back One by one the 'refilled' beer bottles were 'passed' into the front seat to Titch who in turn due to his 'DT's'spilled most of them on Brent O'Lee before pouring them over an unsuspecting French shepherd in the Valley below.

'Ello Ello its peezing down again!' moaned the Frenchman slipping into his sheep-skin jacket and anti-Wellington boots.

The Ringtone stopped and was replaced by a Text message sent from a Welsh Dragon symbol. How R U LUV …U No answer! I knew she'd push me over the edge one day thought Titch.

Back home in Wales, Titch's wife nose was twitching her psychic senses had a vision of Sue Barker and Princess Grace.

And that meant only one thing……Cliffs……and she didn't want her marriage to be on the rocks. She rang Direct Enquiries, and due to the length of time she usually spent on the phone they knew her personally. 'Alpen Headquarters…. please send help!'

'You're still too heavy in the back ...!!!' raged Titch. 'But how? ...asked Mario ....You've had all the piss-bottles, the last of the food...even our shoes and Perriers box of ribbed condoms...we've given you all the heavy items...there's nothing left in the back...' 'It's the 'Gold' in the boot...it's weighing us down'...sighed Titch.

'Eureka!!!'...he cried suddenly after moving Des feet.

'Brent reach in the back gently and see if you can reach Des' wallet...it must weigh a ton.....!'

The Sight of Brent O'Lee taking money from his wallet really shouldn't have bothered Des after all these years but it was the directness of it this time that set him off. Still half-cut and the sight of a hairy `hand reaching into his heart pocket in the French Alps was too 'gaul'ling even for the mild-mannered Des Res. Some primeval fear was awakened in him and uttering one audible word...Darlo....he struck out sending Brent backwards in doing so jamming his behind in the steering column.

The resultant wedgey that Brent received for his efforts stabilised the car...but sent the 'Gold' label beer in the boot further to the back and had also sprung open the boot mechanism. Des 'snoring resumed although one decibel lower this time...and the wind too started to shake the car. With Brent disabled and Titch DT'd Mario was asked to reach into Des' pocket but they were wedged tighter than one of his home –made roll-up fags. Titch reached inside his pocket and took out his faithful tin of tobacco. His head cleared as he relaxed. It was always the same when he rolled his own.

In his head he was thinking of ways to get out of this mess...what would his Welsh Rugby heroes do in such a situation…he thought. He started to hum internationally …thinking back to his days as a boot-boy at the Arms Park…not an apprentice…just a hooligan ….The Rugby songs did the trick as the car rocked to the tune of Bread of Heaven…..the boys prepared to meet their maker in some style.

Suddenly out of the mist appeared a giant St Bernard dog, which bounded onto the bonnet of the mini stopping its descent to the valley floor.

Reaching out of the open window Titch grabbed the brandy cask from around the dogs collar and pinched some of the dogs 'St Bruno' and smoked and drank deeply.

'L'Eau De Chien….' He spluttered spitting out the spring water like it was Allbright.

Bread of Heaven…L'Eau De Chien he was divinely inspired.

Reaching up to the roof he pulled down a bread stick and asked Mario to open the rear seat flap. With all the skills acquired from a mis-spent youth he used the breadstick to 'pot' the yellow and pushed the Gold Label and full bottles of water out into the deep blue yonder causing an avalanche in the French village below that had not been seen before. The mini righted itself with a bump waking Des Res with a start.

'Morning Boys!'…I had a lovely dream about Wales and some Angel…. Charlotte Church… was singing Bread of Heaven…. pointing at the St Bernard….. where did we acquire the nodding dog in the front?'

After their narrow escape, the lads were glad to be alive and felt privileged that God was Welsh. Dog was God backwards and they were singing Bread of Heaven…this meant only one thing in the Rugby fans eyes…they could not lose the match or finish last in the Six Nations table.

Divinely inspired…… with Rugby songs blaring Max Boyce met Max Speed and the sound of 'Hymns and Arias' abounded around each hairpin bend or narrow Alpine pass. Determined to hang onto his 'Yellow Jersey' he drove with the Welsh Front Row motto stuck in his head… 'They shall NOT pass.'

The Mini's heathen brethren did not share Des Religious stance and became increasingly concerned that the distances between some continental Lorry Drivers and the Mini were less than a Yorkie in length. The passengers in the back had had enough of these European Roads and poor Perrier had became in-continent himself due to Des'erratic driving. Looking in the rear view mirror Des liked what he saw not just his bronzen face, neatly trimmed 'Pepe Di Marco'goatee but the other great love of his life. Approaching from behind was a Porsche Carrera with a flashy female driver with a face and body to die for. This Lady in Red was now tailgating Des and he flashed a smile at the 'Demi-God' behind. The smile was reciprocated to reveal perfect film-star white teeth. The challenge had been sent by eye-mail and the race was on. A straight road ahead meant she could make her move. After accelerating to 150 KMH the Mini flew up the road outstripping the stripper.

After checking the rear-view mirror Des assumed he had lost the Porsche.

Suddenly as if using his 'Sixth Sense' he looked to his right …less than two Yorkie's away from him sat Demi Moore who flashed a chase-me smile usually only reserved for pursuing paparazzi. Des for a split second

thought that it was a trick of the light as he saw his own image in the passenger seat next to the Hollywood star.
Bruce Willis just looked and pointed at his doppelganger driving the Mini.

The spell was broken by Mario's interruption. 'Des we drive on the right in Europe'

The two Bruces almost had 'CAR'mageddon as Des spotted the roadblock of cars up ahead. Standing up on the brakes the skid-marks on the road were six inches deep…narrowly beating the skid- marks and Yorkie Bars to be found on the back seat of the mini. Demi and Bruce zig-zagged through the fleet of black sedans at break-neck speed….they proved they did Die-Hard. As the Mini screeched to a halt inches from the first sedan, Des was furious leaping out and shouting and swearing at the dark-suited men who stood silently at various positions on the road and mountain-side. 'Do you think you own the road….?' raged Des like a modern-day Basil Fawlty. Titch opened the door and tried to calm the irate Estate Agent.

He hadn't seen him this angry since his business rival appeared on telly and he wasn't exactly 'Over the Moon' then either. 'Why the violin cases and dark glasses?' asked Perrier 'Are they the Blues Brothers?!' 'They are the Cosa Nostra …and yes they do own THIS Road…!!!!' explained Mario. Titch disappeared around the back of the car and produced a long thin packet of his own. Instinctively the Mafia raised their weapons training them on Titch and the purple Des. 'Leave me negotiate this deal…. Des…. I'm going to make them an offer they can't refuse!!!' said the brandied Brando. The assumed leader met Titch up close. Scarface to Scarface.

As the men embraced each other, the three passengers emerged from the Mini wondering what on Earth was going on. Introducing Mario as the Merthyr Codfather. Ancient rites were exchanged between first and fourth generation Italians.

As Titch handed over the Vacuum blueprint in exchange for a bag of unmarked bills the henchmen backed up the sedans and the Mini was allowed to pass.

The car moved in silence passed monasteries and convents alike towards border control. Des broke the self-imposed vow of silence as he spotted the Porsche parked –up in a lay-by yards from the Frontier. He raced to the finishing post arriving simultaneously with the Porsche. Looking down at the two vehicles the Italian official was confused. Checking the passport photographs of both the Bruces he could not tell them apart.

Finally noting the words 'Walters 24 hour' on the back of Des passport he handed back the passports. In the confusion that followed both men were asked to confirm that they were not planning on 'Moonlighting' again with any Shepherds. And the passports were switched as the official waved both cars through. Looking at the crossroads sign Perrier asked the reason why 'All Roads seem to lead to Rome?'

'We'll guide by the stars…' declared Des following the Porsche as it raced like St Elmo's Fire towards the Capital City of Italy. Pedal to the metal, the Mini raced towards Rome. After what seemed like an eternity of touring passed Turin and roaming towards Roma they reached the outskirts of the Ancient Roman Capital.

Arriving on the Appian Way they munched their way through some vermicelli purchased from the 'Spartacus

Pizza Hut'. Soon the pasta masters had even some linguini as Mario attempted to ring his mother back home in Wales announcing his arrival in the other land of his fathers by mixing cultures declaring his emotions in two languages…Mama Mia…. Mam I'm Here!!! As they raced through the streets they soon realised that they weren't the only Welshmen in town for the game.

The streets were lined with red and white scarves all with Anti-Anne Robinson slogans and other red dragon emblems thereon.

Looking around at the olive-skinned dark haired beauties in tiny designer Tee-shirts, Des, Titch and Co were in their oils.

Looking at the straining Gucci Perrier said longingly- 'See Naples and die!!!'

'I don't see what you see in those girls – not one of them is ginger!' moaned O'Lee disappointedly. Drinking the rich exuberance of the Eternal City the Union-Jack flashed past the windows of the designer shops-Armani, Gucci, Pravda and Derek B Phillips (Rome) Limited.' 'I bet their expensive in there!' moaned O'Lee.

'Yes, Lacoste of living is greater out here!' laughed Titch 'Next stop Vatican City …I've got some business with the Pontiff!' said Des scattering the pigeons in St Peter's Square quicker than a hungry St Tydfil Square Busker.

'Only be a tick…I've got a confession…I planned this trip to cover my own acquisition of an Old Masterpiece!' Des told the boys about his promise to buy a priceless collaboration work by Renaissance-men Michelangelo, Raphel, Leonardo and Donatello. As he left the car he was escorted by the Swiss Guard to the gate.

After Des had flashed his Gold Medallion of St Peter previously hidden beneath the Bee Gee Chest hair he was granted an audience with his Holiness. As he greeted the Pope he bowed and handed him a business card. 'We have a mutual friend-a papal knight- you have a palace …he has a castle.' 'So you've come for the Nazi War treasures Kurt Waldheim gave me have you…?' asked the Pole.' Do you have the Reddy money?' After handing over the Lira to His Crookedness the Pontiff unscrewed his Papal Staff and took out a curled up masterpiece. 'Do you want to see it' …asked the Pope…. stooping towards the sweating Des.

'We have a saying in the Estate Agency business …In God We Trust…everyone else pays cash or goes to sealed bids……. and you're the closest thing to God I'll ever meet!' laughed Des placing the painting into a cylindrical protector.

'I've a hunch …..chuckled the Pope swigging from his hip-flask…you've been Framed!!!'

As he skipped through St Des's Square, the Patron Saint of Estate Agents punched the air. He'd clinched the greatest deal ever and he was happy.

Happier than the time he sold that 5th Floor Flat to Stephen Hawking because he told him that his Guests would Sound like him on the intercom.

Booking into a cheap hotel next to the Coliseum the Tour Party arrived at reception.

As Brent stood on the room balcony, the rest of the lads unpacked their gear.

'I always said I would bring Christian here!' he mused looking at the Arena Brett thought it an omen that the Welsh 15 Gladiators would win the battle of Rome.

Looking back into the room O'Lee noticed the floor was alive with cockroaches… 'Caesar's Palace it ain't' he said 'I reckon we got the animal quarters…..' Titch 'Well it's thumbs down from me…. and the Coliseum smells!'

Perrier told him to stop moaning. 'At least the neighbour's don't have pot-bellied pigs!' He chuckled. Mario raised the team spirits by turning the subject to Rugby.

'Well boys, we're in Rome and we must do as the Romans do!' 'What …pinch handbags and arses…?' asked Brent.

'No, drinka Di Vino!'

Half an hour later and the likely lads were out on the Town resplendent in their tour Tee-Shirts of Wales 22 England 21 Twickenham 1998 as they joined the throng of Welshmen heading for the stadium. A red and white army white Giant daffodils, massive top hats and blow-up sheep everywhere.

As they urinated against walls, trees and into the fountains…even the Trevi fountain had its share of leeks were there too!! Welsh fans adorned every café club and wine bar. Carrying an armful of tins from the off-licence was thirsty work and Titch, two cigarettes in each corner of his mouth decided to cool off in the Trevi fountain.

After choruses of Volare and just one Cornetto he was removed from the Fountain by a local policeman who objected to the song 'Three Cans in a Fountain'.

As the fans made their way to the ground they had their customary argument over the best Welsh player ever.

Perrier, like Welshmen of his age, remembered the halcyon days of the 70's when HAD a rugby team and Triple Crown wasn't just a type of beer.

After the good old days Welsh Rugby had been divided into two Provinces to save money…. North, South, West & Mid Wales and Cardiff.

He nominated Gareth Edwards. Des couldn't separate JJ or JPR. Brent O'Lee was un-swayed. 'Jenks for me! Professional, accurate and of course ginger!'

The cry of Wales went up as they entered the stadium. Brent O'Lee felt for his digital camera remembering his promise to the Editor that he would get a photo for the Depress. Showing his Press Badge, he made his way together with his assistant Titch to the touch-line behind the Italian goal. The rest of the crew made their way to the VIP seating. As the two teams took the field, led out by the Band of the Royal Welsh Fusiliers and a ceremonial goat, Mario, Titch and Des could make out the shapes of Little and Large sitting behind the goals relaxing on the grass.

After a circuit of the ground the band and goat left the stadium.

The game kicked—off and went well for the Welsh team as the reliable boot of Jenkins raced them to a 9-3 lead. 'See…'slurred Brent ………. 'That Jenks is magic!'

'I know how he is so accurate'…laughed Brent my mate works for 'Just Mental' and he told me his secret………………See those ears…. he lines them up with the posts and keeps his foot and head still when he kicks……..!….and he was taught by the Maori Chief that each tackle was a spiritual battle… 'A modern-day War of Jenkins Ears!!!' laughed Brent falling over into the grass'. 'That's bullshit!'…laughed Titch falling over into the same grass and then sniffing his hands. 'Goatshit…actually!' wiping the second-hand grass of his digshital camera.

Brent was having difficulty focusing on his camera…he had double vision.

'Titch, take some photographs…will you, or my editor will turn into a head-hitter on Monday morning otherwise!'

Up in the stand the balance of power was turning. Des like his wine was in vintage form. 'C'mon pass the bloody ball out wide', he bellowed turning claret.

He was a very passionate supporter…mentally tackling, scrummaging like he was on the pitch.' At last…I've been looking for you all over the stadium….!' Called a sweet American voice from behind him. For the third time that weekend, Des looked deeply into Demi Moores' eyes and the Welshman lost track of the game, or his surroundings. He was in Elysium fields…like Russell Crowe's Gladiator he was oblivious to pain, noise or the scoreboard. Demi-God and Demi-Moore stood motionless, as Des' 'pause button' went on and he stood like a ghostly figure Des hands turning an imaginary Potters Wheel. The slap across his face brought him back to Earth as he suddenly realised that he had in fact found Silicon Heaven.

As he was forced by the Steward to remove his hands from her fake breasts, Des' face turned a patriotic red then white. 'Miss Moore…more please!' he pleaded like 'Oliver' with a finished bowl!!! As the stewards dragged the sex attacker away towards the pitch his 'phoney' passport fell onto the grass.

Des explained that he only wanted to go the touch-line again and was further restrained by the security-man.

The Passport was lifted off the floor and hand to the rightful owner Bruce Willis by a 'Die-Hard' fan.

Mario and Perrier left the ground in shame hoping to rescue their friend.

They were gutted to miss the final score but realised that as the Welsh Team were leading 9-6 and in their own- half.

Suddenly the Italian side raised one last effort and the ball was hoisted high into the air to the pre-arranged call of '99'.

The ITALIAN LOB was on.

This was the one moment all game that the Welsh Forward Robert Sidoli had dreaded.

His loyalties between his Welsh and Italian Roots were divided.

Did he catch the ball for Wales or miss it for Italy?
A swift glance at the Mafia Hitman in the stand made his decision for him.

His legs turned to jelly and Sidoli's hands to Ice Cream as the ball conveniently slipped from his grasp.

The ball bounced into the hands of Italian forward Hugo Bastardo.

All that stood between Italy and victory was Jenks.
All that stood between Italy and the wooden spoon was Jenks.

All that stood between Titch and the 18 stone Italian forward was Jenks.

As Jenks and the Italian forward collided with the squatting six stone frame of Titch squatting on his heels the noise was deafening.

For a split second…only Titch knew why the rugby ball had not been grounded by the Italian Forward.

The supreme sacrifice made by the Welshman for his Country.

The playback on the Stadium screen showed that the recently neutered Titch had put his testes on the line for Wales forcing the player to touch down in the 'Dead-Ball Zone'.

The jubilation of the Welsh Fans when the Try was disallowed was matched only by the screams of Merthyr's latest eunuch.

Brent O'Lee comforted his pal's 'Betty Swollocks' and then asked him if he had taken the close-up picture.

The answer was in the negative…..and Brent began to sob.

'You know that suitcase of money you had…. Sobbed Brent…I bet it on Italy to win!' They didn't have time to reflect, as the Italian Mob knew that Titch's tackle-bags had robbed them off the match and they wanted more Welsh Blood!

The sudden streak of Perrier across the pitch stark naked distracted the stewards sufficiently to enable Des to escape from the clutches of the stewards.

The talented Perrier had 'Pole-vaulted' over the stadium fence and created a distraction –copied from like his Tour Idol -David Edwards- creating a 'Dia –Version'

As quick as the flash, Mario backed the Mini into the ground and collected the now 'Famous Five' from the pursuing irate Roman mob and mobsters.

As the Mini sped through the narrow streets, lanes and piazzas the sight of a Union Jack clad Mini threw the sight-seeing Michael Caine into a dementia panic.

Escaping the City via sewers and football stadia roofing, the Polizia pursued the Mini without relent.

Exactly how they escaped their 'close encounter' with an Alien Police Force was a Mini-mystery ...but the Fiat cars strangely couldn't cross the cattle-grids leading to the Alpine passes.

Back home in Merthyr, the Con Club buzzed with the Tour tale and the sight of Titch's bruised Testes on the big screen made him into a local Heroine!

As the newly acquired Renaissance oil painting was revealed to the Committee. Grey smoke emanated from Des Res. The Old Master had been framed by an Old Master.

'There's gonna be a new Pope in Rome soon...!' snarled Des like Arnold Schwartzenegger...I'll be back John Paul!'

As the green faces of Leonardo, Donatello, Michelangelo & Raphael stared back at the red face of Des he sobbed ....

He was having 'Turtle Recoil'.

'Sharing'

Ken James

Delia and Mat were both in their 60s and retired. Mat, being a man who liked an occasional drink with the lads, was carefree and content in his retirement and Delia, who loved her television, gardening and Sunday church, had nothing to complain about. They both were young at heart and rarely thought of the inevitable. If they should decide to fly abroad once or twice a year and a timid friend warn them of the disasters of air travel, they would dismiss the unnecessary comment with their life long philosophy which was, 'When your time has come there will be nothing you can do about it. So enjoy life while you can.' But one day when they both walked down the road to the Spar for a newspaper and a few groceries, the delicate subject of the departure from this life to the other side was brought to them on a subject they had not considered.

It was Mrs. Southgate who had approached Delia and Mat in the village with the news that she had heard the council had stopped burying people in their beloved Pant

Cemetery. 'It's true, I'm telling you', she said with a very serious tone. 'There are to be no more burials in Pant. They're thinking of opening a new cemetery near the Gurnos, or somewhere.'

The well-groomed Delia felt betrayed. 'I can't say I've thought about it, really,' said Delia, softly. 'It's always been a foregone conclusion that I'd be buried here. After all, I've always lived in Pant,' she added.

'I've been lucky,' continued Mrs. Southgate. 'I went to the Civic Centre six months ago and bought a used plot. I'm seventy. I like to know where I'm ending up.'

Delia turned to Mat. 'We should be thinking about the inevitable, you know.' Mat stroked his grey moustache but said nothing. Delia turned back to Mrs. Southgate. 'Mat and I are both in our 60s.'--Delia paused as a huge juggernaut making for the Spar drowned her voice--'You never know when it will happen, do you? I've always thought I'd be buried in Pant.'

Mat suddenly realised the situation. 'I don't want to be buried in the Gurnos. Are you sure all the grave spaces are gone?'

Delia pulled on Mat's arm as a car raced down the road. 'Get on the pavement. You'll be buried before your time,' she said.

Mrs Southgate stared hard at the fast driver as he sped away. 'They look at you as though you shouldn't be out and about, and the fumes are enough to gas you.' She tightened her headscarf.--'All the new spaces are taken, Mat,' she said, coming back to the subject. 'But there maybe an old grave with just one body. They are opening such graves for people who don't mind being buried in the same plot. I don't mind being buried with somebody as long as it's in Pant.'

Delia looked at Mat. 'I wouldn't mind that, would you, Mat?'

Mat puckered his lips. 'I want to know who's down there. Could be a mass murderer.'

Mrs Southgate shook her head dismissing the remark. 'Get down to the council offices,' she ordered. 'They're very nice people down there. Very helpful. You might be lucky.' She looked up and down the road, raised her hand as a farewell gesture, and then crossed when she thought it safe. 'Take my advice now or you'll miss out,' she called, as she was half way across, then had to hurry as a motorbike came roaring towards her.

Mat smiled on one side of his face, 'I think she's wise booking her place early,' he said, a cryptic tone in his voice.

'What do you think Mat, seriously?'

'Well, I must admit, I'd feel more at home being buried locally, I suppose. And it's near the Pant-Cad-Ivor Inn,' he smiled. 'I could always nip out for a pint.'

'Will you be sensible for just one minute? What shall we do?'

Mat looked to the grey sky and imagined the blue vastness beyond the clouds. 'We'll make arrangements, my love.'

The following day Delia and Mat visited the Civic Centre and made enquiries at Reception. The receptionist, an attractive dark-haired girl, kindly telephoned the relevant department who said they could give the couple an interview. The directions the receptionist gave took Mat and Delia down to the basement and into a peaceful room where three elderly ladies sat behind their individual desks in silence. They all looked up and smiled but said nothing. The lady behind the nearest desk peered over her dark-rimmed glasses and beckoned them to sit in the two chairs opposite her; they obeyed, slowly and quietly. In a very soft voice, she said, 'What can I do for you?'

Delia looked at Mat, wanting him to take the proceedings.

'Just making enquiries, really,' said Mat, feeling uneasy about the situation. 'We were told by a friend that the council has stopped burying at Pant Cemetery. My wife and I have always lived in Pant, and though we...we're not thinking of departing just yet, but we were hoping to...sort of...stay in Pant.'

'My family have always been buried in Pant,' said Delia. 'I'd feel a stranger if I was buried elsewhere.'

The lady smiled kindly again and spoke in a sympathetic calmness, 'My name is Mrs Llewellyn. We have many enquiries from people wanting to reserve a grave space. Lots of people are far younger than you. It is true, however, we have run out of *new* grave spaces. But we do have a few *used* graves left. If you wish to purchase a shared grave I maybe able to arrange that for you.'

Mat was encouraged by the lady's gentle tone and accommodating manner. 'Would I be indelicate if I wanted to know who was down there?'

Delia looked at Mat. 'Mat!'

Mat puckered his lips and his face turned a rosy colour. 'Well,' he faltered...'I really would like to know whose company I'd be keeping.'

Mrs. Llewellyn gave a broad smile. 'That's all right.

You'd be surprised what people say when they reserve a grave space. Some want to know if there is a killer down there.'

Mat shuffled awkwardly in his chair. 'So it would be against the rules, then?'

'I will be able to inform you of the occupant when I have located a space. I'm afraid there will be no choice, however, because there are only a few left.' She paused and smiled. 'You'd be surprised how funny and fussy some people are. I had one old gentleman who purchased a space and told me, 'I hope my grave won't be too far from the main gates because my legs aren't very strong.' I thought he was joking, but he was very serious.--Anyway, I'll take your details and make a search for you. When, and if, I find some room, I will write to you. I need to have your name, address and the required fee, I'm afraid.'

'Oh right,' said Mat and gave their names and address. 'How much do we owe you, Mrs Llewellyn?'

'That will be £130 please.'

Mat unconsciously made a nervous throaty sound. 'Will a cheque be all right?' he asked, not having that amount of cash on him.

'Yes, yes, that will be fine,' smiled Mrs Llewellyn.

When the business was completed Delia and Mat thanked her for her time and kindness. As they left, the three ladies gave a final smile. Mat ensured he closed the door quietly, not wanting to disturb the tranquillity that pervaded the room. Outside he showed his chequebook to Delia with a frown on his face. 'Oh for goodness sake,' said Delia, 'I'll give you half if it will make you any happier.'

'But we don't know if we'll have a grave space,' he

said.

'The lady is bound to find a grave with only one person in it.'

'I think I'll have to go for a drink tonight, love.'

'Surprise, surprise,' said Delia.

A few days later a letter arrived from the council allocating Delia and Mat a grave space, ZXIV in Pant where a young child had been buried over a hundred years ago. Mat was reading his newspaper and put it down and was amused by a receipt for the cheque attached to the confirmation, it was headed Merthyr Tydfil County Borough, *Leisure Department.*

'We'll be there till Armageddon, I suppose, so it needs to be leisurely,' he said.

He handed Delia the letter and sat on the settee where he resumed reading the newspaper.

Delia sat at his side, her slight figure still wrapped in her thick red dressing gown. 'I wonder who the child is,' she thought aloud.

Mat lowered his paper, 'What child?'

'The child who's buried there.'

'They won't tell you that,' he said. I'm just happy to know it's not someone with a violent past.' He rustled his broadsheet as he lifted it again and began reading.

'It's a nice thought knowing you are going to keep a child company. I wonder if it's a boy or a girl.'

'Does it make any difference what sex it is? The poor thing is just a bundle of bones now.'

'The spirit is still there, waiting for company.'

Mat lowered his paper again. 'Waiting for the resurrection, I suppose.'

'We're both Christians, Mat. That's what we are taught to believe in.'

'You wouldn't like to make me a cup of tea, would you, love?'

Delia got the message. Making an absent-minded move towards the kitchen, still thinking. 'It could be. It could very well be, you know.'

Mat ruffled his paper. 'What now? What could be?'

'It doesn't matter. Do you want a biscuit with your tea?'

'That will be fine.'

'After you've had your tea and read your paper, we'll take a trip up the cemetery and try and find this grave. I'd like to know where it is.'

Mat put his paper down, deciding to get into the spirit of things. 'I hope it has a pleasant view,' he called. 'I wouldn't want you complaining.'

His facetious remark made her smile. She took off her glasses and cleaned them after the kettle had steamed them. Carrying a cup of tea to Mat, she placed it on the coffee table at his side.

'I'm going to get ready for the cemetery,' she said. She turned and smiled at him. 'I hope the neighbours are nice.'

Mat chuckled and sipped his tea. 'There'll be no barbecues or noisy parties, anyway.'

As it was a fine autumn day but a bit chilly, they dressed in warm clothes and walked to the cemetery. They called into the office behind the cemetery church and asked the supervisor for directions.

'It's a little complicated,' he said, taking his glasses off and standing up. 'But I've got to go and see the boys, so

I'll take you there.'

He was a short man of slight build, but walked sprightly. Too quick for Delia and Mat, for they had to make haste to keep up. The three climbed a steep tarmac path with a tall stone wall on the left, and an array of pitted headstones, grey and lichened, on their right. There was not one gravestone which stood erect and straight. Arched pieces of granite tilted to all points of the compass. Huge stone crosses leaned forward looking tired and worn, oblong tombs subsided sadly. At the top, the path wound around to cross-roads. There, the supervisor stopped and pointed to a piece of rough grass between two crumbling headstones. There was no sign of identification, and the long lumpy couch grass was turning autumn yellow.

'It doesn't look much, I'm afraid. It's been abandoned for a long time. I'll leave you to it and check on my diggers over the other side.'

'Thank you,' said Delia.

'It's a pleasure,' he said, and went on his way.

Mat looked around him, taking in the scenery. They were at the top all right, gravestones all around, sloping down on all sides. Scattered here and there, standing proudly among the old crosses and tombs, like new boys on the block, were shining black granite headstones indicating the recently interred. There was a fine view of the bleak Twynau Mountains and the wind-swept ridges. Down the slope he could see a piece of ground covered with fresh wreaths and sprays. Delia just stood gazing at the unkempt piece of six by three.

'Mat, can you feel an atmosphere?'

Mat pulled at his flat cap. 'What atmosphere?'

'Well, you know, as though there's something about the plot that's drawn us here.'

'£130, that's what's drawn me here. We've had our money's worth. There's a fine view and the neighbours are quiet'

'Fate. I feel as though fate has drawn us to this spot for some reason.'

Mat turned his back on her, not to ignore her, but to shelter his behind from the strong chilly breeze. Coming through the gates on the Brynau side was a hearse accompanied by the funeral cortege.

'Here we come. In a few years they'll be bringing us in like that.'

'Us?' questioned Delia. 'We're going to die the same day, are we?'

'I didn't think of that. If you want the top bunk you'd better hope I go first. They won't remake the bed once you're in.'

'Try and take things seriously, Mat.'

'You've got to think of these things.'

'I'm going to buy some flowers for this grave,' said Delia.

Mat turned to her. 'There's nothing wrong with you, is there?'

'We'll have to tidy it up. Make it look respectable.'

'It's a grave, not the front lawn.'

'Somebody is down there, Mat. Alone and neglected. The little darling deserves respect.'

'Mrs Southgate will think you're mad.'

'I don't care. I have a feeling about this grave. A very deep feeling indeed.'

Mat wasn't one to argue. He turned his attention back

to the funeral. The open grave was surrounded with mourners looking to the sky, their lament riding strongly on the breeze.

'Let's go,' he said. 'I don't want to see them shovelling the earth in.'

As the weeks went by the roughness of the grave was transformed into a neat and tidy rectangle: All grass had been removed and a concrete kerb surrounded the fresh brown soil. Three urns of flowers, equally spaced, made it stand out brilliantly.

The grave diggers passed there on occasions, their brains trying to figure out who had suddenly been buried there, for not one of them could remember who had opened it up. Furthermore, it was too early for a gravestone to be mounted to give any clue. They began to suspect that their supervisor had, in an emergency, contravened union regulations and had opened it up with the help of management when the men had had a dispute some weeks ago. Wanting to make sure they had their facts right before taking any unofficial action, they decided to take turns in keeping an eye on the grave. If they could find some relative visiting the grave they could diplomatically ask when the recent burial had taken place. As nobody seemed to attend the grave on weekdays, straws were drawn for someone to do a Sunday ritual. It was on the second Sunday afternoon that the chosen sentry saw Delia arranging flowers and tidying up the grave. Tentatively, the gravedigger, dressed in his Sunday best, approached Delia and complimented her on the neatness and colourful patch of ground. After tactfully asking a number of questions, to which Delia seemed surprised at the personal nature of them, the man discovered the truth. To the relief of his workmates the mystery was solved and all was well

In the meantime, Mat had given up on Delia. She had become obsessed with the grave and was attempting to trace the history of it. Week after week she would attend the grave until Mat just let things go over his head. Then one day he realised she was more relaxed about the subject, though she still went up the cemetery once a month to tidy it. He wanted to know why her enthusiasm had subsided, but didn't like to mention it in case it might re-kindle the fire. Nevertheless, one Sunday having a quiet lunch at home, he decided it was time to be logical about it again.

'Is it this Sunday for the cemetery, love?'

'Next week. I'll get some flowers on Friday.'

'You've given up the atmospheric peculiarities of the grave then?'

'I know who's buried there now, don't I?'

Mat was shocked. This was the first he heard of it. 'Who's buried there? Who is it?'

'I told you some force had drawn us there. Well, you didn't share my intuition. But if you remember, years ago, I told you about a young child who died in our family at the end of the 19th century. My grandfather told me it was his younger sister. She was only four when she passed away. It's her.'

Mat was staring at her in disbelief. 'How do you know it's her?'

'I researched my family. My grandfather's sister was buried in Pant cemetery, and the grave we bought was first opened the year of her death, down to the month. So it must be her.'

'There must have been lots of graves opened the same time.'

'I dare say. But I had a dream two weeks ago. I saw the cemetery the way it would have been over a hundred years ago. I saw a child's coffin being lowered into our space. And then, I had a clear picture of my grandfather.'

Mat looked up at the ceiling, and then stared her straight in the eye. 'You're serious, aren't you?'

'My grandparents were never ones for spending money on graves.' She finished chewing on a piece of chicken and pointed her fork at him. 'My relative is buried there. I know it! I know it!'

'Who am I to doubt you, love?' And then he carried on with his Sunday lunch.

'And do you know the irony of it? They have now stopped selling used graves. Fate waited for us to purchase our grave.'

Mat suddenly felt a chill. It was the phrase, 'Our grave.' It all seemed too close for comfort.

'When Heroes Walked'

Celia G Thomas

Merthyr Tydfil was a boom town in the 1800s, a town humming with the industries of iron and coal, criss-crossed with quarries and coal levels and canals that transported iron and coal to Cardiff, then one of the busiest ports in the world.

It was a bustling town of tramways, clusters of cottages and tai unnos (one-night houses) and labyrinthine alleys flanked by lodgings houses and brothels. Near the centre of the old village of Merthyr were the Crawshay settlements, close to the River Taff. This was a 'no go' area known than as China, which had its own laws and its own emperor. At night, sparks from the blast furnaces lit up the skies and these could be seen from miles around.

Terraced houses, built between tips and mines, were mainly of stone with two rooms up and two rooms down and with a privy at the bottom of the garden. As most families were large, the cottages were woefully inadequate and amenities were sorely lacking. Most houses did not even have taps so water had to be carried from wells or stand pipes. Sanitation and drainage were absent so outbreaks of cholera and other dangerous diseases were frequent.

Work was back-breakingly hard and hours in the mines and ironworks were long. Small wonder then that these workers found solace in the cwrw bach, the pub which was the social, political and cultural centre for men who wanted diversion from their work, a forum in which to air the views, and a place where they could sing, make music and hold eisteddfodau. Some of the most popular inns were the Dynevor Arms, the Miners Arms, the Three Horseshoes and, central to the town, the Castle Inn.

For those who renounced strong drink, the chapel was the focus of their leisure time. Here was the venue for the eisteddfodau revived by Iolo Morganwg and supported by his son, Taliesin Williams, who ran a school for middle-class children. He also organised concerts and poetry readings.

For those who preferred sports, there was plenty to choose form. Running had been a tradition since fables exploits of Guto Nyth Bran of Llanwonno. Fighters were very popular and one of the best was red-haired Shoni Sgubor Fawr who rules as emperor in the notorious district of China.

Outdoor pastimes included hunting and horse-racing which were often accompanied by the refreshing brew of cwrw bach (small beer). Glebeland was the setting for fairs frequented by circus performors, magicians, hucksters, ballad singers and harpists. A day at the fairground was a day when workers could forget their miserable working conditions and wives, with their children, could escape from their shabby, in-sanitary homes.

Not all houses were slums though. On a rise on the outskirts of town at Cefn, William Crawshay II had built a mock medieval folly in 1825 at the cost of £30,000 – a huge sum in those days. This was set in beautiful parkland with a long, wide drive leading up to the house – actually, it looked more like a castle. So it became known as Cyfarthfa Castle and often referred to as 'The Castle'.

The rooms were large, many oak-panelled, with beautiful furniture and opulent furnishings. An army of servants were employed to clean the mansion, to cook for the family and to tend to their needs. These were cooks, kitchen maids, parlour maids, ladies' maids and char women who did the rough work.

There were gardeners with assistants to look after the extensive grounds. There were grooms to take care of the horses and a coachman to clean and maintain the carriages. There were odd-job men to see to the smooth running of this luxurious mansion. Williams Crawshay was very possessive of his castle and woe betide anyone who tried to enter his grounds illegally.

One of the maids who worked at Cyfarthfa Castle was Marged Price who lived in Merthyr's main street near the Castle Inn. Her father, Huw Price, was a puddler at Crawshay's Ironworks. His job was to stir the molten wrought iron by expelling the carbon. It was hard and skilful work and could be dangerous. Huw had worked for Josiah Guest at the Dowlais Ironworks, but he'd left because he resented the Guest Truck Shop system which kept workers in debt.

At Crawshay's the men were allowed to elect their own doctors who would be more sympathetic in cases of compensation for injuries sustained during their work. William Crawshay senior had always tried to avoid labour troubles and was not opposed to trade unions as long as they did not become too powerful or too demanding.

Marged was very close to her father, especially since her mother had died. He was always very protective of her and warned her to be careful whenever she visited her friend, Dwynwen Jones who lived in China.

Marged had always known that this part of Merthyr was very rough. Street fights were frequent and knives were often used, but there seemed to be an unwritten law that women were not to be molested and Marged never was.

She had been frightened once though when she'd gone to China to call on Dwynwen. As she'd walked down the street near the River Taff she'd seen a crown outside one of the small cottages. They were shouting and cursing in Welsh which Marged understood. There was a chorus chanting 'Come out, Ianto Sedd Fawr, you hypocrite. A deacon of the chapel you are but you beat your wife and everybody knows it.'

Some men broke into the house and dragged the miscreant out into the street. There on a make-shift sled was the ceffyl pren (the wooden horse) and on it was an effigy of Ianto Sedd Fawr. They thrust him onto the sled and pushed him through the streets, naming and shaming him for the bully he was.

They stopped at the riverbank and held him down in the water, almost drowning him, but not quite. They set fire to his effigy and warned him not to lay a finger on his wife Gwyneth, a little mousse of a woman who had endured his beatings for years – too terrified of him to complain.

Whether Ianto ever beat his wife again, Marged never knew. What she did know was that she had been witness to the rough justice melted out in China. The following week the disgraced deacon was driven from his chapel and ostracised by his neighbours from that day on.

Marged's home was conveniently on the main road opposite the house of Thomas Darker who owned a grocery and drapery shop. Marged was a good needlewomen and sewing was her way of earning extra money to out by for her 'bottom drawer'. She often bought materials, laces and cottons from Darker's shop and one day Mrs. Darker invited her into the parlour for a cup of tea.

Marged was most impressed by the lovely furniture, beautifully polished to a smooth and glossy finish. After tea, Mrs Darker played Welsh tunes on her pianoforte and was eager to show the new organ which she admitted she had not quite mastered as yet.

When it grew dusk the lady of the house lit the gas lamp which gave a soft glow to the room – unheard of luxuries in a town where most people had to use candles or oil lamps except, of course, for Cyfarthfa Castle which had all the modern conveniences.

One day Marged was returned home from work at the castle to find her father sitting very disconsolately by the fire.

'What's the matter, dad?' she said. 'You're looking quite upset'.

'Crawshay has closed down one of the furnaces', said her father, 'and scores of men are out of work'.

'I'm sorry', declared Marged. 'Are you one of them?'

'Thankfully no', replied Huw, 'but the price of iron had dropped and several other furnaces in Merthyr have also closed down. There will be hard times ahead, I'm afraid'.

A few weeks later Marged was coming from the market when she saw people crowding outside Margaret Rees's house. She heard the men shouting and the women crying. Then two bailiffs came out carrying a bed. They were jostled and pushed by the crowds who grew angrier by the minute. There were cried of 'for shame' and 'how can you do this to a lady who is so sick?'

One of the bailiffs, red in the face and obviously embarrassed, spoke quietly. 'We have to do this. It's our job. If we refused, someone else would take our place so please let us pass'. This seemed to mollify the crowds and they stood silently for a few moments. The Marged asked if she could enter the house as she knew Mrs. Rees well. She went in and found her lying on straw in the throes of a serious illness.

She looked up at Marged. Her face was etched with suffering and her once bright eyes were full of sadness.

'The bailiffs have come', she said quietly, 'and we had no money to give them. We are so deeply in debt. They've taken my son's watch, some furniture and now they've taken my bed'.

Marged tried to comfort the old lady. 'I'll bring you some cawl tomorrow, Mrs. Rees. That will make you feel stronger'. When she called the next day, she was told that Margaret Rees had died during the night. Her son was distraught with grief and anger. 'Down with the Court of

Requests!' he shouted. 'We must rid ourselves of this unjust system that robs us of even the basic essentials of life'.

When Marged reported the incident to her father he was furious. 'There's going to be trouble over this, Marged', he exclaimed. More furnaces are being shut down so more men will be out of work, and those who are still working will be on short time. Then the bailiffs will be busier than ever. We must put a stop to it'.

Months passed. A new year dawned – the year of 1831 and black clouds were gathering over the hills of Merthyr Tydfil. Already a quarter of the furnaces had been shut down. Wages continued to fall as the price of iron dropped and to make matters worse, the cost of food rose. By April, Plymouth Works had blown out town furnaces and later, in the summer, three furnaces at Dowlais and one at Penydarren closed down.

On May 2nd there was a meeting of workers at Riverside near China. Effigies were burnt and tempers grew hot. On May 23rd miners pay was cut and Crawshay sacked eighty-four puddlers. On May 30th there was a large meeting at the Waun where the workers put forward a four-point resolution. They wanted to abolish the hated Court if Requests and with it imprisonment for debt. They wanted to stabilise food prices to prevent hardship. Lastly, miners wanted rules about taking over a stall vacated by another miner; they could do so only at an increased rate of pay.

Huw Price was at the meeting and told his daughter that the following day he would visit his brother, Tom, who lived in Penderyn and had been active in local affairs concerning the miners and men who worked at the Hirwaun Ironworks.

The next morning Huw rose early, had a large breakfast then walked over the mountain to Blaen Cadlan, reaching his brother's house in the afternoon. The street was black with people and his brother was there holding a man against the wall and pinning his arms so that he could hardly move. Other men were doing the same to persons who were obviously bailiffs, and these were driven off by the crowd.

This was a victory for the people of Penderyn. They had succeeded in stopping a Court of Requests distraint on one of their neighbours. Lewis Lewis, known as Lewsyn yr Heliwr, Lewis the Huntsman.

When all the fracas had died down, Tom Price introduced his brother to Lewis. They chatted for a while and Huw became curious about this man who had not only defied the iniquitous Court of Requests but had also aroused the villages to support him.

Later, when questioned, Tom told his brother all he knew about Lewis Lewis. He was a native of Penderyn, born in Blaen Cadlan in Cwm Cadlan. He had been a haulier but was now a miner at Penydarren, earning eight shillings a week to keep a wife and four children. He was bilingual but preferred to speak in Welsh and when he spoke men listened to him. He was a natural born leader whom people were prepared to follow however dangerous the situation became.

Lewis Lewis' stand against the bailiffs and the support he received from his neighbours were the first known resistance to the Court of Requests which proved successful. Only two days later, in the evening, a mob attacked the house of Joseph Coffin, President of the Court of Requests, and it was there that Lewis the Huntsman saved the life of John Thomas, the constable who was trying to protect the property from damage.

It was when the mob attacked him that Lewis saved his life. In doing so he was injured himself but declared that he did not want to shed blood. John Thomas never forgot this brave act.

June 2nd, 1831 was a truly momentous day. In the morning Huw Price joined bands of men who marched through Merthyr carrying banners blazoned with the word REFORM. They hoisted a red flag with a loaf of bread on top. Crowds of women and boys joined them as they tramped along Brecon Road. They turned off past Bethesda down towards Jackson's Bridge.

In the town shopkeepers boarded their windows and locked their doors, while many bailiffs hid from sight, fearing retribution which they thought would surely come, and come it did.

After the attack on Jospeh Coffin;s house that evening when windows were smashed and his property was looted then burned, Williams Crawshay sent for soldiers, Highlanders from Brecon, the yeomanry from Llantristant and the High Sheriff from Neath.

Now there was no stopping the crowds. They headed for Cyfarthfa and stopped the works, then they marched to Penydarren and Dowlais Ironworks.

Marged Price knew that her father was with Lewis Lewis and she feared for him. She was always up early and was always breakfasting before seven o'clock. Her father had not returned but as she looked out of the window she saw him marching in the crowds. She went to the door to call him but the noise of the shouting mob drowned her frantic cries so she went back inside the house, very worried now as she guessed that soldiers would soon be arriving.

Marged hurried up the street towards Cefn to Cyfarthfa Castle to report for work. As she hurried along she heard a strange, strident sound. It was the music of the bagpipes played by the Argyll and Sutherland Highlanders. As she turned the corner she caught sight of them. Their kilts were swinging as they marched and women, standing at their doorways, mocked them and shouted, 'Go home and out your trousers on'.

Despite the seriousness of the situation, Marged could not suppress a smile and she caught her breath when she saw how young some of these soldiers were.

Some of them smiled at her as they passed but many looked away. Most were from working class homes themselves and did not relish coming up against miners and ironworkers who had rebelled against their masters only because their conditions had become intolerable.

As if to set an already dramatic scene, thunder boomed across the valley and black, ominous clouds hid the sun. By now Marged had reached the iron-wrought gate of the castle. Several soldiers were guarding the entrance and one of the officers questioned her. When she told him she worked for the Crawshays, he ordered her to return home as conditions in Cefn were likely to become too dangerous.

Marged retraced her steps and, as she was nearing her home she saw troops gathering outside the Castle Inn and hundreds of workers pressing close to them. Some were shouting 'Caws gyda bara! (cheese with bread!)'.

Major Falls, fearing bloodshed, asked the people to fall back. His troops had already been instructed to point their bayonets up and no one was to fie unless ordered to by an officer. The situation was very tense and growing worse by the minute.

Ann Harries, a neighbour, called Marged and said, 'Look, there's Lewis Lewis. He's the leader and the young man standing next to him is Richard Lewis. They call him *Dic Penderyn'*.

Marged nodded, 'but where's my father?', she asked. 'I'm desperately worried in case he will be injured or even killed.'

'There's nothing we can do, Marged. My man is there too but all we can do is wait', murmured Ann.

Then the Riot Act was read and Major Falls asked the people to keep calm. Twelve delegates were chosen to hold talks with the ironmasters. They put forward the four point resolution already decided at the Waun meeting, but the masters would not consider any of these conditions until the crowds laid down their arms and disbanded.

By now the Riot Act's hour was over and Sheriff Jenkins told the men to disperse. Ann Harries watched as Lewis Lewis urged the men forward towards the soldiers. The hurled clubs and stones and four soldiers fell wounded but the attackers were driven out. Some rebels were already dead.

One soldier, Donald Black, lost his musket and was stabbed in the thigh. Major Falls was bleeding from his head and neck. Growing more confident the crowds forced their way up the steps of the inn but again they were driven out.

By now the soldiers were angry but they dared not fire until given the command. At last one officer, afraid for the safety of his men, yelled 'Fire!' and then the shooting began. Four men fell and lay bleeding on the street.

Ann Harries saw town men being carried off to the Tramroad and later she watched as John Hughes, a miner, fell mortally wounded. Then through the gun smoke she saw her husband limping towards her, being helped along by Huw Price whose arm was covered in blood.

'Thank God you're safe! Thank you Huw. Bring my husband into the house. I'll tend his wound and yours. Then go home. Marged is frantic with worry'.

With his right arm bandaged, Huw picked his way through the stone and cudgels which littered the street past several corpses that lay in pools of blood. He passed a woman weeping as she cradled her dead son in her arms. He knew the woman. She was Mrs. Robinson and her son was only seventeen.

Huw learned later that many of the wounded had died in ditches alone and untended. Others had their wounds washed and bandaged in kitchens where small frightened children looked on in disbelief. Man, enraged by all the suffering of their families and friends, paraded through Merthyr and beyond calling men to arm themselves and join the fight.

The next day during talks between the twelve delegates and the ironmasters, Josiah John Guest and William Crawshay, it seemed as if a settlement had been made, but before a definite conclusion could be reached, a large crowd marched to Cefn waving guns and firing in the air. They approached the gates of Cyfarthfa Castle then stopped. Many went back to the town and many more stayed in the Brecon Road. The crowds split and melted away.

By Twelve o'clock an unearthly quiet had settled over Merthyr Tydfil. After all the shouting, banging and tamping of feet and the whistling ricochets of bullets, peace descended on the troubled town. Many hundreds of men had lost their nerve and wanted to settle. Many felt that they could do no more. Whatever the reasons were, the insurrection had lost it momentum.

On Sunday, June 5th it was the military that was now on the offensive. The stipendiary, J. B. Bruce, declared that the ring leaders must be caught but there was still shooting from the men at Dan-y-Graig. Between twelve o'clock and two o'clock the firing stopped and the rebellion collapsed. Only hours later two of the rebels leaders were captured.

All Roads Lead To Merthyr

'Mrs Prosser Saves the World'

Nigel Roberts

Teel sat alone in the cockpit of his spacecraft, a curious dome shaped contraption that resembles a small bubble car. Amazingly this is the vehicle that will carry Teel, travelling faster than the speed of light, to the chosen destination of the elders.

Teel is a Rilder, a space traveller, the most experienced Rilder on the planet Trey. Teel has travelled back and forth to many planets in his long life. But this time it is different, he is travelling to another solar system, to a planet that is a mirrored image of Trey. A planet whose atmospheric composition, mean surface temperature, and surface gravity are exactly the same as that of the planet Trey. Teels destination is the planet Earth.

Trey is a planet half the size of Earth, but apart from its size it could be its twin. It has rivers, oceans, trees and mountains. Trey even has its own sun. The inhabitants of Trey are also very similar to human beings. Their molecular structure and internal organs are almost exactly the same and their digestive systems also work in the same way as a human being. Treyans facial structure is also identical to a human, except for one small detail everyone on Trey looks exactly the same. Everyone on Trey looks the image of Norman Wisdom.

Trey is a victim. A victim of its own good health. There is no illness on Trey. There are no drugs, no tobacco, no alcohol, and there is also no consumption of animal fats on Trey, (probably because there are no animals). The inhabitants of Trey consume only one food, this food gives them all the nutrients they need, The Kour, a boring bland tasting plant that resembles a giant carrot and of course they drink water.

The inhabitants of Trey live a long life, a very long life, generation after generation, now there is just no more room, they need another place to live. A planet like their own in every way a planet like earth.

A Treyans life does end, they die of old age, and old age only they cannot be killed, (or so they think) and they suffer no disease. Their bodies are virtually indestructible. Their skin looks no different from a human's, yet it is a trillion times denser than steel. Their brains, although the same size as a human's can handle more data than Earths largest computer, they can learn an alien language in seconds.

Treyans have only one weakness, high pitched noise, it can alter the composition of their brains, causing extreme pain, and eventually causing the brain to explode and ultimately death, but because there is no high pitched noise on Trey, they don't know it yet.

Teel tensed himself ready for take off. His mission was simple, land, observe, and report back to the elders of

Trey how much resistance the Earthlings would give before their eventual extermination.

The spacecrafts engine roared into action, Teel, Trey's greatest Rilder was on his way.

Mrs Prosser sat on the pre-second world war armchair that was pulled as close as possible to the open fire, and stared deeply into the shimmering flames. She had sat in the same spot and looked into the flames of the same fireplace since she was a toddler.

She was born in this house at 29, Castle Street Dowlais. On the 7th of January 1901, today is the 7th of January 1963, its Mrs Prosser's Birthday. She's 62 years of age.

Mrs Prosser's life hadn't been an easy one. To be born in a terraced house in Dowlais at that point in history wasn't exactly being born with a silver spoon in her mouth.

Dowlais was an old industrial community, and had been so over a hundred years before Mrs Prosser was born. Welsh men and Women from all over rural Wales came to Dowlais In search of employment and a better way of life. They found employment, but also times of mass unemployment and short working hours. There were accidents at work running into double figures every day, and because of the mass influx of people, it produced overcrowding and disease.

Mrs Prosser's father died in an industrial accident when she was just Twelve years old, so to make ends meet and put food on the table, she finished school and followed her mother into the age old trade of pub cleaning and at the time in Dowlais there were many.

Up until the age of twenty, Mrs Prosser's life had been a sheltered one. From the age of twelve, her life had been a constant routine of cleaning pubs, and on her days off cleaning the house. There was nothing in-between.

Then it happened. Whilst cleaning the urinals, of the Camarthen Arms public house in Elizabeth Street, in walked Ponty Prosser, a man who couldn't wait to point Percy at the porcelain. Ponty was the kind of a man that took no notice of the sign saying 'TOILETS BEING CLEANED' 'DO NOT ENTER' pinned to the toilet door.

Ponty was a giant of a man compared to the majority of Dowlais males. His five feet, three inch frame resembled a miniature Battleship. Ponty worked days regular at the Dowlais Steelworks 7am to 11pm six days a week, and on Sundays he fought bare knuckle fights on the fields just above Incline Top, Penyard where he also lived.

Ponty was a hard man, the hardest in Dowlais so it was said. He was also known as a man who could hold his drink, a quick pint of ale to most would mean a quick gallon for Ponty, and he always said, he would like to die with his lips wrapped around the tap of a barrel of scrumpy. Yes Ponty was an extraordinary man, he was the quickest man casting moulds in the mould casting department in the foundry at the Dowlais works, he had the quickest left jab in Dowlais, he was the quickest shuffler of a pack of playing cards probably in the world. Which were amazing feats for a man with only one arm. Ponty lost his right arm in a bet with his mates that he could steal a couple of pork chops, from under the nose of Mister meat cleaver Chang, the local Chinese butcher. He lost the bet.

Ponty could do almost everything with his left arm, but he always struggled with his fly buttons. Ponty smiled at the girl kneeling on the floor in two inches of dark yellow water, (the urinals were blocked yet again) and with a wink of his dark brown lazy eye said 'give us a hand girl'. It was love at first sight, and after a whirlwind romance they were married six months later, and Ponty moved into 29, Castle Street Dowlais.

Things weren't easy for the couple, as two months after they were married, Mrs Prosser's mother ran off with Dai Goldie, the door-to-door goldfish salesman from Treorchy.

Soon after Ponty was put on short time at the Dowlais works, and many of the pubs Mrs Prosser cleaned stopped employing cleaners, because most of the regulars were so drink sodden, they didn't know or care if the pub was clean or not.

Times were tough for Mrs Prosser. Ponty had time on his hands that he needed to fill, and he filled his time and belly with rough cider at the many pubs dotted around Dowlais. It even came to a point where if he was in a pub where his wife was working, he would take her days pay and drink it back to the land lord.

The year was 1923. Mrs Prosser was 23 years old. At last brightness came into her life, she gave birth to a daughter Bronwen.

The house in Castle Street was cold, as were her feelings now towards Ponty, as his drinking tore them further apart. But it was Bronwens smile that warmed her and kept her warm for the next two years.

Then it happened. The lowest point in Mrs Prossers life. While she was collecting her pay in the Bush Hotel in the High Street, Dowlais. Bronwen was stolen from the pram, by a gang of Rumanian gypsies from Newcastle on their annual baby stealing jaunt to Dowlais and was never seen again. Mrs Prosser was distraught, but survived, she had always been a survivor. She threw herself into even more cleaning. As well as the pubs she cleaned in Dowlais, she ventured farther than she had ever been before and started cleaning pubs in the Town of Merthyr. Only two miles from Dowlais but to Mrs Prosser a different world.

She survived, just. Day followed day, week followed week, year followed year. Nothing changed, Mrs Prosser cleaned. Looked after Ponty who was now suffering from deep depression. And Cried.

The year was 1930, Mrs Prosser was 29 years old. The previous five years came and went in a blink of an eye, with no laughter or happiness.

Ponty was now on permanent short time at the Dowlais works. When he had money he would drink it all away. He was getting more depressed day by day and the couple barely spoke a word. It was 4th February 1930, when Ponty received the earth shattering news, that the Dowlais works were to be closed with only a months notice and there were to be 5000, Redundancies. This news was the final straw for Ponty. On the night he received his notice he broke into The Cardigan Arms, in Victoria Street, Dowlais, at 3 a.m. He stuck a half pint glass up his up his rectum, wrapped a lace from his left boot around his Penis and tied it tightly in a double knot. He then put his mouth over the tap of the scrumpy barrel and turned it on. The cider poured into Ponty and with no means of escape, his stomach expanded, bigger and bigger until his stomach couldn't take any more. Ponty then stabbed himself, just below the belly button, with a lemon knife he had taken off the bar. He burst. There were bits of Ponty all over the bar, walls and ceiling and completely covered the four stone pub cat Montague, who had observed Ponty breaking in but was just to fat and lazy to move. Death by cider. It was the way Ponty wanted to go. At his funeral, Mrs Prosser didn't shed a tear.

Mrs Prosser stared into the flames, contemplating the past, the disappearance of her two-year-old daughter Bronwen, the death of her husband, and what she had done with her life since Ponty's suicide. Tears fell onto the recently polished oil – cloth, as she whispered to herself, 'what a waste' But if nothing else she was a survivor.

By Mrs Prossers standards the past four years hadn't been so bad. She had become good friends (her first ever friend) with Mrs Jordan from Mary Street, who was a bar maid in the Hollybush Hotel in Market Street Dowlais, one of the pubs Mrs Prosser cleaned. Mrs Jordan was of a similar age to Mrs Prosser and initially they didn't have much in common but over the years they became very close.

Mrs Prosser had never been one to socialize but Mrs Jordan had convinced her to go out with her once a week, on a Friday night, to the Blue Boar Inn, a pub situated on the far end of Castle Street.

They didn't drink much, only a couple of milk stouts, and they sat in the snug, because the bar in the Blue Boar, had a strict men only rule. Mrs Prosser always sat next to the door of the snug leading to the bar, because she loved to listen in to the men's conversation. Some of the stories made her laugh. In fact, listening to the jokes and stories of the Blue Boars regulars who were a bunch of weird and wonderful characters, helped Mrs Prosser to learn to laugh again. One of the Blue Boars regulars, Father Mc'Cormack, Dowlais resident Roman Catholic priest, always sits in the bar near to the door of the snug, and Mrs Prosser can hear every word he says.

Father Mc'Cormack, after a few pints of Real Ale is a joker, a comic, a comedian and he makes everyone in the pub laugh. Especially Mrs Prosser.

Laughter evaded Mrs Prosser for so many years, she seemed to be making up for lost time, for when she laughs, she laughs louder than anyone in the Blue Boar, she laughs louder than anyone in Dowlais Mrs Jordan swears she laughs louder than anyone in the world.

Mrs Prosser's laugh isn't thunderous it's high pitched, it starts as a titter, then the pitch gradually gets higher, so high humans cant hear it, it's at this point Blackie the pubs alcoholic Labrador starts howling, when Blackie stops howling, Mrs Prosser's mouth is still open, and Mrs Jordan swears that Mrs Prosser's laugh is so high pitched, at it's highest point, dogs cant even hear it. 'it's a laugh beyond this world' she chuckles.

It's the 7th January 1963, it's a Friday, and it's Mrs Prossers Birthday. At 7pm Mrs Prosser and Mrs Jordan are going down The Blue Boar to celebrate, maybe have one more milk stout than usual, and maybe a laugh or two.

The same day, numerous people observe a small bubble shaped flying object around Maysville Kentucky U.S.A. three F-51 jets were dispatched to investigate, at a height of 15,000 feet two of the planes left the chase because they were not equipped with oxygen. The flight leader Captain Verdun Roberts disregarded the danger and relayed a commentary back to the ground, until according

170

to one observer his plane seemed to explode in the air, and the strange bubble shaped object just seemed to disappear. Seconds later a flying bubble shaped object appears directly above Castle Street Dowlais, and lands in the five feet high grass at the garden of number 29.

Teel opened the bubble shaped dome of his space craft and breathed in the crisp winter air. It felt good as his lungs expanded. 'No time to lose' he thought to himself. Teel knew before he could observe the Earthlings he must do three things. He must disguise himself not to look out of place, quickly learn and understand their language, find a place where many gathered. Concealing the spacecraft would pose no problem as it was designed that it could be flattened to the size of a corn flakes box and easily be hidden in the long grass.

Teel was suddenly jolted backwards, as a booming voice echoed from a building twenty feet away. The deafening voice was Rev Protheroe delivering his daily sermon at the Chapel in Mary Street.(the rear of the chapel was positioned in Mrs Prossers back garden). Teel listened intently, it would take him only minutes to learn and speak the Earthlings language.

'Is it true'? Roared Rev Protheroe. I ask you children of Babylon, 'Is It True'. His voice rose even louder. 'There as been vicious rumours on the streets of Dowlais recently that some of the flock has been having relations with a ghost, yes you miserable sinners, a ghost. Now I ask you? He thundered, is there any truth in these ridiculous rumours, is there anyone in this congregation having sex with a ghost'? A hand raised slowly, the hand of Mister Rhys Morgan, the partially deaf pig farmer from Pant.

'Mister Rhys Morgan' screamed Rev Protheroe 'Is it true? Have you been having sex with a ghost'?

Rhys Morgan lowered his hand slowly and sheepishly answered 'Oh ghost, I thought you said goat'. Everyone laughed, except Rev Protheroe.

'What a weird lot' Teel thought to himself, as he was now thinking in the language he had just learnt. Ghosts, goats, 'who are these people'?

Teel turned sharply, as his acute hearing detected a flat monotone drone the other side of the garden. It was Dinny Probert the local drunk, trying to sing Molly Malone in Welsh. He was totally inebriated, he had been drinking all day in the pubs around top Dowlais, and was taking a short cut through Mrs Prossers garden heading for his final destination of the day. The Blue Boar public house. Teel walked slowly towards Dinny. Dinny never reached his final destination. His final slurred words were, 'cor butt you look just like Norman Wisdom'. Dinny's clothes fitted Teel perfectly.

Teel hopped over the garden fence and into the narrow Alley that led into Castle Street. 'Is the whole of planet earth like this place' Teel thought to himself. The streets were empty. It was five minutes to seven o' clock on a Friday Evening. Teel walked slowly down Castle Street, and as he reached the Blue Boar Public House, he could hear the creak of the pub door opening. It was seven o, clock it was opening time and it was Friday night.

As the blue boar's door opened, so did almost every door in Castle Street, and people started to pour out of their houses, all walking in the same direction to the open doors of the Blue Boar. Teel looked in amazement at the faces of the people walking towards the pub, because they all looked different. No one looked like himself, or anyone else on the planet Trey. (Not one looked like Norman Wisdom.) 'What a ugly lot' he thought.

Teel concealed himself in a doorway and watched the Earthlings all filing into their place of gathering. He thought he already knew how weak the race was. The killing of Dinny Probert was as easy as picking a bunch of Kour. But he needed to know were there any stronger of the species, were there special ones. He would soon find out, by observing at their place of gathering.

Mrs Prosser sat in her usual spot in the snug of the Blue Boar Public House. Mrs Jordan was at the serving hatch ordering their usual milk stouts. The pub was packed, more than a usual Friday night, Mrs Prosser thought. 'Maybe they know it's my Birthday' she said to herself, then thought better of it. Mrs Prosser looked around the pub, where she sat in the snug, near the door leading into the 'Men Only Bar' there was a large pane of glass, with the words Mitchel And Butlers printed in the centre. Through this pane of glass she could observe everyone in the pub.

The bar was full of regulars, men from not only Dowlais, but from the whole of Merthyr. The beer and scrumpy in the Blue Boar was legendary. The pub's regulars were real characters, the hard men that always stood by the bar renowned for holding their drink, and the drunks that always sat down they liked their drink but couldn't hold it. Conversation was never limited in the Blue Boar; the regulars were as diverse as doctors, factory workers, those without work and tramps. The pub certainly had a varied clientele.

Mrs Prosser looked around the snug, it was the same old faces that looked back at her, the same faces, sitting in the same places, that they sat every Friday night. Except for two, one a woman in her late thirties that stared back at her intently, the other a man with an expressionless face that looked for all the word like Norman Wisdom. Mrs Jordan sat opposite Mrs Prosser and handed her a milk stout, 'happy birthday love she said' and meant it.

Father McCormack turned from the bar with a pint of Real Ale and a whisky chaser, (Irish whisky of course). And sat in his usual seat. It had been his fourth journey to the bar and he had only been in the pub twenty-five minutes. It took Father McCormack at least three pints to warm up, after the fourth pint the jokes came thick and fast and the regulars loved him.

Father McCormack was fifty-eight years old, and came from an extremely poor area of Dublin an area that was no more than a ghetto; it was a place where there were only two ways out, either become a thief or become a priest, he chose the latter. Father McCormack was a good man, a caring man, he cared about people. The strange thing about father McCormack was although he was a Roman Catholic Priest he wasn't exactly religious, he had always had the opinion that religion got in the way of God. He couldn't comprehend why in poor areas of Naples, Italy, people were starving, while the Vatican City had unimaginable wealth. He always thought 'God wouldn't like that'. But he always helped when people needed help and he would always listen to any one that needed a kind ear.

Teel studied everyone in the Blue Boar and thought to himself, 'extermination of the inhabitants of earth is going to be easier than he or the Elders of the planet Trey could ever have imagined, this race has no intelligence, no strength, no power' and smiled to himself as he sipped on his half pint of scrumpy.

'I could get used to this' he thought.

Father McCormack finished half of his fourth pint and knocked back his whisky chaser in one gulp. Mrs Prosser gestured to Mrs Jordan that that for some reason the pretty woman sitting in the corner was staring at her. Mrs Jordan turned around and then back again, to face Mrs Prosser, 'I don't know who she is but she looks just like a younger version of you love' she chuckled.

Mrs Prosser stared into the strangers eyes, but her attention was diverted, as an Irish voice in the bar starts cracking jokes. Father McCormack had warmed up. 'What are the poles doing in Russia' he asks. 'Holding up the telephone lines' he answers himself. Mrs Prosser begins to chuckle. 'A blind man walks past a fish shop, good morning ladies says the blind man' quips the comedian priest. Joke after joke follows in quick succession, Mrs Prosser's laughing gets louder and higher pitched with every joke Father McCormack says.

Teel starts to feel a strange sensation inside his head, a sensation he has never felt before, Teel is feeling pain. He looks at Mrs Prosser and connects the sound she is making with the unbearable sensation he is feeling inside his head. The pitch of her laughter gets louder, he feels that his brain is about to explode. Just as Blackie the pubs alcoholic dog starts howling he realises he can't take the pain any longer, the pain will kill him. He thinks to himself 'Is this human the only one that can make this unbearable sound, if I kill her, will the pain go away'. Then he realises the woman in the corner, the woman that was staring at Mrs Prosser is making the same sound, even more high pitched, even louder. He can stand no more and rushes out of the door of the Blue Boar, 'cor didn't that bloke look like Norman Wisdom' says Big John Shag, the pub's landlord.

Outside the Blue Boar Teel takes in a huge breath of the cold night air. 'How many on this planet make that unbearable noise' he thinks with the only part of his brain that isn't muddled with pain. 'It could be everyone, the chance is too great, they cannot be conquered'. Teel makes his way back to the long grass at the rear of 29, Castle Street, Dowlais, climbs into his bubble shaped spacecraft and takes off for the journey back to Trey. His task of observation is complete. The elders of Trey, will have to find another Planet for it's overspill to live on. Planet Earth cannot be conquered.

The woman in the corner with the high-pitched voice, walks towards Mrs Prosser. Mrs Prosser knows who she is. 'Bronwen'? 'Yes mam' replies the woman. How did you find me'? Wept Mrs Prosser.

'A Rumanian gypsy from Newcastle, who I thought was my mother, for all these years told me the truth on her deathbed' she replied 'she told me my real name and where I was stolen from, I asked the landlord at the Bush Hotel, and he told me where I could find you'. They hold each other for what seems like ever. Mrs Jordan cries.

Its January 7, 1963, It's Mrs Prosser's Birthday, she has just received the best Birthday present she will ever get she has her daughter back and although she doesn't know it   MRS PROSSER HAS SAVED THE WORLD.

All Roads Lead To Merthyr

'Children For Sale'

Jan Caswell

When Owen got back to his own kitchen, his mother was preparing to go out. It was not usual for his mother to be going out to town at this time of the day, and he was interested to know what all the fuss was about. On the table, there was a basket covered with a white cloth. Owen knew from past experience that someone was in trouble, and his mother, a God fearing woman herself, was going out to help. 'Don't take your coat off, Owen, you're coming with me. Your Dad will meet us later.'

'Where are we going Mam?' asked Owen, being bustled through the doorway, he'd only just entered.

'There's trouble down at the Pugh's.'

'The Pugh's.' Owen had heard the name, probably from Chapel.

'They live down by Bethesda. They lost everything to the Court of Requests, the other day ‑ at least that's what Morgan Thomas, the Deacon, told your father this morning. Mr. Pugh lost his job several months ago. He

179

was lucky enough to get a job down in the pit, but, not being used to pit-work, he was run over by a train of coal trams and killed.

Owen had heard about the accident but did not connect this with the Pugh's name.

'And now with no money coming in the family are in more debt - lost everything, and poor Mrs. Pugh with five little ones to keep. It's a dreadful place that Court of Requests. Joseph Coffin should have more sense. He's a hard man – always was. Even as a boy he had no heart. He'd kill any creature that crossed his path. The wicked good-for-nothing rascal – and he the President of the Court of Requests. It makes you wonder how on earth he got the job in the first place.'

Mrs. Jenkins shook her head in dismay. 'Come on Owen. There's no time to waste. Let's get down to the Pugh's and see what we can do.'

Owen and his mother hurried along the gravel lane down to the Brecon Road. The warm Spring sun had dried the rough surface of the road, but rancid, stagnant water still filled the rucks made by the cart wheels that ploughed up and down.

Sad, poorly-dressed people, with worried faces, frequented this part of town. It was an area built by Crawshay for his workers and so attracted all types of people, who attempted to scratch a living from those who had a regular job in the works. The Cyfarthfa Iron Works provided for many families. Owen had been told that, with full employment, came scores of people from all over the surrounding areas, all expecting to get some kind of work. Thousands had come into the valley and many of these poor souls had found themselves living in hovels, cellars or on any waste ground they could find. Their lives became a constant search for food and warmth. Many spoke neither Welsh nor English. The Spanish and Irish people formed close-knit communities with others down by the river, at a place they called China, a place where Owen's mother forbade him to go. No respectable person would put life or limb at risk by going there. However, Owen paid furtive visits down to the town in which he used to live. He knew his way around. He was a local boy and knew exactly where to go and what to avoid. Life down by the River Taff and over by the Glebeland during market day could be very exciting. Traders, gamblers, shysters, hustlers, pedlars and those with plenty of money to spend mixed freely together on market day. There were drunken brawls in back streets. Blackened eyes, skinned knuckles and bad heads had to be treated the following day. Owen had thought that on Sunday mornings, many were grateful for a day of rest for completely the wrong reasons.

Owen followed his mother along the road, snaking their way around the rubbish and human waste that littered the place. Owen knew what his mother would do when she arrived at the Pugh's. She would give everybody something to eat. The children first, and then Mrs. Pugh. Then she would try and comfort Mrs. Pugh, who had been admitting to everyone that she did not know where to turn. The Chapel people were always very good on such occasions and although the Pugh's were recent additions to the congregation, everyone had taken to the family and were shocked at the death of Mr. Pugh.

Approaching Bethesda, the noise of barking dogs, screaming babies and noisy children reached their ears.

The children seemed to be going around in gangs, just like packs of dogs. Poorly dressed , dirty people shuffled about. The smell of decay filled the air. It was a place where days were hungry and nights were cold. Dark passages led to a maze of hovels. It reminded Owen of the China that he had heard about in town. A place where vagabonds, rogues and thieves lived openly, and where unseen eyes watched from every corner. Bethesda was another place you kept away from at night. Owen did not feel too safe during the day time. His mother, however, felt she was on the Lord's business and believed that no harm would come to her or her son. She was probably right, but Owen kept very close to her, just in case.

The Pugh's lived in one of the smaller houses around Bethesda. Mr. Pugh had been a puddler at Cyfarthfa before losing his job. Nowadays it was so easy to plunge from plenty into destitution within a matter of weeks. It was a shabby two-roomed house standing on the edge of the road. Behind, there was a large cinder tip and in the hollow formed were even more dwellings, cellars and one roomed hovels. Every lodging was full of people. Stagnant water and household waste lay every where. These dwellings were built below the level of the road and were entered by rickety ladders leading here and there.

Owen could not believe that anyone could live in such a place. They seemed no better than rats.. The whole place was unfit for human occupation, but no one would move. Where would they go? If they did move, others were only too ready to take their place. People were only too pleased to have somewhere to call their own.

As they neared the Pugh's house there were several women standing outside the door sobbing and very distressed. The women stood around in small groups whispering and wiping their eyes with the edges of the shawls that were draped around their thin shoulders.

Mrs. Jenkins was quite unprepared for what greeted her in the small room of the Pugh's meagre home. Mrs. Pugh had been under great stress and in despair had taken her own life, leaving five small children. She had drowned herself in the River Taff.

The five small children were sitting around an empty fire place. Cold and hungry and all alone in the world. Nobody knew where the Pugh's had come from, and so there was no hope of a family or relatives coming to claim Merthyr's latest orphans.

Secretly, Owen hoped that Mrs. Pugh's body was not in the house. He had heard of tales of dead bodies creaking and groaning in their coffins. He had no wish to hear any mournful sounds. A cold shiver ran down his spine. 'Someone's walking over your grave,' were the words he recalled. But Mrs. Pugh had not been brought home.

Mrs. Jenkins quickly pulled herself together. She wasted no time. There were small mouths to feed. She busied herself emptying her basket. Owen was set to light some kind of fire. Neighbours, who before their visit hung around in small groups, now saw to the children and the house. They had just needed someone like Mrs. Jenkins to spur them on.

In no time, the children were reasonably clean. Clothes had been begged and borrowed from the sympathetic neighbours who could spare them. The house furnishings, a table and a few chairs were acquired and soon the children sat eating the food brought by Owen's mother. Mrs. Jenkins was certain that they had not had a square meal for several days. They ate up every crumb of bread and morsel of cheese. Some of the neighbours shared in the meal. These kindly souls were also short of food and were only too pleased to be offered a share of such a feast free of charge.

They discussed with Mrs. Jenkins what to do with the children , as she was not yet prepared to let them be taken anywhere. The Poor Law Guardians boarded -out orphaned children, children deserted by parents, or those whose parents had been jailed for some crime, and had left their children to run wild on the streets, where they hunted for food like animals and often they became scouts for the thieves and rogues in China.

Mrs Jenkins was very aware of this. She had heard and seen for herself how cruelly the children, farmed out to unscrupulous child-minders, had been treated. They were often hungry and dirty, but they provided a little extra money for the minders. These pauper children seemed to Mrs. Jenkins condemned to a life of misery and were forced into crime in a vain attempt to change their lot .

Mrs. Jenkins was determined that the Pugh family, until tragedy struck them and twisted Mrs. Pugh's disturbed mind, would not be lodged with anyone willing to take them for a few pence. She would first want to know all about the prospective parents. She had a chance to do her best for these children, and she would.

News of the tragedy quickly reached the ears of the Minister and Deacons of Mrs. Jenkins's Chapel. The Deacons in their starched white collars, black Sunday suits and black hats had unfortunately little time for this tragic family. Mrs. Jenkins could not understand this attitude. It did not seem Christian to her. But according to all the Deacons, Mrs. Pugh had sinned by taking her own life and leaving the children orphaned. Criticising poor Mrs. Pugh did not help the poor little souls left without a mother or a father. On the other hand, Mrs. Jenkins felt it was her Christian duty to help anyone in need, and in this case, the need seemed very great in deed.

Fortunately the Reverend Watkin Thomas felt more kindly towards the children. He knew Mrs. Jenkins was right and the Deacons, on this occasion, should have shown more Christian charity. But this was no time to quote the scriptures to anyone.

Three pairs of sad innocent eyes looked over the table at the Minister and Mrs. Jenkins. The twin babies lay fast asleep on a rough cot.

'Five little ones,' said Mrs Jenkins. 'Two would be too many, but two would be easier to place.'

'Poor little souls,' commented a neighbour, rushing out of the room, tears in her eyes, overcome by the plight of the children.

'This is no time to be tearful,' said Mrs. Jenkins. 'Action we need, not tears. We'll shed tears of joy when these little ones have a new home.'

'It'll not be easy,' added the Minister. 'Five extra mouths to feed. No, it'll not be easy. It's not a task you should take on alone. Finding homes will be difficult. Times are hard.'

'I'm not doing it alone,' replied Mrs. Jenkins.

'No, not alone, my dear, the Lord is always with us.'

'The Lord will certainly play a part, for I have a plan.'

'What do you mean, Mrs. Jenkins?'

'We have seven hundred and fifty members in our Chapel. Our members call themselves Christian. Well, you, Mr Thomas, are going to see just how Christian your congregation is.'

'I don't understand, Mrs. Jenkins.' 'I want you to announce next Sunday in Chapel the plight of the Pugh children. We need a home for five small children. They must not to split up. They must remain a family.'

'But Mrs Jenkins, surely that's impossible. A home for five children— two merely babies. It's asking a great deal.'

'Christian people, Reverend Thomas. Christian charity is what you preach and now is the time for your congregation to prove themselves. There are enough orphans roaming the streets as it is. Show Christian charity to them and they will eye you with suspicion, hurl abuse at you, throw stones, spit at you and then run off. Well as long as I am able I will not let this happen to the little Pugh children. Their parents were God-fearing. I know they wanted them to have a Christian upbringing and I will try to provide it for them and I hope you will help. We will pray to God to ask him for his help. With His help, all is possible.'

'Amen.'

The following Sunday, after a sermon on Christian charity, the Reverend Thomas related the story of the five Pugh children. With his gift for words he had the women of the congregation close to tears and the men had a surprisingly large number of colds that day. Noses were blown into snow-white handkerchiefs by grave Deacons. White stiff collars became uncomfortable as the Reverend Thomas asked and prayed for some member of the congregation, in this corner of God's vineyard, to come

186

forward and accept the Pugh children into their household.

The next morning, a fat, shabbily dressed woman, wearing a monstrous hat and carrying a wicker basket over her arm, waddled up to the door of the Reverend Watkin Thomas, and knocked sharply with the brightly polished brass knocker. Martha, the housekeeper, answered the door. She was used to the many odd callers at this door, but even she was taken aback by the strange sight. Apart from the woman's threadbare clothes, she was dirty and did not smell very good.

'I want to see the Priest,' she demanded in an Irish brogue.

'The Priest?' repeated Martha.

'There's no Priest here. This is a Baptist manse.'

'I don't know about 'hat,' replied the woman. 'I want to see the man who 'as the children for sale.'

'Children for sale. We have no children for sale.'

'Yes, 'e 'as,' said the woman, roughly, worming her way into the hallway, past Martha, who had stepped back from the dirty woman, to avoid the appalling smell. 'Where is 'e?'

Her high pitched voice had disturbed the Reverend Thomas, who appeared at the top of the oak stairs. Martha was much relieved. The two women looked up the staircase at the Minister.

'I 'm looking for the Priest with children for sale.'

'Children for sale. I assure you my good woman, I have no children for sale.'

'Don't you good woman me, with your smooth talk. It's all over the town. You said so in your Church yesterday.'

'Were you there?' asked the Minister.

'No I wasn't 'ere,' she said. 'I'm a good Cafolic, I am.'

'If you say so. But if you had been there, you would have heard me ask for a good Christian home for five orphaned children. I have no children for sale.'

By now the Reverend Watkin Thomas had descended the stair, and, as the woman approached him, he caught his breath. The woman had not washed for quite some time. Her black teeth showed in a scurvious smile, as she tried to bargain for the children.

'I must ask you to leave,' he said. 'I repeat, I have no children for sale here. Would you see this woman to the door, Martha?'

'Don't be 'asty. Don't be 'asty,' said the woman, holding the sleeve of the minister's jacket with her grimy hand. 'I'd give 'em a good 'ome, I would. Plenty to eat, a nice warm, clean 'ome, I would.' She smiled her horrible smile.

Martha pulled at her basket in a vain attempt to dislodge the unwelcome visitor. The Reverend tried to pull in the opposite direction, and they swayed to and fro on the bottom of the

stair like the pendulum of a grandfather clock. But they could not dislodge this alarming woman. Suddenly there was a knock on the door.

'Oh dear, what shall I do Sir?'

'Answer it, Martha. I'm in no danger. She just wants to bargain for the children.'

Martha let go and hurried along the hallway. She was very conscious of the abominable smell left by the woman. It seemed to linger everywhere. She wiped her hands down the sides of her spotless white apron. She sniffed gently, for she was very upset by the whole affair. She opened the door.

'Good morning Martha, is the Reverend in?'

'Oh Sir, yes Sir,' replied Martha, relieved to see William, Meyrick, the solicitor, standing outside. 'Please come in Sir, and help us to get rid of this horrid woman.'

'What horrid woman?'

'There, Sir,' pointing up the hallway.

'Good gracious, Molly O'Grady.'

William Meyrick approached the couple on the staircase. As soon as the woman spotted the visitor, she let go of the minister's sleeve, rushed down the hallway, straight past Martha and with a rude gesture, left. But her smell lingered. Martha slammed the door, rattling the brass door-knocker.

'What was she doing here?' asked William Meyrick.

'You're not going to believe this William, but she came to buy the Pugh children,' said the Minister. 'In fact, to barter for them, if you want to know the truth.'

'She did, did she?' uttered William Meyrick. 'Well, she would, wouldn't she?'

'You seem to know all about everybody,' commented the Minister, smiling. 'My work as a solicitor brings me into contact with all sorts. She is Molly O'Grady, well known drunk and child minder, if she can get her hands on them. She used to be employed by the Poor Law Guardians, who paid her a shilling a day to look after children. Sadly, she kept them in a cellar. They had little food, no warmth, but she made sure that they had the syrup.'

'The syrup?'

'Syrup of poppies, one spoonful keeps children quiet for hours. They sell it down in the market, if you know where to look. She's not supposed to have any dealings with children, but she obviously ignores the Courts. But let's forget her for a moment, where are the children?'

Owen Jenkins was looking after them. He was thoroughly enjoying himself. He had acquired five new little friends. Needless to say, his mother would not leave the children down at Bethesda and had brought them home. Owen had never had any brothers or sisters to look after. The presence of the toddlers had been a novel experience for him. The three older children slept in his room. He slept on a makeshift bed on the floor, and children had his bed, but every morning, they would be found snuggled up with him on the floor. They followed him everywhere. It reminded his mother of a mother duck being followed by her ducklings and it made her laugh to see them. She made sure that they did not occupy too much of his time, for she knew how tiring children could be, but Owen was coping very well.

However the following afternoon, the Reverend Watkin Thomas was bringing along two ladies who were prepared to accept the children into their families. James Abbot, the Sunday School superintendent, had been approached by Peggy Price and Annie Williams, two sisters of the Parish, who wanted the children. Peggy was keen to have the three toddlers and Annie wanted the twins. The sisters lived next door to one another and felt that in this way the five children would not be split up. Mrs. Jenkins believed that their prayers had been answered and that no better solution would be found.

Mrs. Jenkins was busily getting the children ready for their new mothers. Owen sat with Tom and Ben, while his mother placed a large pink ribbon in Mary's fine hair. She did look pretty.

As Owen watched, the door opened. A black, wet nose pushed its way into the room and Meg, the mongrel dog padded her way in, wagging her tail. She was delighted to find her master and his new little friends. Tom and Ben struggled off the horse-hair sofa to grab hold of the small dog, they had come to love.

Meg flopped down on the floor, only too pleased to be fussed over by two pairs of small hands.

'See that the boys don't get dirty, Owen. I want them to look
their best for the Reverend Thomas and the ladies.'

'They're only playing with Meg. They won't get dirty. She just wants to be stroked,' he assured his mother.

'I'm relying on you, Owen. Don't let me down.'

'I won't Mam. I'll keep an eye on them.'

The Reverend Thomas arrived with the ladies exactly on time. The sisters were dressed in their Sunday best and they stood excitedly on the doorstep outside, as the Minister knocked on the door.

Mrs. Jenkins greeted them warmly. The two sisters were very keen to meet all the children as soon as possible. There was not much about the children that the sisters did not know already. William Meyrick and the Reverend Thomas had done a thorough job. The ladies were expecting five forlorn little waifs, but when Annie saw the twins and Peggy the three toddlers, their hearts warmed to them instantly. They were indeed five little souls, very pale and very thin, but Mrs. Jenkins had dressed them in the clothes provided by the Chapel people and they looked simply angelic. Peggy put both her hands to her face in sheer delight. Who would not find a place in their hearts for these three dear little orphans?

The children stood in front of Peggy Price and Annie Williams. Gradually, the three children raised their eyes slowly, from the polished shoes of Peggy, up passed her long black skirt, and then to Annie's high-necked, home-made blouse and the black shawl draped across her shoulders. Finally, they observed the bright, smiling faces of the two sisters. Catching their eyes for an instant the children bowed their heads quickly, not daring to stare. The inspection was interrupted by Meg, the dog, who once again sneaked her way into the best room, much to the delight of the children. She was closely followed by Owen, who did his best to remove the dog, before his mother came in with the tea. He failed in this, but his mother allowed the dog to stay, just for this special occasion.

The dog stayed close to the youngsters, always happy to have little hands fondle her hair, rub her nose or pull her ears. She had never had such constant attention and she loved it. Her tail wagged to show everyone that she was happy. It was just what the children wanted at this moment. Meg wanted the five children to stay. Mrs. Jenkins had made a very nice tea of Welsh cakes and buttered scones. Everyone tucked in politely. Not many people could provide such a tea, but then the Jenkins's were in a privileged position, for they lived within the grounds of Cyfarthfa Castle. Mr. Jenkins was a farrier. One thing the ironmaster believed in was to share his castle fare with the employees who served him. In fact, he treated all his work force fairly, although many would disagree. He believed in a good day's work for a good day's pay, but like all workmen the world over, it would never be enough to satisfy their needs.

Talk around tea, like much talk in Merthyr at this time turned to the dreadful things the Court of Requests were doing. According to Peggy Price, Joseph Coffin would take the bed from under the dying.

'The Court has the law on its side and we must respect the law. Laws are laws, and rules are rules, and that is what he's obeying and that's what he's paid to do,' added the Reverend Thomas. 'Nonsense,' uttered Mrs. Jenkins, no longer prepared to remain silent. 'Rules are for fools to obey, but for the guidance of the wise. Surely he can see the plight of the people he condemns? He must have some Christian charity in his bones. He goes to Church, doesn't he?'

'Every Sunday, we pass him on the way to chapel.'

'And much good does it do him.'

'He'll get his come-uppance one day,' added Mrs. Jenkins.

'Enough of this,' said the Reverend Thomas. 'I think it's time we made our way home. You ladies will have much to do in the next few days.'

'Indeed,' agreed Annie Williams with a smile.

'The children will soon settle down to a normal life. We'll get plenty of support from our own families.'
Mrs. Jenkins smiled warmly at the Reverend Watkin Thomas. The Pugh children were no longer orphans. Today they belonged to a loving Christian family. They were certainly not for sale and never had been.

All Roads Lead To Merthyr

'A Big Night'

Leslie Norris

I used to train at the Ex-Serviceman's Club three nights a week, Tuesdays, Wednesdays and Fridays. Training began at six, but I was always late on Tuesdays and Wednesdays because of homework. I used to like getting there a bit late. As I hurried through the long passage that ran beside the room where the old, dry miners – hardly any of them ex-servicemen – were drinking away their age and disappointment, I would hear above me the slithering feet of the other boys as they moved around the ring or the punch-bags and the pungent smell of the liniment would come greenly down the stairs to meet me. I would watch them working out a bit first, looking particularly for my friends Bobby Ecclestone and Charlie Nolan, before going into the dressing room to change into my shoes and shorts. I used to wear black shorts with a yellow band round the waist and a yellow stripe at the side of each leg. In Warrilow's Sports Emporium they had satin boxing shorts, immaculate and colourful. Mine were home-made. Most of the time I used to skip. I loved that rope and I could do some very fancy skipping, very fast and for a very long time. Tiredness was something I'd only heard about. Then I'd box a few rounds with Charlie and Bobby, and sometimes with one of the older and more skilful boys. They were always very kind, showing me how to slip a left lead, or how to move on the ropes. I hardly ever used the heavy, shapeless punching bags; when you're thirteen years old and weigh eighty pounds it doesn't seem very necessary. Then I'd do some exercises on the mat and finish off with another burst of skipping.

Boxing with Charlie Nolan was best of all. Charlie had been in school with me, in the next desk, until he'd moved to another district. He was almost the same age and size as I was and his footwork was a miracle of economy and precision. His feet brushed the floor like a whisper as he moved perfectly about me, in a kind of smooth ritual. I, on the other hand, would jig up and down in a flashy and wasteful way, careering around the ring at top speed and not caring very much where I got to. But Charlie's hands were slow. They would sit calmly in front of him, now and again mildly exploring the space between us, and I would hit him with a variety of harmless punches that left him blinking and smiling. As he passed us, Ephraim Hamer, our trainer, would say, 'Well done, Charlie!' He rarely said anything to me. After we'd showered we'd sit about listening to the bigger boys, or boasting quietly between us. Bobby Ecclestone would tell us about his work in a grocer's shop; he was errand boy in the shop where we bought our groceries and I often saw him sweeping the sawdust boards, or staggering out with huge loads to the delivery van. It was

Bobby who had first brought me to the Ex-Servicemen's Club. He was fifteen and the best boxer among the boys.

One Friday evening after we had finished working out and we were sitting warm and slumped on the benches, Bobby asked me if I was going to the weigh-in the next day. I didn't even know what it was. I was always finding that there were whole areas of experience, important areas too, about which I knew nothing and other boys everything.

'Where is it?' I said carefully.

'Down at the Stadium. One o'clock,' said Charlie. 'I'm going.'

Everything fell into place. Next day at the Stadium our local hero, Cuthbert Fletcher, who everyone said would have been feather-weight champion of Wales except that he was coloured, was to fight Ginger Thomas, the official champion.

'Are you going?' I asked Bobby.

'Of course,' he said. 'It's my dinner-time. See you outside at ten to.'

All Saturday morning I hung about in a fever of anxiety in case my lunch wouldn't be ready for me in time to meet Bobby and Charlie at one o'clock outside the Stadium. But it was, and I was the first there, although Charlie was not long behind me. He hadn't had his lunch and was eating a huge round of bread and jam which he'd cut for himself from a new loaf. Bobby wouldn't let us go inside the Stadium until Charlie had finished eating. A few men hung about in a corner of the empty hall, their hands deep in their overcoat pockets. They whispered softly and tunelessly and they all carried an air of vast unconcern, but when Cuthbert and Ginger Thomas appeared, they hurried forward to greet the boxers, talking excitedly to them. It was exciting too. I don't know why it should have been so, but we all felt a curious tightening of the air as the boxers smiled formally at each other. Cuthbert stepped on the scales first, and a great fat man adjusted the weights, flicking them up and down the bar with finicky little movements of his enormous fingers before he called out, in a high voice, 'Eight stone and twelve pounds, gentlemen'.

Cuthbert smiled, ducked his round, crinkly head at his friends, and moved away. Ginger Thomas was a lean, pale man, elegant and graceful, his mahogany hair brushed smooth and close to his head. He, too, stood on the scales and his weight was called in the fat man's brittle tenor. Everybody shook hands and at once the place was deserted.

'That's all right then,' said Bobby.

'Nothing in it for weight,' said Charlie.

We stood together silently, for a long time.

'Are you going to the fight?' asked Bobby.

'No,' said Charlie, 'my father won't let me.'

Bobby looked at his shoes as they scuffed the ground in front of him, first the right shoe, then the left one.

'I can't go,' he said. 'Don't finish in time on Saturdays.'

'I expect I'll go,' I said, 'if I want to.'

'Will you?' said Charlie, his eyes big.

'I expect so,' I said, although I knew I couldn't.

At eight that evening I was in Court Street, one of the crowd milling around the Stadium, knowing I could not get in. Slow, comfortable groups of men with money and tickets moved confidently through towards the entrance, talking with assurance about the fights they had seen in the past. On the steps near the door Trevor Bunce danced up and down, his wide, cheeky face smiling as he asked the men to take him in with them. An arrogant boy and leader of his gang, Trevor Bunce was bigger than I was. You could see him everywhere. Incredibly active, his string-coloured hair hanging in his eyes, he bounced with energy through a series of escapades wherever you went. The street lights came on suddenly, and we all cheered. I knew with certainty that Trevor Bunce would get in somehow.

Now the whole road was thick with people and the few cars prodding thought the outlaying districts honked and revved with impatience and frustration. I moved cautiously to the pavement. I saw that, prudently, they had built a temporary barrier of corrugated sheets of metal above the low wall which separated a little yard, belonging to the Stadium, from the road. On lesser occasions many daring boys had climbed this wall - an easy feat - and run through a nest of little rooms into the hall itself. There was even a large door, always locked, which led directly into the raucous noise where even now the first of the bouts was being decided.

As I looked at the new metal sheets, Trevor Bunce threw himself past me, leapt on the wall, and, with unbelievable strength, forced back the ling edge of the barrier. For a moment only, it was wide enough for a boy to wriggle through and Trevor Bunce did just that. But before he was half clear, the inexorable metal wall snapped back, pinning him at the waist, his legs licking wildly; and even as we looked, we heard clearly and without mistake, a sound as of a dry sick breaking. Then Trevor Bunce began to scream.

In seconds, it seems to me now, we had ripped away the corrugated wall and its wooden framework, and men's gentle arms carried Trevor away. I saw him as he went, his face white and wet, but his eyes were open. He cradled his right forearm carefully, because it was broken.

By this time many of us were in the yard itself, aimlessly stacking the six-foot sheets of time in an untidy heap near the wall. There must have been forty or fifty of us; boys, young workless men, and a few older men who were there by chance, it seemed. Yet, haphazard and leaderless as we were, we suddenly lifted our restive heads and, like some swollen river, streamed for the door that led to the Stadium's lesser rooms.

I didn't want to go with them. Some shred of caution tried hard to hold me back, but my treacherous legs hurried me on, gasping. We met nobody, except in a corridor an old man wiping saucers with a wet cloth. He pressed himself against the wall, his mouth wide open, and we were past him before he got a word out. And then we were in the great hall itself, our force broken against the huge weight of the legal customers. We lost ourselves among them at once.

The noise, the heat, the immense, expectant good humour made the whole place intoxicating, but I could see nothing except, high overhead, a blue, unshifting cloud of cigarette smoke. Agile though I was, I could not push or wriggle another inch nearer the ring. It was Freddie Benders who came to my help. Freddie didn't fight much, because he was nearly thirty years old. His ears were rubbery and he had few teeth, but he often came down to the club and sometimes he'd let us spar with him. You could hit him with everything you had, right in the chin, even, and he'd only laugh.

When he saw me he shouted out, 'Make room for the boy there, let the boy get down to the front'.

Grumbling and laughing, the men inched more closely together and I squeezed my way almost to the ringside.

'That's right,' shouted Freddie. 'That boy is going to make a good 'un. Keep your eyes on Cuthbert tonight boy!'

I saw the fight. I saw every moment of the fifteen rounds, and it was a great fight, I know it was. Yet all the time it was on, all the time incisive Ginger Thomas moved forward with a speed and viciousness I had not imagined, what I really saw was Trevor Bunce's white face, what I heard was the stark snapping of his bones. When the fighters moved around the ring, the crowd was silent and absorbed and at the end of each round there was a great sigh before they clapped and shouted. I think Ginger Thomas won, but at the end the referee held Cuthbert's arm up and we all cheered, with relief and pride rather than with certainty. Ginger Thomas stood in the centre of the ring, aloof and unmoved; his pale eyes glittered in the arc-lights, and then he turned and swaggered easily away. His lack of emotion disturbed me more than the terrible, precise fury and venom of his attacks.

When I got home my parents had nothing to say to me. I was so late, my crime was so enormous, that all they could do was to point to the stairs; I hurried up to my room to shiver gratefully under the icy sheets. I knew I should never sleep again and, even as I realised this, fell at once to sleep. When I awoke all was dark and confusing, and my right forearm was throbbing with pain. Struggling with darkness, I found the fingers of my left hand tight in a cramping grip around my right arm. The pain made me think of poor Trevor Bunce, in hospital surely, and I felt with quick relief the whole, frail bones in my own arms.

The following Tuesday I was late getting to the Club, but only because I found my French homework particularly difficult. I waved to the boys, changed eagerly, and soon had the old skipping rope humming away. Everything began to feel fine, it wasn't until I put the gloves on to spar with Charlie Nolan that I realised that something was wrong. I kept on seeing Ginger Thomas, destructive and graceful, his hands cocked, moving into Cuthbert, as he had on the Saturday night. I could see his face, relaxed and faintly curious, the sudden blur as he released three or four short punches before sliding away. I knew too that I was doing this to Charlie, but I couldn't stop. Charlie was bleeding from the mouth and nose and he was pawing away with his gloves open. I could tell he was frightened. Yet I kept on ripping punches at him, my hands suddenly hard and urgent and the huge, muffling gloves we used no longer clumsy. I could hear Mr Hamer shouting as Charlie hid in a corner and then somebody had me around the waist, throwing me almost across the ring. Charlie was crying, but in a little while Bobby Ecclestone put an arm round Charlie's shoulders, talking to him softly. Nobody said anything to me and I sat on the bench. I thought I was quivering all over, but when I looked at my legs they were all right. I felt as if I were going to be sick. Nothing seemed to matter very much. I walked to the dressing room and began to change. I was so tired that it was an effort to take off my ring clothes, and when I pulled my vest over my head I could feel my face wet with my own tears. I took a good look at the room before I went out, then I shut the door behind me, very quietly. It sounded just as it always had, the slithering of the shoes around the ball or the heavy bag, the rhythmical slapping of the rope on the boards as somebody did some lively skipping.

Nobody saw me go. As I went down the stairs I could see through the window little groups of quiet drinkers in the room below, but they could not see me in the dark passage.

I never went back there. Sometimes when I went for groceries, some cheese maybe, or some canned stuff, I would see Bobby Ecclestone in the shop. He didn't say anything to me and I didn't say anything to him. It was as if we had never been friends.

'Have Your Cake and Eat It'

David Edwards

Do you remember, not so long ago, when the pubs did not open all day Sunday?

Rugby club players and members of Troedyrhiw Rugby Football Club, based in the lower Merthyr valley, tended to follow a weekend routine that had been followed for years previously, in hundreds of rugby clubs, in dozens of towns, throughout the valleys. Play a game on Saturday, pints and songs after, meet the wives and girlfriends about half seven, then out for the night.

Up on Sunday morning (or afternoon, depending on alcohol intake), down the club to discuss the events of the night before, sink a few pints then home for dinner by 2 o'clock (3 o'clock in later years) and a few hours sleep, then back out by seven for the evening session.

After a few more pints, they would decide on what to do that night. Look for a pub in Merthyr to see a band or the odd pub singer banging out the old favourites, visit the local club disco night or just 'go to town'. Obviously, this would be followed later by a visit to Mays for special curry and fried rice to take home, or, on a special occasion, a sit down meal with the compulsory fried egg in Hing Hongs.

Dai Cake and his mates from the rugby club liked the Cricket Club on Sundays. After town and Brandy Bridge on Fridays and town and Dollars on Saturdays, the Crick made a nice change and it wasn't far to go and easy to walk home.

You had all the Pentrebach boys, who played rugby for Hills Plymouth and seemed to lose every week. All the boys from the Black would be there, up for crack as per usual. Best of all, the Treharris boys would arrive in a Transit van that would do credit to the Tardis. They could get more bodies in the back of their van than a meat factory can get Portuguese workers in one house today.

The 'Crick', as it was (and still is) affectionately called, was legendary. The disco played the same songs every week, so you knew when your favourites were coming. The Treharris boys drank all the Strongbow, and then woke Lippy to dance around to Nellie the Elephant. The Boat dance was a favourite at the end of the night, along with the compulsory Bunny Hop, the worse dance ever invented, ever. As always, it would be followed by a few slow smoochies, when all the people who had been eyeing each other all night could get close for a slow dance.

Best of all, if you pulled one of the local lovelies, there was the cricket pitch or the lane behind the club to try out new positions. Silly leg off tended to have a different meaning then. This was great in winter in the dark, but not so clever in the summer, when the rest of the club watched from the veranda.

However, after months of this, Dai Cake got bored. Dai was what is commonly known in Merthyr as a 'character'. They are everywhere, every pub or club has got at least one character.

Dai had been married for twenty years and never been faithful in all this time. If there was a trip anywhere, any time, Dai would be on it. He played rugby, bowls, darts, and pool: anything to get him out of the house and into a pub. Any rugby tour, international game, darts tournament, Dai would be there.

Dai had one redeeming feature. He was very protective of his mother, fairly typical in Merthyr, and nobody could say a word against her. Dai had been in the rugby club a few weeks previously, when a call came to say his mother had been taken to Mardy hospital as she had fell in the house.

Dai had drank about eight pints but jumped in his car and shot up the hospital. As he pulled up outside in a panic, in his drunken state he accelerated instead of braking and drove straight through the new glass patio doors. He jumped out of the car and told the shocked porter that he was visiting his mother and would pay for any damage. When he was arrested later, Dai was most indignant because the porter had not believed him and called the police.

Dai had been quiet for a while after this incident and was getting bored with the weekend routine. He was always looking for new women to grope or ogle and the attractions of the Weather Girls in the Crick or the Brandy Bridge crew on Fridays had worn thin.

Dai moaned to the boys, as they queued in Mays Chinese, that he was bored and wanted a change, but they all ignored him as he was always unhappy when he was on his way home to his wife. The following weekend it was all forgotten as they followed the usual routine.

However, on Sunday night, when Gwyn's minibus pulled up at the club at the usual time, they were in for a surprise.

'Where to boys? Town or the Crick?', asked Gwyn.

Dai Cake held up his hand. 'Tonight Gwyn, we are going to the Spunk Shop in Pontlottyn!', he declared solemnly. All the boys were amazed. They were actually leaving the valley for the night, but had no idea where Dai was leading them.

'It's Pontlottyn Legion he is taking us to', said Mikey. 'I've heard of this place from the boys in work and it filled with women, wall to wall. It's supposed to be really great there'.

The boys were pacified because Mikey was always sensible and knew his way around, being much older and experienced than the others.

'How much will this cost?' asked Snidge. 'I don't want to waste money on bus fare and not have my tenth pint, because I only had five lunchtime, as I had to take her to the Scala to see Grease'.

'It is 50p each, as usual', said Gwyn. 'So, for the 20 of you, plus the 2 on the roof and Vincent hanging on the back door, that will be, uuuh, call it a tenner'.

Gwyn charged 50p per head on any night of the week, to wherever you wanted to go and however many people were in his bus. Through the 1980's and into the 1990's the price never altered. It could be down the Globe in Ponty on Friday (Sweaty Betty's for Indian meal after), the Tara Club in Glynneath or Caerphilly Social, it was always 50p per head each way.

There was much excitement on the bus as they passed up the Bogey Road, throwing empty beer cans at the 'gippoes' sitting around their fire. There was a hitch at the top when the minibus could not get up the steep bit and Gwyn's bus looked like the Anthill Mob from Wacky Races, with everybody pushing and Dopey Gerald running behind, drinking slops from discarded cans.

They got over the top and past the Tunnel Tavern. The older guys looked wistfully at the Tavern as they passed, because this is where they would take their girlfriends for an illicit night out, telling the wives that they were rugby training.

The bus arrived safely in Pontlottyn, which was good going for Gwyn. The last instruction from Gwyn was to tell the boys the bus would leave at exactly 11 o'clock, so they could all be back in time to catch Mays for curry.

The mist was down and it was dark and gloomy. The Legion stood concrete and forbidding and looked as inviting as the Haunted House in Porthcawl fair.

'What a poxy dump this is Dai', exclaimed Vincent. 'I would rather have stayed behind to play darts in the Railway!'

'Just come and have a look inside, we're here now till eleven anyway, so you may as well make the most of it', cajoled Dai.

Inside the Legion, it was absolutely bouncing. Glyn got the round in and they went into the 'lounge' to have a look around. It was full of women! They made their way across the sticky carpet towards a group of ladies standing around their handbags near the one armed bandit.

'It's better than Star Wars bar! Look at all the lovely ladies!' shouted Dai Cake.

The boys had to agree that it was looking promising. Not as good as Caerphilly Social on a Friday night, mind you, but very promising for a little Sunday night excursion.

It was standard valleys dress night for the women – bottle blonde hair, red lippy, white top and tight jeans, fag, tattoo and Bacardi and coke (or pints of 'bow and black to impress the boys).

Dai was grinning happily and groped the first girl to pass and got a slap, then a smile. 'I'm in boys', he shouted.

All the others looked on in disgust. She was about 55, with a light moustache and sagging boobs, and tobacco stains on her fingers, but Dai was oblivious. He held her hand and whispered in her ear.

'Face like a rat catcher's guard dog comes to mind with her', muttered Glen, sarcastic as ever after a few pints of cider.

Dai ignored him. 'Have a dance, love?' he asked, as he started to twirl her around her handbag.

A committeeman came over and told Dai they were in the 'lounge' and dancing was only allowed in the main hall, as they did not want to lower the tone of the club.

Dai grabbed the girl by the hand to take her to the hall and she fell straight over. Unknown to Dai, she was still a bit pissed from the lunch time session and she only had one leg. Her left leg was made from metal and strapped at the thigh.

Dai stood there with his mouth open, in shock, as she lay on her back with her plastic leg caught on the holes on the carpet and laying at right angles. Everybody looked on as the boys helped her up.

'Ugly AND disabled' muttered Glyn. 'Nice one Dai'.

Mikey turned to Dai. 'Come on Dai, don't panic, it's OK, it was an accident, like'.

Dai was in a trance. 'Mike, she's only got one leg! I've never shagged a girl with one leg before'.

Dai helped the girl up from the floor and gave her a big hug, whilst he straightened out her leg. She was a bit cool with Dai but he pleaded with her how sorry he was. When he bought her a Bacardi and coke and a pint of Bow and black, she came round a bit.

'Come and dance', said Dai. 'What is your name?'

'Peg', replied the girl. 'Peg Legge. Help me strap on my false leg properly and I'll show you how to do the Boat Dance because I can do that one nice and easy'.

That was the last the boys seen of Dai, sailing on the floor of the dance floor with Peg sat between his legs, oblivious to everybody else. Snidge did Nellie the Elephant instead, as there were no Treharris boys in the Legion. They played the same songs as the Crick and everybody was happy.

Glen drank loads of cider and got pissed again whilst Jeff stayed on the Allbright and got just as pissed. They all managed a few smooches and a couple of gropes and were going home happy.

End of the night and Gwyn was waiting to go at 11 o'clock.

'Wait just a few minutes Gwyn, he'll be here now', said Jaffa, who was Dai's older brother. 'Donna will kill him if he's not home again' After ten minutes of waiting, Gwyn pulled off with Dai nowhere to be seen and all the others boys deep in their beer and not really caring.

Meanwhile, Dai was over in Fochriw in Peg's council house, drunkenly trying to undo her leg straps. He was besotted, although she was coyote ugly, with a row of bluebottles in her mouth where her teeth used to be.

'What a turn on this is', said Dai. 'I love these silver buckles holding your leg on' Peg tried to bite Dai's neck in a drunken state of frenzy and Dai thought she was trying to kiss him, which excited him further. All thoughts of his wife, the bus home and the rest of the boys faded into the distance.

He managed to get her leg un-strapped and tossed it to the floor, whilst at the same time trying to pull off her pink knickers, ignoring the pee stains underneath. Peg wrapped her good leg around Dai and he was totally ecstatic.

The pigeons next door woke Dai early on the Monday morning. Dai was befuddled with the drink from the night before and memories of his sexual fantasyland with Peg came flooding back, especially when he could see her leg discarded on the floor, gleaming in the sun shining through the window.

He turned over to see Peg, snoring next to him with her leg draped over his and her black teeth showing against her white face and, for a moment, Dai was in love. The he remembered he was married, his wife Donna would be frantic and he was in the back room of a poxy house in the next valley, with a one legged nymphomaniac.

'Oh shit, ooh shit, shit, shit', groaned Dai. 'Donna will kill me this time. This is the end. What am I going to do?'

Peg stirred and farted, filling the room with a rotten apple smell, a remnant of the weekend Strongbow.

'I need to go home', shouted Dai. 'Wake up and help me find my clothes'.

'You want to go now and all last night that's all you wanted to do was come. You really are mixed up, Dai', moaned Peg. 'Anyway, the first bus from Pontlottyn is not until midday on a Monday, because the driver is the doorman in the Legion, so you will have to get a taxi or walk'.

Dai didn't have money for a taxi and after last night sexual Olympics, he could not face the walk over the mountain. He sat there feeling sorry for himself until Peg started to strap on her leg, with the buckles still shining in the sun. Dai jumped on her and all thought of self pity went out of the window.

'Let me hold your leg, Peg, I love these straps and the silver buckles. Can you show me that trick again with your nipple piercings'?

Any guilty feeling disappeared and Dai and Peg were lost to the world for a few hours. Peg went out to the local corner Spar and came back at half past ten with a load of cans of Strongbow. They drank these in bed, between trying various sexual positions involving one leg and straps.

Suddenly, Dai spotted a bus coming over the hill and came to his senses. 'I've got to go Peg, my wife will be going ballistic and the bus is coming', pleaded Dai. 'I would ring you but you haven't got a phone so perhaps I'll see you next week, is it'.

'Piss off Dai', screamed Peg drunkenly. 'You men are all the same, taking advantage of me because I am disabled'. She started beating Dai with her leg as he pulled on his shirt and ran from the room.

On the bus back to Merthyr, Dai started to sober up and realise what a mess he was in. Deb would not believe anything he told her after the last episode where he did not make it home and he would be out of the house. He had to think up a really good story this time.

Being hospitalised, locked up by the police, lost memory after bang on the head, got on the wrong bus and ended up in Swansea, playing poker and onto a big win – these were all excuses he had used before, amongst others, on more than one occasion. This time he was dead, the excuses would not come.

Dai got back to Merthyr and walked down the canal bank to Troedyrhiw, trying to conjure up a good reason for going out Sunday night for a 'quick pint' and arriving home at half past three on Monday afternoon. As he got to the Dynevor he considered whether to have a quick pint.

As he stood debating with himself he could see Smoko at the bottom of the hill, opening the rugby club to let in the brewery delivery. The club usually did not open until Monday night

'Great, I'll go to club and have a few pints with Smoko to give me more time to think', thought Dai. 'Perhaps he may have a few ideas'.

Dai walked in the club and Smoko started shouting. 'Where have you been, everyone is looking for you, Donna is going berserk, the police have searched the river, where have you been?'

'Smoko, I have been to Heaven and back', said Dai. 'Give me a pint of cider and I'll tell you all about it'.

Dai told his story, elaborating about the silver buckles and Peg's stump. 'You have always been a pervert', said Smoko, 'ever since that time when the Alsatian bit you'.

'But this time it is love', said Dai. Smoko reminded Dai that Donna was still looking for him and was really on the warpath this time.

'Please Smoke, just pretend you have not seen me and I will sort it out', pleaded Dai, full of self-pity.

The door opened and Dai Caravan came in. 'Shit, Dai, what are you doing here? The police are dragging the river by the bridge, looking for you. Donna is in the street going berserk and you are in here having a quiet pint with Smoko'.

Dai Cake decided it was the time to face the music, as he could not think of any more excuses. This was the end. He would be out of the house within the hour.

As he left the club, the brewery driver was just finishing loading barrels into the cellar under the rugby club.

'One minute whilst I have a quick pee', called Dai to the driver, as he ran into the toilet next to the cellar. 'Don't wait for me'.

As he stood there having a pee, the driver of the dray started to pull away. Sudden inspiration came to Dai on a shaft of light shining through the barred window. An idea sank into his drunken brain.

The driver called Smoko and told him the delivery was complete. Smoko went downstairs to the cellar and locked the door, then locked the roller shutter door to the cellar and changing rooms, and also, the toilets. Dai was now locked in, under the rugby club, with no way out.

He sat on the toilet, working out a story to tell Donna. The cider and the lack of sleep from the previous night took its toll and Dai fell asleep.

Suddenly, he woke to the sounds of footsteps in the bar above. Big A was opening the club for the night, so it must be about seven o'clock, thought Dai. He waited for ten minutes, and then started shouting. 'Help! Help! Can anybody hear me? Please, I need help!'

A few minutes, Dai heard the roller shutter door clang open and voices down the corridor. 'Help me, please!' shouted Dai.

The door opened and Big A and Harpo stood at the door, mouths open and wondering what the hell was going on. 'Thank God. I've been hear all night', sobbed Dai, as he collapsed to his knees. 'I went to the toilet for a crap last night, after eating those pork scratchings, and some silly sod locked me in. I have been here all night and frantic with worry. What will Deb think!?'

'Harpo went for a glass of water as Big A helped Dai to his feet and up the stairs. 'Stuff the water and give me a pint of Bow', said Dai. 'What a nightmare'.

Big A and Nigel explained to Dai that a search party was up searching the Lido, the police had dragged the river, and Donna had searched the field and all the lanes around the Cricket Club looking for him. Nobody was admitting to seeing Dai the night before.

'Oh no. I was locked in all night by mistake and Donna, my poor dear, will be beside herself with despair', wailed Dai, as he necked his pint and signalled to Harpo for a re-fill.

Big A was as sympathetic as ever. 'Don't you worry now Dai. I'll phone her to explain the situation' he soothed. He phoned Donna. 'That stupid bastard that you call your husband is here in the club. The drunken arse managed to get locked in the toilets for the night', Big A told Donna. 'He is in a right state, you had better come and see'.

A few minutes later, the door burst open and Donna, followed by her sister and her mother, came storming into the club. Dai went for the Oscar performance.

'Donna, Donna, I thought I would never see you again, the mother of my children, the love of my life, the centre of my existence. I was locked in on my own, with rats and spiders and mice. I could not stop thinking of you as I became more and more dehydrated. I thought I would never see you again!'

With this, Dai fell to his knees off the stool. Deb thought he was emotional and exhausted after his nightmare but Harpo and Big A could see he was completely and utterly pissed.

'Oh Dai, what a relief! I thought that you had gone with some other tart again', sobbed Deb. 'I thought you had left me for another'.

'Never. How can you think that, my love', groaned Dai. 'You make the best Welsh cakes I know of. I feel really dehydrated after my ordeal, real thirsty'.

Donna ordered Dai a pint of cider and a pint of lager for her to celebrate Dai's safe return. A couple of boys came in from training and bought more cider for Dai after hearing about his nightmare ordeal in the toilet.

By nine, Dai was in a right state again and hadn't spent a penny. 'Take me home Donna, I need to sleep', pleaded Dai. 'I did not sleep a wink last night, with one thing and another happening'.

Dai and Donna got up to leave the club, arm in arm, with Donna looking lovingly into Dai's eyes. Harpo and Big A looked at him suspiciously, wondering how he managed to get all those footmarks on his arms and back, as he had been locked in the bog all night.

'All's well that ends well', sighed Dai with a sly wink to the boys, as he staggered away, with Donna holding him up.

At least until next weekend when it starts all over again.

'Winter Malady'

Eira Williams

I was gently awoken with the in-flight announcement, in Maltese, by Captain Charles Polidano. I understood him before he gave the English translation, after all I'd been 'flying' this airline for over thirty years.

As we descended into Cardiff International Airport, my spirit also went lower and lower; we were in thick dark grey clouds. When the airliner's wheels touched onto the waterlogged runway, I wanted to shout 'Abort landing, take me back!' I had gone to sleep gazing from the window on summertime, somewhere south of Sicily and woken up to see winter had arrived in my country.

Within an hour I would be home, no longer kissed by the sun but embraced by the rain and the mist of the Brecon Beacons, sent south on a regular basis, with the additional gift of sleet and snow thrown in over the next few months.

It is at this cheerless time of year that we feel hibernal, our bodies cry out 'Let me lie dormant and be torpid.'

The Establishment doesn't help; it turns the clocks back confusing our metabolisms even more, and if that is not enough it then bombards us with adverts stating 'Influenza can kill but have a 'flu' jab anyway!' and we in our meek and disorientated state do so.

'You should not feel ill after this jab!' the butch nurse said, as she stabbed me in the arm with World Class Darts Championship precision.

She was wrong. I'd now been ill for two weeks, grudgingly I went to the Doctor, who greeted me well enough although her abrupt 'Good morning' followed by 'come in, come in,' spoken in quick succession, made me feel I was intruding. This stern large woman hunched over her desk and monitor, her computer more the patient that I. As I spoke she barely glanced at me and never touched me at all, adeptly prodding various keys with her fat fingers. Her gaze at the machine devout-like, as if it would giver the answer to my query of feeling dreadful.

Then the diagnosis. 'You are suffering from S.A.D. – Seasonal Affective Disorder', she again said into the screen. 'I will give you some anti-depressant tablets.' The fat finger in action once more, then out of a convenient slot pops a prescription. 'Don't stop taking them until we say, you'll need another script in a month's time.' By now my malady is easing and I am suffering from mild irritation. She hands me the script and, with a clearly dismissive look and a slight tilt of her head, glanced towards the door indicating that I should follow it.

I didn't move. I couldn't. With great calm I looked her in the eye. 'You did say S.A.D. Doctor?,' 'Yes S.A.D.'

'Well, I disagree…'

I knew perfectly well what S.A.D. was. A friend of mine, a professional man, had been diagnosed some years ago. This illness completely devastates him. In winter he becomes a different person and even with medication, which has become stronger each year, he now sits in a chair unable to do up his own shoe laces.

From somewhere I found courage and a sliver of humour. 'Well, I disagree. I'm more likely suffering H.A.D. – Holiday Affective Disorder. You see Doctor, I'm missing my good friends and their infectious humour. They always have time to sit over a meal or drink, to chat, telling you of their good and bad days and wanting to know of ones self. I miss their hugs and kisses when greeting, planning get togethers with all the family and friends. I miss the colours there too; the calm creaminess of the stones that make the flat roofed biblical houses, the breathtaking wide unclouded lapis lazuli sky and the soothing azure and turquoise sea. But mostly the comforting familiarity of old friends.'

'You may not understand, Doctor, how much I miss the warm patina created by those friendships. So thank you, Doctor. Keep your prescription. Perhaps you can press another button and push it, along with your limited attention, back into that machine. Good day!'

I made my way to the shops still picturing her face paralysed with shock and I hoped a jarring jolt. I stocked up on paracetamol and cleaning materials. My theory: have a week in front of the fire, rest and let this horrid virus make its copy within my body. When recovered I will spring clean early. Then in February it will be on with my nail polish (Mediterranean Pink, of course), and I'll head for the airport in the knowledge that on my arrival those friendships will start again, just as if I'd only left them an hour ago.

'Roses in December'

Wendy Grey-Lloyd

A gentle tap on my bedroom door announced the beginning of my working day. I turned and saw through the half-opened curtain, the morning mist slowly meeting the grey snow-laden sky. As I luxuriated in the warm bed, streaks of pink and blue splashed the horizon where the winter sun fastened its feeble rays on the barren hillside known locally as 'The Darren.'

Snow had not yet fallen this year- the winter of 1940- but there had been a hard and sharp frost in the night and the roofs of the houses were iced like Christmas cakes and the pointed icicles completed the decoration by draping jaggedly over the Landers. I felt a rush of cold as I left the warmth of my bed so I washed and dressed quickly.

A voice called up the stone stairs, 'Are you ready for your breakfast Miss Thomas?'

'I'm on my way down Mrs. Hughes. Just collecting my books for school.'

'It will be snowing by this evening,' pronounced Mrs.

Hughes. 'I wonder how many children you'll have in school today?'

'Well if the bus is running they should all manage to be there. Mr. Parry can be relied on to collect the children from the outlying farms even when the weather is unfit for walking. I've known him to drive into the farmyards, scattering the hens, in order to pick up the children. Besides, today we will be serving the school's annual Christmas dinner. Few children will want to miss that treat.'

'Here's your coat. Wrap up warm now. I'll have a hot stew ready for you when you return.'

Since most of the men in the teaching profession had joined the armed forces at the onset of the Second World War, women had been recalled to the profession order to fill the vacancies. Before the war, married women were not allowed to hold a teaching post. I had recently qualified as a teacher and was fortunate to be able to return to my home county of Merthyr Tydfil, where I was fortunate to have been offered a post in Treharris. It was a church school built in the last decade of the nineteenth century and named 'Graig Beth Llwyd.' I was the only qualified teacher there but I did have the help of a young pupil teacher who took charge of the infants' class under my supervision.

During the week I lodged near the school with Mrs. Hughes who cooked for me and did my laundry. At the weekends I returned to my home in Dowlais to be with my mother and young sister. Mrs. Hughes' terraced house was near the long winding road that led to the school. The churchyard lay to the west of the school, so both buildings nestled in a remote cwm.

The children ambled daily to the school through the rows of tumbling tombstones and ancient crosses. They chatted and laughed through the churchyard and were not troubled that here life and death walked together.

When there was a wedding in the old Church, we abandoned our lessons and went out to watch the proceedings, the children eager to catch the thrown pennies. It was a custom in the area for the best man to toss coins to the onlookers for luck. However if there was a funeral, we stayed indoors and offered a prayer for the departed and then continued with our lessons.

Today, as I trudged up the frost-rutted path, a robin sang from his perch on an ivy-covered headstone. I noticed that in this old grave, surrounded by low rust-railed spears, a spindly rose tree was growing and its thin branches bore some delicate blossom. J.M.Barrie's lines came to mind; 'God gave us memories so that we may have roses in December.'

I smiled to myself and pushed open the creaking school gate; the wind and weather on this exposed hillside had taken their toll on the original iron gate. Because it framed a school the gate had not been removed for Lord Beaverbrook's request for scrap in order to build machinery for the war.

Inside the classroom, a fire was burning brightly in the Victorian grate, which was piled high with red -hot coals. Even if there was rationing for food and clothes, being a mining area, at least we had warmth.

I heard the school gate open and through the high window of the classroom I saw the children crunching in their heavy bots over the frozen yard. Some of the boys had been trying to form snowballs out of the thin layer of snow that had fallen on the high ground and as they came into the classroom, they took off their wet gloves and scarves and left them hanging like whimsical Christmas stockings on the metal guard that surrounded the fire. Soon the smell of warming wet wool filled the classroom, and the school day began.

I lifted the lid of my desk and removed the register. Suddenly the outside door blew open and a small girl stood against the skyline. She must have been about eight years old, dressed in a faded blue serge dress with a finely knitted fawn shawl draped about her thin shoulders. Her black boots were tipped with white as if she had walked through heavy snow and her dark hair curled in damp ringlets.

She did not move, so I made my way to where she was standing and invited her into the room. There was a faint aura of roses about her person. I extended my hand, she hesitated, looked around and seeing the other children, she smiled. I indicated a vacant desk by the window and she sat down.

'What is your name?' I asked her. 'Rose', she replied. 'Where do you live?' She pointed to the window ad whispered quietly. I could only catch one word 'Coed.'

Freddie Roberts, a precocious eight year old, announced that she was probably one of the Romany children camping on the Common for Christmas.' My mam says we'll 'ave to watch our chickens . They 'ave a 'abit of disappearing at Christmas.'

'That will do Freddie.' I said, 'Come, sit by the fire Rose and warm yourself.'

She walked to the front of the classroom, her blue eyes smiling, her dimpled cheeks already less wan but smell of roses still surrounded her person. She sat on one of the small stools and stretched out her pale hands to warm her frozen fingers. Suddenly, she gave a squeal of joy and rushed towards the old wooden box of toys that that was kept in the corner of the classroom. Since the war, we had very few new toys. There were several knitted soft toys, a few hand made wooden playthings and surprisingly some outgrown toys of previous generations. Rose picked out an old china doll that someone must have given to the school many years ago. It's age was indicated by the style of dress, that of the late Victorian period. The high-necked red taffeta outfit was trimmed with faded and tattered lace, and hair that once shone like silk was now matted with age. Only the small black leather boots had survived the years of children's play.

Rose at first stroked the doll, then cradled it, and rocking back and fro, sang a song that was not familiar to me. I asked her to return to her seat. She went, still clutching the doll and humming.

'What a baby,' I heard Margaret Jones whisper. This nine year old appeared much older than her contemporaries, probably because she had five siblings younger than herself and had been given responsibilities beyond her age.

'Now children, let's mark the register. Anyone missing today? I wonder whose dinner we'll have to share if they are not here for our Christmas meal.'

'Will there be enough for 'er?' asked Freddie pointing to Rose.

'I am sure there will be plenty for everyone, even you Freddie Williams!'

Everyone laughed and I then called out their names. All

eleven children responded with a loud 'Present Miss.' There was one extra today of course --Rose--making up a class of twelve Junior pupils.

'Now everyone take out your sum book and we'll do some subtractions, but first let us recite our tables. The whole class groaned, as was the custom when 'Tables' were mentioned and then the chanting of the tables began.

'Muriel, will you say the five times tables please?' Muriel was a quiet, unassuming little girl but she was very good at sums. She repeated the exercise with ease.

'Now children, I shall question you on your tables. Put up your hand if you know the answer. Five times seven equals?'

Rose's hand went up immediately and she gave the correct answer in a quiet voice. At every question Rose's hand was raised first, but of course I had to allow the other children a chance to air their knowledge.

Soon it was time for a break from lessons in order for the children to drink the fresh milk that had been delivered that morning in individual milk bottles. On chilly days, the cold milk bottles were placed by the fire, in order to melt the frozen liquid in the necks and of course, it warmed up the children in such wintry conditions.

An orderly queue formed and every child took a bottle and a drinking straw and went off into little groups to drink and chatter. Milk was free for the children and it was an important part of the their diet.

Rose refused a drink and went to sit near the door, still holding the doll and smiling as she gazed at it.

After break- time, the children moved back to their desks. No one had ventured out into the yard. It was too cold. The warmth of the classroom kept them willing prisoners indoors.

'Now children I want you to take out your writing books. Write your names clearly on a new page, and then tell me what presents you would like for Christmas. Rose dear, I'll give you a sheet of paper on which you can write.'

There was silence for some time as the children indulged their imagination. As I passed between the desks, I read silently some of their requests. Dear Freddie had asked for a bicycle, but his father was missing in the war, presumed dead, and his mother was struggling to bring up three children on a pittance. Little chance of a bicycle for him this Christmas.

Suddenly, the dinner bell was being rung. This was the moment they had been waiting for all term---a warm Christmas dinner complete with a plum pudding made from a wartime recipe that managed to overcome the many restraints of rationing. I led the children into the infants' class where the dinner was to be served. The old tables had been transformed by the covering of colourful paper tablecloths made by the children in their craft lessons. The festive aroma of roast chicken filled the room. Freddie sniffed the air and said, 'Ooh, Miss, don't it smell luvly?'

'Yes it does, Freddie, now come along and sit down. Mrs. Roberts is ready to serve us.'

I settled my class onto the benches around the tables. I found a place for Rose and called her name but she wasn't in the room. Hadn't she followed the rest of the class to the dining area?

'Has anyone seen Rose?' I asked, looking around the

room.

'Probably gone 'ome to a chicken dinner. It's likely one of ours,' said Freddie with his mouth full of crunching sprouts.

'Oh dear, I hope she's all right. I'll go and check to see if she is still in the classroom.'

'I expect she's still clutching that doll. She seemed to be very attached to it, Miss,' pronounced Margaret Jones in her usual matter -of -fact voice.

I went into my classroom but it was empty. The fire was still burning brightly and the old Victorian doll had been placed neatly back in the toy box. The smell of roses still filled the air. It was the perfume that surrounded Rose on her first entrance. Perhaps she had gone home as Freddie had thought. I opened the outside door and stepped into the yard. A gentle wind blew around my face. How odd! It was bitterly cold but suddenly I felt quite warm. I called out 'Rose?' No reply. There was no sign of her. The school gate was fastened, as it always was when all the children were safely inside. I closed the door and returned to supervise the meal.

In the afternoon, the children returned to the classroom, replete and bubbling with laughter and excitement. I was going to read them the Christmas story but before that, the unavoidable register had to be marked, in accordance with education board regulations.

Suddenly, I saw Rose again standing by her desk, her sober woollen dress covered by the lacy shawl. She smiled as I called out the names of the children but did not answer when her name was called. I started to count the heads but Muriel was quicker than I. 'Eleven children all present Miss.' I opened my mouth to say something but when I looked again at Rose, she wasn't there. I must have been dreaming or Mrs. Roberts must have put extra stout in that Christmas pudding!

The afternoon raced by and home time came quickly. The children were to meet the bus at the bottom of the hill and from there they would be delivered safely to their house or farm.

'Come along everyone, time for hats, coats and gloves. The bus will be waiting to take you home.' The class formed a neat crocodile line and I accompanied them down to the waiting bus where I wished them good afternoon and hoped that they would be on time for school in the morning. I waved to them until the bus disappeared over the brow of the hill with dear Freddie waving to me until the bus was out of sight. I returned to the school to tidy the classroom and prepare for the next day's teaching.

I went to my desk and stopped suddenly, my heart missed a beat. There on top of the register were placed some branches of the small pink roses that had framed the tombstone by the church. I touched the delicate petals and at once the scent of musk roses filled the room.

Who could have put them there? The children had been with me in the classroom all day and no member of staff had left the building. The infant teacher had escorted her class down the hill and had gone home. The cook had departed soon after lunch had been cleared. Anyway, they would have surely told me if they had left the flowers.

I puzzled on the matter as I tidied my desk and then my eye was drawn to the Christmas letters written by the children. The top letter was written in crisp copperplate handwriting a style not commonly used by children of the present generation.

The letter began, *'My name is Rose Arabella Maud Marriott, and my home is called 'Plas -yr- Coed', in Treharris. I would like for a Christmas present the doll dressed in red taffeta with lace trimmings that I saw in Mr. Peacock's Christmas bazaar when my papa took me in his carriage for a visit to my Grandmamma in Cyffatha Castle, Merthyr Tydfil. Also, I would be grateful if my cough would get better in time for my cousins' visit on Boxing Day so that I could play games with them and not become tired and..........'* Here the letter trailed off and before I could consider the contents, there was a knock at the door and the Reverend Michael Evans, the Vicar of 'Graig- Beth- Llwyd' church entered the classroom.

'Good afternoon Miss Thomas, I saw a light in your room as I was leaving the church and I thought you might require a lift in my car to your lodgings. I have been preparing for the service tomorrow that the children will be attending.'

'Thank you, Reverend Evans, that is most kind,' I replied, 'I have just finished. I'll get my coat'

His eyes moved towards the roses on the desk. 'Oh, tut, tut Miss Thomas, I notice you have been taking roses from the graves,' he gently admonished me, 'on the other hand, did some child wish to thank you? Some of these children are so poor that I do not mind if they take a few flowers to give as presents. Times are difficult in these valley villages what with so many men at the front and with tight rationing. Surprisingly, only one tree blooms at Christmas in our churchyard each year and that is the one on the little Marriott's grave.'

'Did you say, Marriott?'

'Yes, the family lived in the old 'Plas' in Treharris for many years, and their heiress, a little girl, died of consumption at the age of eight and is buried in the churchyard. The family were regular worshippers and gave money to build this school for the village children. When their only child died, they were broken-hearted and left the area soon after her death. I know from my predecessors that a trust fund was set up to keep her grave in good order but that was many years ago and the money has long been exhausted. It is a shame because the stone needs cleaning and the weeds should be cleared. However, most of the inscription can still be read quite easily. Come, I'll show you.'

I was just locking the door when again the waft of rose scent filled my nostrils. I remembered the flowers and returned to collect the branches from my desk.

The Vicar waited by the gate and we walked into the churchyard together. As we approached the grave, I saw that the old rose tree was now dusted with frost but bare of blooms. I knelt down and arranged my rose branches near the headstone.

'There' said the Reverend Evans, pointing to the inscription, 'you can just make out the words,' and he began to read aloud:

'*Here Lies Sleeping Rose Arabella Maud Marriott, departed this life,* I can't make out the actual date, but I think it's *December 1892 aged eight years. A clever scholar, a gentle child*'

'Fifty Christmas's ago,' I murmured, 'I do hope her short life was a happy one.' 'You can be sure of that,' replied the Reverend Evans. 'She lacked for nothing.' I began to shiver in the late afternoon air and the Reverend noticed my discomfiture. 'Come,' he said, 'let's get to the car. It's becoming very cold here.' As we walked back down the icy path in the half-light of a winter's afternoon, the vicar continued to enlighten me on the tragic short life of this young girl. 'When she passed away, the family sent all her toys to the Rectory for distribution. The Governess of the school at the time received the more expensive ones so that every child was able to share the gifts that had been given. You probably still have some in the school although I should imagine they would be well used by now and quite battered.'

'Yes,' I said, 'I think we still have her doll.'

'Well, when I have seen you safely home I must finish my sermon for Sunday morning. I want the congregation to believe that even in these dark days of the war God has not forgotten us and that one day we shall all be reunited. God sent his only child to show us the light and the way. Dear me, Miss Thomas, I'm so sorry, I'm practising my sermon on you.'

I dismissed his apologies with a smile. What was the message, I wondered, that this Victorian child had brought?

One thing was certain, 'The rose still grows beyond the grave!'

'The Reception'

Chris Sullivan

The reception at Merthyr Tydfil's Jubilee Club had all the finesse of a Mongolian army feeding station, as guests jostled at the bar for their free glass of Asti, while the large table of grub at the far end of the hall peered at them with bad intent. Resplendent with relics from a forgotten gastroenteritis age, I at once understood the meaning of the phrase, 'running buffet', that is used in Wales to describe this style of spread, most ran away from and not to.

Spam reigned supreme like a towering culinary colossus, while innocent sausages were impaled on sticks between tinned pineapple chunks. Sausage rolls, slimy to the touch, eyed up the salted peanut; next-door naive prawn cocktail flavoured crisps promised an evening of good old Merthyr heartburn, while the cold *Quiche Lorraine,* lonely at the end of the table, had been included for the posh girls from, *The Walk* who worked in the Tax in Cardiff.

The girlfriend looked at the assembled cuisine and walked away totally un-amused. 'I thought you said there'd be food, but this is *grubbish*,' she spat with all the venom of a narked cobra. And to that there was no reply.

So as I wondered what was so wrong with the spread, I hastily jammed as much as I could down my throat in as short as time as possible, filled my pockets with peanuts and made a full frontal assault on the bar. For her sins, I left my good lady to the ravages of my elderly female relatives and pretend aunties, who steamed right in from all the sides with an unrelenting interrogative ear bashing; the gist of which was why, and more importantly how, we were childless.

One such 'auntie' actually sang my praises. She told of how l was such a good boy, a good athlete and a good student. 'But,' she declared eyes half closed, head aloft. 'Still not a patch on my Maldwyn,' who, according to her, had the mind of Patrick Moore and the looks of Brad Pitt. Or was it the other way around? How he had managed to avoid the hallowed halls of Oxford and leave school at 16 with not even a spirit level to his name was anybodies guess. And just how he deigned to marry the most ugly, foul-mouthed female in the town is a mystery that still keeps the nations intellectuals awake at night.

But Maldwyn, as far as his good old ma was concerned, was a svelte, multi-talented genius, still waiting for the right opportunity to come along. She was so proud of the fact that he played goal in the school football team but, little did she know that when he stood between the posts there was little room for the ball to pass by. Over the course of a good half hour 'auntie' Rose re-counted the magnificence of her offspring. Mal, while holding the wife's wrist with one hand and knocking back gin and orange cordials (supplied by her ever attentive but understandably cowering husband) with the other. And the more she drunk the tighter her grip became until her double G and O's reached double figures and she dozed off only to awake again, in a split second and begin her tales of Maldwyn The Magnificent, all over again.

At the bar drinks were served that I had completely forgotten about. Requests for rum and pop, vodka and lime were aplenty - drinks that make your gums recede and your pee turn a funny colour. While boredom gnawed at my other half, whose hand was visibly turning blue, I tried to interrupt but couldn't get a word in upside down, inside out, or even edge ways.

'Shut up Christopher!' belched Auntie Rose.

'Stop interrupting… I'm talking to this lovely girl.'

And so I skirted the crowd peering over - fashion intense - trying to look as if I was looking for someone very, very important. Thus postponing the inevitable.

As I looked over the crowd I saw the bride's parents. The wife, Janice, putrid in pink. Her fifteen stone bulk encased in a crimpolene suit, in a particularly innocuous shade of said colour that tried desperately to contain her five foot two inch frame. A brave but minuscule bolero jacket failed miserably, to cover one of her many rolls of not so common or garden fat, that shuddered majestically like a wave of crepe paper. In contrast her hair was a definite dyed blue black, that, ever so reminiscent of Elvis circa 1967, was certainly inspired, while her bright pink lipstick failed to reach the corners of her mouth, causing me to ponder, for just a moment, on the fate of Scott of the Antarctic. She looked like a brick with lipstick.

She saw me; she stood still for a second like a squirrel, checked both sides then rushed towards me like an angry prop forward. A shiver ran up my back, my hair stood up on end and my mouth dried up like a summer puddle, but luckily, her husband - a right Brahma - intercepted her. Already pissed on the cider he was still on the Teddy boy vibe and sported the Brylcreemed coiffure of Ducks Ass and elephant's trunk in a mottled grey and black, freckled with pavement stone sized chunks of dandruff that, hung tough on his jacket collar while his general incongruity was exacerbated by his attire. His suit all very Kevin Keegan a product of Hepworths in the High Street circa '77 and with fat lapels and flares that perfectly derided his purple nineties long collared shiny shirt, the buttons strained to the max at girth. Added to the staggering ensemble was a slim Jim leather tie, an item that he was obviously extremely proud of. He had the head of a Teddy boy and, due to his humongous beer gut, the body of a pregnant sixty odd year old bird but otherwise he was quite slim. He was indeed a walking talking contradiction. But a really nice chap.

Caught off guard I stared for too long and felt a tap on my shoulder. I turned around.

'S-s-still in the smoke 'en; too busy to visit you mam an' dad like; too busy see the real people.'

Looking down, I saw my cousin Michael with the same centre parting cutting through his foul, lank greasy ginger hair, while his eyes, dulled by constant alcohol, wallowed in yards of bloated sweating fat.

'Dew, dew, I'd say you're bit of a twat like,' he added, really believing that to speak his mind with such candour was an admirable trait but really was just immensely rude.

'Where's you bit 'en?' he continued in true snide mode.

'Real smart like; proper tidy, I'd give her what for anyway'.

I slowly looked him up and down, his shit brown suit and purple tie just covering the compulsory beer pot. All my childhood memories of his temper tantrums - his crusading mother to whom he could do no wrong, his 'it's my ball and I'm going home' attitude - came rushing back.

'Please just leave, go away' I pleaded

'Life's too short for the likes of you. You really are a waste of a human body .You really are.'

And as he loitered, thoroughly confused by my outburst, his tiny eyes struggled to focus.

'Dew, dew,' he said laughing. 'Ha, Ha, well you still ain't lost your sense of 'umour then have you? Bloody 'ell mun, you always liked to wind us up didn't you? Well aye mun. Ell of a boy, dew.. Fucking dew.'

He staggered off, a pint of Strongbow in each hand, and swayed over a table full of familiar faces. He moved towards Janice, his beloved, and spilt half his pint over her dress. Her answer was to clout him right around the ear. He hit the deck, she stormed out and her mother was on her tail. Sniggers and blasphemies peppered the hush, until Dewey a local wag, quiz champion and ferret fancier broke the silences 'Ding, ding,' he shouted. 'End of round one.'

Realising that as old rivalries and petty family disputes reared their now intoxicated heads; the altercation was but a taste of things to come, so I fought my way to the bar. As I waited and looked up to order I saw in the reflection in the mirror behind the optics a gang of strangers nudging each other and pointing my way, as if espying an extremely rare bird while the bravest (or thirstiest) of the bunch walked over.

'Hallo butt, 'how're you doing?' said he.

'Staying at mams are you? An't seen you mam in a fucking long, long time, and 'ow are you - okay? I go to London every couple a years. Up to Twick'nam like; bloody mad up the smoke; they'll stab ew for tuppence mun, all 'ose chocolate drops, fucking coons, dew, dew not safe mun, not safe; but you look well on it. Anyway good health.'

He drained his glass and not without a certain drama, plonked it down on the bar and looked at me nodding.

'Get 'em in then but.' he said.

'Pardon' I said.

'Your round like,' he said.

'What are you drinking?' I said.

'Pint of Strongbow' he answered, smiling smugly while looking round to his pals, as if to say 'see boys this is how it's done.'

'How you can drink that I don't know. It is so bad for the liver' I said, my Guinness now ready and walked off.

Rather more pleased with my self then the occasion warranted, I looked in the side bar, once known as the *snug* and spotted an oasis in the form of Bill Beynon, sat in his usual chair, that he occupied most days from 7-12 midnight weekdays and 11-3pm and 7-12pm Saturdays and Sundays. The Jubilee is what one might call Bill's local and he is there almost always. In fact, apart from one holiday in Porthcawl in 1970, he, having packed his wife and kids off to Butlins in Barry Island, has spent every vacation there day and night since 1967.... supping large.

As I made my way to his table, he spotted me and stood up. 'Fucking hell,' he shouted swirling every syllable around his mouth like a fine wine, 'Look boys its old golden bollocks come specially to get a round in.'

Now these were the blokes I didn't mind getting the drinks in for. They were what some London types call Diamond geezers and I had borrowed money from each one at least twice when, as a teenager, I needed to take a girl out or go on hols. This was when Bill, his brother Bob and their best pal Jimmy Spoons were all in gainful employment at the Merthyr Vale Colliery, pulling in good wages. Now all were un-employed but, due to a bit of poaching and general skulduggery, could still find the price of a pint or ten. Bill was the oldest and the most tattooed, his knuckles and fingers like a toilet wall in an uncared for pub, but he was beyond the price of gold per ounce.

'Eh, golden bollocks 'he said as I sat down having supplied a round.

'You've been around a bit. You're sophisticated like - well travelled and stuff but can you tell me one thing? It's been bothering me for a long, long time.'

'I don't know,' I answered seeing his cohorts' stern faces.

'What's the definition of a lesbian?'

Now I pondered this loaded question for quite a while, especially as his wife, Muriel, had recently gone over to the other side or as he put it, 'started supping at the furry cup.'

'I don't know,' I said taking the fifth.

'One slip of the tongue and you're in deep shit!'

I could've spent all day with Bill and the boys but my mobile rang. It was the wife. 'Save me,' she pleaded. 'Save me now!'

As I weaved my way through the crowd, my Aunty Violet collared me and Uncle Vince, who immediately quizzed about the delights of 'Les Miserables', for what seemed like the rest of my life. At first, I thought 'Les' was perhaps a legendary local moaner but, after a while, I discovered that they were talking of the famous musical of the Victor Hugo novel and that, on their one and only visit to London they'd seen it.

'Bloody Marvellous that Les Miserables,' said Vince pronouncing the name in full on Brit fashion. 'Absolute falubous' agreed auntie Vi. It seemed that, *Les Miz,* was the highlight of their lives and after I had taken an initial interest - thinking it was this interesting local character - they let rip with unbridled, *Les Miz'* recollections coupled with less than sparkling renditions of the productions most popular ditties. After sitting there, eyes glazed over, jaw open, for what seemed like months I blurted out the horrible truth: I hadn't seen, *Les Miz*. Silence enveloped the conversation and the world. They looked stunned. They looked at each other. They looked at me. They looked at each other. They looked at me.

'How can you live in London and not go to see Les Miz?' they asked almost in tears.

'Well it's different when you pass it every day you don't bother' I answered desperately trying to let them down gently.

Then a light bulb appeared over Vi's head, she smiled and said with uncommon calm, 'Well that's okay we can tell you all about it from the beginning can't we Vincent.'

I sank into the leatherette chair, and resigned myself to my fate. But miraculously, like a drowning man desperately clutching for anything that could float, I produced the totally twattish, vomit provoking words.

'Oh please don't tell me, it'll spoil it, after all you've said I *must* go see it.'

I shuddered, smiled, grabbed the moment and stood up 'Oh, sorry I must go, my girlfriend is waving to me,' I said. 'I can't abandon her, she's on her own and she really is a stranger,'

'Oh yes,' they said in unison and I trotted off only to hear Violet mutter,

'Dew, Dew, what's the matter with him? He must be twp.... imagine livin' in London and not going to see Les Miz- bloody craaazeee.'

'Absolute insanity,' whispered Vince disparagingly.' Absolute insanity.'

I moved to the edge of the dance floor and looked around and watched the intoxicated throng doing the birdie song, complete with hand movements as young children, in their dickie bowed Sunday best, ran between the dancers playing touch.

One such child, short in stature but gigantic in bolsh, knocked into Janice the mother of the bride, using her as a shield to avoid the touch of his playmate, while Janice reeled around precipitously like a weeble that would most definitely fall down. I cringed as I imagined her 15 stone flattening the two stone boys. Regaining her balance Janice eyed the culprit, Christopher, and grabbed him, shaking him like a rag doll, shouting at him, 'Behave now,' she said. 'BEHAVE!

Now this young lad was from the other side. He was from the family of the groom. Pikeys to the last. His mother, a certain *Moira The Hun* - the hardest landlady in the world.

Realising her enormous breach of etiquette, Janice turned a lighter shade of pale and shrank into her torso like a tortoise, as the badly tattooed habitual jailbird and notorious lesbo, Moira of 'The Clink' stormed through the crowd like a refugee in search of a food parcel, frothing at the mouth, dribbling with intent saying:

'What do ewe think you are fucking bastard doin'?' her voice rising to a strangled scream head lolling back and forth a tattooed finger prodding the offender sharply. 'I will fuckin' rip you're head off and shuv it up your cunting arse. I will, I will…. I'll kill you where you *fucking* stand you, you , you shitehock !'

She followed up by delivering a splendid head butt that Mike Tyson would have died for. The blow had all the force of a two ton oak door slammed in one's face and promptly splattered dear Janice's nose akimbo. Blood spurted out left and right as the barbaric Moira followed up with a knee to the stomach and an elbow to the back of the head grinning like Jackie Pallo. But fair play Janice stood her ground; eyed Moira like a gal possessed, grabbed her hair and pulled for all her 190 pounds was worth. They both fell; exposing acres of market stall panty hose punching in a most admirable fashion, shoulders behind the blows not wasting a shot, while knickers provided the temporary relief. It was a proper ruck. As my admiration for Janice went up about 10,000 per cent fools rushed in where angels fear to tread, in the form of their husbands, who tried to separate the two ladies, now rolling on the floor, pulling lumps out of each others hair, screaming obscenities, while clawing morsels out of each others blotched and bruised faces. It was class. I started to feel homesick.

Eventually, after what seemed like far too long, but was actually only a minute, they were separated and both combatants were pulled to neutral corners, while the two sides (that is the brides family and the grooms family) detached themselves, stopped mingling and started to console the pugilists.

The music came back on, albeit apologetically, as Talwyn Roberts, DJ of the Loony Toons Mobile Disco, tried to ignore the fact that the mother of the bride had been butted by the sister of the groom and put, *Making Your Mind Up*, by Bucks Fizz on the decks. This was an entirely redundant choice as both sides had made their minds up at birth. But as time went on alcohol, slowly but surely, anaesthetised the proceedings and things returned to thinly veiled animosity - the two families now distinctly separate - facing each other like rival football firms waiting for the merest hint of disrespect to steam right in to their sworn enemy.

Within minutes everybody was talking about the incident, so I, like every other close observer, retold what I'd witnessed in minute detail suitably embroidered for dramatic effect.

'Are they all like this, weddings I mean?' asked the Mrs.

'Oh yes,' I answered enthusiastically most proud of my home towns idiosyncrasies, 'Funerals as well.'

'Girl on the Viaduct'

Mike Jenkins

She perched herself there surprisingly comfortably,
waiting for the night train, the ghost train.

When she was a teenager she'd never have considered
it. Her recurrent dreams of falling. Constantly on look-out
for her little bro' Bri (Bri for Bright she always said).
Down, down......even though she could swim through air
most times.

And now, it didn't matter.

The town had spat her out, rejected her. Where was her
notoriety now? Front page, the 'Merthyr Gazette'. She'd
made it. She had lost it.

This viaduct was nicknamed 'The Arches'. Her dad had
bored her with stories about railways. She'd ignored him
then. But now he was gone she heard his voice more
clearly, enthusing about connections, junctions and
decrying closures. Her mam, with that jolly Italian smile,
teasing him.

'Trains, Daveed! The only trains you get here are ghost ones. Have you seen them, my Katie?'

Her Katie. Her mam up with the birds, a flight of geese going south to warmer climes. Her dad pacing along the missing line, sleeper to sleeeeper, but with nothing there.

Her sight swooped down to the little river, the Taf something. No dizziness, just a sense of power. All that was left. She dangled her legs onto the solid surface like a puppet. No god pulled her strings.

She faced away from town towards the Beacons, towards the winding river which cut deeper than its width would ever suggest. The flat plains of grassy banks resembled kept lawns, between rocky waters and steep slopes of thick woodland and bushes.

The town had expected so much. And then those songs.......Chrissy, the guitarist had written them, but Katie knew they told the truth. They weren't what people wanted to hear. They were tales of pettiness and a people who wouldn't stand up, but turned upon each other to rob or grab what they could.

She hummed one of them, but it was the lyrics which burned inside. She wanted to forget them, every one, to drop them into the tumbling, gushing froths of the Devil's Punchbowl downstream from the viaduct.

'Ey! Yew orright?'

From the other end of The Arches' path a bulbous man called out.

Katie nodded and flapped her arms, as if ready to take off. He seemed alarmed by this and strode rapidly along the rubbly line.

'Don' worry love. I'll be there in a tick. Sorright!'

Katie thought he was about to yank her back into safety, so she acted quickly.

'I'm jest admirin the view. It's lovely up yer,' she tried to sound placid.

The toad-faced man with large black-rimmed specs leant near her strategically.

'Thought yew woz abseilin or summin.......The missis seen yew. I'm the lan'lord up there,see. No abseilin allowed yer now. Not since....it's the rools.'

'Na, I'm jest waitin. Sooner or later my train'll turn up.'

He frowned at her, suspecting madness. What to do next?

'Look love,it's too risky. Yew get all kinda nutters up by yer. Boyz on booze 'n' drugs,all sorts.......'ey could take advantage......why don' yew come up my pub an I'll buy yew a nice drink. There's an even better view from-a beer garden.'

'Are yew tha desprut f' customers?........Look, yew're very kind an 'a, but I don' need no Samaritans. No way I'm gunna jump.'

The landlord weighed her up. Attractive girl : deep, dark eyes. Too pale and tatty though. Didn't eat properly. Standard denims, but attitude nose-rings. He couldn't work her out. Something hidden.

'Yew shewer? My missis ull.....'

'Onest. There's no problem. I'm on'y sittin.'

He shook his head, unsure. Peered to the top of the slope for a semaphore message from his wife. Reluctantly, he turned and waddled away, leaving Katie to herself again.

STREET PULSE : it wasn't even that good a name. But then the Stereophonics was naff and what about

Catatonia, a state of paralysis for goodness sake? Next to the 60 Foot Dolls, Street Pulse was positively poetry. And Chrissy had been there from the start. Her other half until......

There were people below waving up to her : three lads with lager cans hooked to their paws, like the landlord's fear made human. You couldn't escape it. Chrissy had said it right in 'Weapons of Glass'........

> *Where alcohol is the fuel*
> *And love is up the arse -*
> *Saturday nights with weapons of glass.....*

There she was yet again. Going back, when she wanted to go down. Down into flight, not drowning or the final crack.

One of the boys took out his plonker and pissed. He shook it while the others gestured at her and pointed at his barely-visible penis.

'Ey love!' he yelled, 'do us a favour, jump an land on me will ya?'

Katie shuddered her legs wide and instantly regretted it. They weren't an audience, just three pathetic lads out to taunt. They reacted with typical excitement, wooahing and corring, while Katie tired to send them up with a snigger they'd hardly detect.

Another man ambled along the viaduct, acccompanied by a woman. They didn't talk. The man was dressed casually, while the woman looked too chic for a country jaunt. As they approached Katie, he stared deliberately at her. As they passed, his eyes followed her, his wife tutting at this all-too-customary behaviour. He stopped abruptly, like a train at fallen boulders.

'C'mon Mart, yew promised me a tidee drink after all this walkin.'

He continued to eye Katie.

'Bloody ell, Mart,yew never give over d' yew?'

'Wise up,Lou, she's an ex pupil.'

At the familiar 'wise up', Katie returned his full focus for the first time. His wife, hands on hips, daring him to be over zealous.

'Sir....I......Ow's thin's?'

She sounded so relaxed given the fact that she was balanced on a viaduct hundreds of feet above the narrow valley floor.

'Mart! Yew comin or wha?'

Katie's former Geog. teacher tried to contain his annoyance.

'Louise, yew go ahead. I'll catch up. I won't be long.'

His wife shrugged acceptance and plodded off, muttering disgust. While Martin leaned close to Katie, examining her eyes for a response.

'Katie, I aven't seen yew for ages. Not since all the......

'I know......'

'I thought yew'd made it Bigtime......Oh God! Yew....I mean.....'

He suddenly contemplated the drop.

'Yew wern thinkin of......What appened,Katie ? Tell me.'

He moved even closer now. She knew he was ready to grip.

She laughed at his concern. He was shocked.

'Yew know, sir........I mean, Mr. Davies.......yew always woz my eero, y'know. Ever since yew took us on tha field trip an bought us all them drinks.'

He'd been a sucker. They'd led him on. He got into trouble when the parents found out. Been given a warning.

'Really? I thought......yew know......I thought the kids always took the piss outa me.'

He'd dropped his pen on the floor deliberately to ogle at girls' legs. 'Pervy Marty' they'd dubbed him. But Katie was pleased with any audience now, even him. He was uncomfortably near, his breath against her neck, puffing.

'The train'll come eventually, Mr. Davies. My dad promised it would.'

Martin Davies was thrown by her sudden distracted talk. He wondered if she'd had
a breakdown and this really was a suicide attempt.

'What happened to the band, Katie? Yew were doin great. I remember goin to that gig in the Kooler Club an.....'

Katie's mood altered again. She reluctantly spat her memories out.

'Yeah, it all changed. Ev'rythin! Chrissy wrote all them songs.......they tol the truth....nobody wanted t' yer it........I got my own manager, tried t' go solo. I woz so fuckin crap Mar.....Mr. Davies. Without Chrissy I wuz nothin.........Thought I could be Cerys Catatonia.........Katie Cefn Coed, eh? All attitude an no fuckin talent whatsoever.'

Martin was scared. This girl now seemed on the edge. He was ready to pounce, to catch her. She stared longingly into the emptiness in front of her. He tried to twist his neck towards her and touched her arm doing so. Excited by her cold flesh. She recoiled : a sudden flashback of grovelling on the classroom floor.

'My mam woz a bird Mr. Davies. I wish I could join er.......But my dad.......maybe ee'll be drivin tha train when it comes.'

'Katie, don't get yewrself all worked up..........if I really woz yewr hero, lissen t' me now. Jest come off there an come with me for a drink or somethin. Meet my wife, then after that we cun jump together......I mean.....'

'Sir....yew wozn my eero, yew woz a right plonker! Now leave me be, will yew?'

Martin backed off, baffled by her wayward nature.

'I....er....'

'Jest piss off, right?.....I int gunna jump!.......Don' feel guilty. Go f'r a pint. Forget it!'

Her eyes were still lusciously exotic despite the haggard features and neglected hair. A swift sense of her legs, under the desk, long and lovely, leading......The girl was obviously deranged. He moved further away.

'Alright! I know when I'm not wanted.'

'Too true.'

He headed for the pub and a tongue-lashing. How far down could you go, he thought. Katie had been up there. Cool Cymru, wasn't it? After the Manics so much was expected. He liked their stuff....Street Pulse. He'd only seen them once. At the very back, leaning against the bar, posing as an A & R man.

Below her, those boys had disappeared. It was gradually darkening. Annoyingly, one of Chrissy's songs revolved in her head :

> *Dark days of boarded-up brains*
> *Of tunnels, tablets, graffiti stains......*

Bleak words, but they matched her mood. She was glad Davies had gone. Creep. Touchy, crawly. The small valley peaceful again. When darkness came.....Shouts from the other side of the viaduct. The three boys cavorting towards her, two swinging sticks, the other calling out.

'Ey,yew gunna jump, or wha? Takin yewer time, in yew?'

The stick-swingers guffawed. She actually thought of moving on, but couldn't. There was nowhere to go.

In a moment they were around her, a dog-pack sniffing. She tilted her body from one side to the other as they beat the wall with their sticks behind her. They were all glassy-eyed, not plate-glass but jagged and knife-like. Each one goaded.

'Yer! Woz tha yewer fancy-man or wha?'

'Yew bin screwin im?'

'Spread yewr legs agen, eh? Like yew done from below!'

Katie stood up on the parapet facing them. A hostile audience. A Club where all they wanted was Heavy Metal covers.

'See them sticks, well suck on them! Coz tha's all yew boyz 've got.'

It wasn't a clever put-down, but the gall was enough.

'Aw, fuck off yew loony-toon!'

They threw their sticks at her and she wobbled, surprising herself by flapping her arms, as though she'd grown feathers. The leader of the pack jeered.

'C'mon boyz, le's leg it. She's mental.'

They ran off down the path, still mocking - 'Loony toon! Loony toon!'

Katie resumed her former posture. Let the light go down with her future. She felt weak and hollow-headed. She fancied she could hear a train in the distance, but it could easily have been a plane overhead.

Then, out of the welcome silence of the line, out of its long throat fading into the tunnel of trees, came her father's voice, informing, declaiming : 'See Katie, love. Wales woz once the centre of steam. We done it first an now.....look at this...nothin ! On'y a bare track t' walk an fill with memrees.'

With his final words an explosion of birds, of starlings rising from bushes and trees
 clattering wings as though her mam's tongue was chiding him for being too depressing.

Katie felt she could remain here, poised on stone. Caught between the ghost-voices of those that mattered most, with no crowd below, in the darkness, waiting for her to drop.

BOOKS TO BUY AT
MERTHYR TYDFIL LIBRARIES

FICTION FOR ADULTS (Set in Merthyr Tydfil)
A BLOODY GOOD FRIDAY. Desmond Barry. £7
BELT OF KINGS. Anthony Bunko. £4.99
THE MERTHYR TRILOGY. Alan Osborne. Play. £6
SIEGE OF EL RANCHO. Anthony Bunko. £4.99
TALE OF THE SHAGGING MONKEY. Anthony Bunko. £4.99

FICTION FOR CHILDREN (Set in Merthyr Tydfil)
CHILD OF DUST. Mike Jenkins. £7.99
IRON TOWN BOY. Ann Ahmed.
LITTLE MARTHA TEARFUL. Coral Smith. £3.99

GROWING UP IN MERTHYR
BAG FULL OF MONKEYS. Evans George. £7.50
DEVON CORNWALL. SHIRT, TIE & TENT. John Durbin £5
WHEN THE KIDS GROW UP. Ken James £6.95

HISTORIES
ABERFAN, OUR HIRAETH. Maureen Hughes. £15
BRIDGES OF MERTHYR TYDFIL. WL Davis. £15
THE DIARY OF CHARLES WOOD. Edited by Joseph Gross. £10
DOWLAIS IRONWORKS. John A Owen. £5.
THE GLAMORGANSHIRE CANAL. Rowson & Wright. £30
HISTORY OF MERTHYR TYDFIL. Charles Wilkins. CD ROM.
£7.50
HISTORIC TAF VALLEYS. Vol 1. Treharris/Quakers Yard. £3
HISTORIC TAF VALLEYS. Vol 3. Cefn Coed to Aberfan. £6
THE MERTHYR HISTORIANS. The Merthyr Tydfil Historical
Society.Vols. 7-18. £7 - £10
MERTHYR TYDFIL IRON METROPLOLIS. Dr Keith Strange.
Tempus. £17.99
OLD GUNPOWDER FACTORY OF GLYNNEATH. £2.
POOR RELIEF IN THE MERTHYR TYDFIL UNION IN
SOMETHING MUST BE DONE. Ted Rowlands. £14.95
STRANGER IN A FOREIGN LAND. Carl Llewellyn. £2
VICTORIAN TIMES. Tydfil Thomas. £10

WORKING IRON IN MERTHYR TYDFIL. R. Hayman. £3.50
WALK AROUND OLD PENYDARREN. Trevor Peasey. £2

PICTURE BOOKS
FACES AND PLACES. MT Historical Society. £4.50
MERTHYR TYDFIL OLD PHOTOS. I & II Tempus. £11.99 Each
MERTHYR IN RECENT YEARS. Lewis Roy. £4.99
THE UNCONQUERABLE SPIRIT. Merthyr in the 1930s.
VALLEY LIVES SERIES. £2
  BOOK 1. Schools and Scholars of Merthyr Tydfil.
  BOOK 2. Valley Champions. Boxers of Merthyr Tydfil.
  BOOK 3. Music and Musicians [Merthyr Tydfil].
  BOOK 4. The Valley at War. Changes due to W.W.I & II.
VALLEY VIEWS SERIES. £2
  BOOK 1. Historic Street Scenes [Merthyr Tydfil valley].
  BOOK 2. Transport.
  BOOK 3 Industrial Life.
  BOOK 4 Coal Mining.

POETRY BY LOCAL AUTHORS
CICATRICE. Siams Fyrsi. £3
INVISIBLE TIMES. Mike Jenkins. £3
LANGUAGE OF FLIGHT. Mike Jenkins. £6
PARTING. Siams Fyrsil. £3
RED LANDSCAPES. Mike Jenkins. £4
THIS HOUSE MY GHETTO. Mike Jenkins. £3
YESTERDAY'S TOMORROW. Alun Rees. £4-95

SPORT
HOWARD WINSTONE: WELSH WIZARD. L Miles. £9.95
JOHNNY OWEN . Murphy Jeff. £15
MERTHYR TYDFIL FOOTBALL CLUB. David Watkins. £9.99
REACH FOR THE STARS. HOWARD WINSTONE. £15
STABLE OF EDDIE THOMAS. Wynford Jones. £11